## PERILOUS DAWN

Major Perry Rhodan, commander of the spaceship *Stardust*, found more than anyone had expected might exist on the moon—for he became the first man to make contact with another sentient race!

The Arkonides had come from a distant star, and they possessed a knowledge of science and philosophy that dwarfed mankind's knowledge.

But these enormously powerful alien beings refused to cooperate with the people of Earth . . . unless Perry Rhodan could pass the most difficult test any human being had ever faced. . . .

The PERRY RHODAN series and characters were created by Walter Ernsting and Karl-Herbert Scheer.

Series Editor & Translator:

Wendayne Ackerman

English Language Representative
of PERRY RHODAN:

Forrest J Ackerman

# PERRY RHODAN

## #1

by K. H. Scheer & Walter Ernsting

AN ACE BOOK

Ace Publishing Corporation
1120 Avenue of the Americas
New York, N.Y. 10036

ENTERPRISE STARDUST

*Introducing*

# PERRY RHODAN
# AND HIS ELECTRIC PERSONALITY

## By Forrest J Ackerman

As Tom said to Jonathan, "The race belongs to the Swift."

Or are you too young to remember Tom Swift? (*In the Land of Wonders,* his *Planet Stone.*) And Roy Rockwood and his Clarke's Tours of the solar system. (*Air Express to Venus*—air?!—*By Space Ship to Saturn.*) The Carl H. Claudy classics, including *The Mystery Men of Mars.* These boys' sf books of a less sophisticated generation never won any Hugos (and not just because they were published prior to the establishment of the annual science fiction "Oscar" awards) but they did generate a great deal of entertainment.

Then there was Gordon, who was flashy, and Rogers, who was always bucking the baddies. You probably heard of Buck and Flash in the movie serials or comics or TV revivals or camp posters.

Now comes, roaring into the 70's—PERRY RHODAN . . . earth-tamer . . . planet adventurer . . . star-seeker . . . Peacelord of the Universe!

America, for once has lagged behind—we are 8 *years* behind the Germans in discovering the world's greatest spaceman. In the pulp era of our past we have had many great continuing characters: Doc Savage, the Shadow, Captain Future, G-8, et al. Savage started in '33 and ended in '49 and is, 20 years after his disappearance, enjoying a renaissance in paperback. But the 16 years of Doc Savage's exploits cannot possibly compare with such an impressive record as Perry Rhodan's because Doc, most of the time, appeared only monthly, sometimes bimonthly, whereas Perry, since the beginning, has been published *weekly!*

Ain't that outasite? (I hope I'm hip to the mod slanguage

because I'm so old that I remember when people blew their noses instead of their minds.) Over 400 adventures of Perry Rhodan, Thora, Gucky (the mouse-beaver), Atlan and all the characters you will come to know and who will grow on you—*over 400*—have already been published abroad!

Every week in Germany a new Perry Rhodan plot appears and sells out an edition of 130,000 copies! (No American science fiction periodical equals that record even on a *monthly* basis.) Germany—with a population of only one-third that of the United States! If Germany had our population it would mean that approximately 400,000 people would be reading Perry every seven days!

A second, reprint, edition of the earlier episodes now runs 50,000 copies a week in Germany.

And the *third* time around on the republication of the earliest ones, they're printing 20,000 copies—to make an incredible total of 200,000 copies of Perry Rhodan's cosmic conquests being read each week! (By U.S. population comparison, *600,000!*)

Plus! Pocketbooks (wholly different adventures) . . . hardcovers (revised from the magazines) . . . comics.

Perry Rhodan has appeared for three years in France, is now in Dutch!

Over 500 Perry Rhodan Clubs flourish in Germany, Switzerland and Austria, complete with membership pins. Regional and national Perry Rhodan Conventions are held annually!

The first Perry Rhodan film, S.O.S. FROM OUTER SPACE, has exploded on the screens of Europe.

To satisfy the demand, a corps of half a dozen or more writers is kept busy creating new plots from the master history—more complex than anything ever dreamed of in the future histories of Asimov, Heinlein or Doc Smith—masterminded by Walter Ernsting (Herr Science Fiction of Germany) and noted sf author K.-H. Scheer.

In Germany, all serious sf buffs claim to hate Perry Rhodan, but *somebody* (in unprecedented numbers) is certainly reading him. When I went to the Science Fiction Film Festival in Trieste in 1965, I also took a trip to Frankfurt, Germany, and when I got off the train at the station, at the depot magazine stand the first thing I saw was an ordinary looking middle-aged businessman buying (you telepathed it!) a copy of PERRY RHODAN!

The PERRY RHODAN series may never win a Hugo. It *may* be panned by both professional critics and in the fan magazines, USA. But if Perry's American reception parallels that of the land of his origin, you are holding in your hands a collector's item that will be sought after by those who, like you, will be hooked on Perry and reading him ten years from now. Which means, if we can get production up to one a month, by 1979 about 130 Rhodan adventures will have been published—and the Germans will be 800 adventures ahead of us! (This could cause an increase in the USA in the studying of German.)

Can we ever catch up with Perry Rhodan? Well, there's no time like the present—and no place like this pocketbook —to start. Ahead lie innumerable encounters with alien intelligences, robots, invisible men, monsters, survivors of Atlantis, zombies, giants, micro-men—all part and parcel of the infinite panorama of the most colossal space opera series ever conceived!

# ENTERPRISE STARDUST

## CHAPTER ONE

At the northern entrance to the center's main underground building, the heavily armed sentries saluted sloppily. Lieutenant General Lesley Pounder, commander of the Nevada Fields Air Base and Chief of the Department of Space Explorations, passed them by, satisfied. Under unusual circumstances like these, he was not greatly concerned with being given an exact military salute. He was interested only in seeing that his men were alert and on the job.

At precisely 1:15 A.M., according to plan, Pounder entered the main control room in the center. With him were Colonel Maurice, chief of staff, and F. Lehmann, scientific supervisor of the project. Lehmann was known primarily for his position as Director of the California Academy of Space Technology.

Pandemonium seemed master inside the center's main building, which housed the electronic "nervous system" of the spaceport; but this apparently senseless commotion was, in fact, a series of last minute preparations for Zero Hour. The general's sudden appearance caused no interruption in the beehive activity of checking, and double checking. The general had arrived; that was all there was to it.

General Pounder, square of body and mind, was well-known for his uncompromising talent for getting things done *his* way. This was cause enough for the admiration of his colleagues and the dismay of those in the Capitol in Washington. Now he proceeded to the control room's huge closed circuit TV screen.

A view that had not been clearly discernible in the press room glistened here at close range on the slightly convex glass of the tube.

Pounder leaned heavily forward with both hands on the back of the swivel chair, motionless, staring intently at the screen. He remained like this for several moments. Professor Lehmann nervously fingered his rimless spectacles. He was boiling inside with impatience. Here the Big Boss was reinspecting all the unimportant little details that had been checked out repeatedly before his arrival, when there were far more urgent things to attend to. He shot imploring glances in General Pounder's direction.

Colonel Maurice shrugged his shoulders almost imperceptibly in a wait-and-see gesture. Pounder was as well informed as any of the team of esteemed scientists, but he obviously still had a few questions that bothered him.

"Beautiful! Breathtakingly beautiful and overpowering," Pounder murmured, gazing at the big video screen. "Something inside me persists in asking if we might not be going too far. The experts in the department still consider it madness to risk a blast-off here from Earth. Not only must we overcome atmospheric resistance, but in addition we must struggle to attain a speed we could have achieved naturally had we departed from a space station."

"You're referring to the orbital velocity of our manned space station, sir," added Professor Lehmann hastily. "That is not the determining factor in this case. If you will only consider the tremendous problems that would present themselves if we should try to assemble prefabricated parts in empty space under zero gravity conditions. . . . Experience along these lines has proved very unsatisfactory. It is easier by far to construct a spaceship here on Earth than to do so some 1100 miles above the surface. Why, the savings amount to more than 350 million dollars per unit!"

"They found your statistics very impressive in Washington," said the general with sarcasm. "Well, it's too late to change anything now. Let us hope that the splendid results of our trial run justify today's effort. Professor, my four best people are going to be on board that ship. If anything goes wrong, you won't hear the last of it."

Lehmann changed color under the general's icy stare.

Colonel Maurice was a cunning strategist at handling the ball tossed eternally between the warring fronts of "scientific concerns" and "military interests." Now he steered the conversation away from such unpleasant possibilities with his usual suave diplomatic skill. "Sir, may I remind you of our press conference? Our foremost reporters are no doubt awaiting you most anxiously. I've passed out no further information."

Pounder suddenly raged like a mad dog. "Is this really necessary, Maurice? I have other things to worry about."

The colonel smoothly eluded him. "Sir, I would strongly advise—"

The astrophysician, Dr. Fleet, shielding his mouth with his hand, coughed spasmodically. He was responsible for the affairs of space medicine and therefore for keeping the test pilots in perfect health.

Pounder smiled abruptly. "All right then, let's go. But only by way of the video intercommunications system."

The disaster, Maurice felt, had grown even worse. The technicians who were standing around suppressed a grin. Wasn't it just like the old man?

"Sir, for heaven's sake! The people expect your appearance in person. I promised them!"

"Then unpromise them," returned Pounder, unimpressed. "Which one of these speakers shall I use? Make the announcement, Maurice."

The chief of staff implored him, "Sir, they'll make mincemeat out of us in their editorials. You know that."

"I'll keep these guys under lock and key until they've cooled off again. We'll see. Switch on, please."

In the sparsely furnished observation bunker, the loudspeakers came to life. Pounder's face appeared on a TV screen. He greeted them with a sickeningly sweet smile and, "A beautiful good morning to you, gentlemen!" (It was shortly after midnight, local time.) Then the general became more matter-of-fact. He overlooked the grim faces of the reporters.

Very briefly, in a tone more appropriate to the reading of a recipe for chocolate cake, he said, "Gentlemen, what you've been seeing on the screen in your bunkers for the last few minutes is the familiar three stage rocket, in which, however, individual units have undergone considerable innovation. The final preparations are under way, and blastoff will follow in approximately three hours. The four test pilots are still asleep. They will not be awakened until two hours before blast-off."

So far, the reporters remained uninspired. Manned space flights were no longer a rarity. His eyes narrowing somewhat at the thought, Pounder enjoyed dealing his trump card in a startling manner.

"In view of past experience, the Space Explorations Command has renounced assembling the spaceship in orbit. The difficulties and failures of our earlier attempts are well-known. Therefore, the first rocket to land on the moon will be launched from Nevada Fields. The ship's name is *Stardust*. The commander of the first lunar landing expedition is Major Perry Rhodan, thirty-five years old, test pilot for the space force, nuclear physicist with a subsidiary specialty in ion reaction engines. You will recall Major Rhodan as the first astronaut to circumnavigate the moon under the auspices of the space force."

Pounder was silent again. He noted with satisfaction the uproar of voices that gave proof of a very high degree of excitement.

Someone shouted for silence, and it became quiet again in the bare room.

"Many thanks," said the general with a polite cough. "You were a bit noisy. No—please, no questions now. My information officer will see to your questions immediately after blast-off. At the moment, I can give you only very brief hints. My time is limited. The *Stardust* will be launched with a select four man team. In addition to Major Rhodan, Captain Reginald Bell, Captain Clark G. Fletcher, and Lieutenant Eric Manoli will participate in the expedition. You are no doubt familiar with all these names. We have here a special military scientific team. Each test pilot has a degree in at least two additional fields, and these men are among the greatest experts in the western world. It is what we call a complementary team. They are adjusted to each other psychologically and in the coordinated employment of their diverse specialties. For them, space has become a home away from home. Photographs and fact sheets concerning the astronauts may also be obtained from the information officer."

General Pounder seemed unwilling to favor his audience with a longer speech. He was already glancing at his watch. Rudely interrupting the noise, he said, "Please, gentlemen, your inquiries are fruitless. All I can give you are basic facts. The *Stardust* has been equipped for a four week stay on the moon. We have designated a research program for the landing team. After the successful remote controlled landings of unmanned space probes, today we risk the lives of four men in the attempt. Let us hope that we have made no mistakes. You know, of course, that this Earthbound launch will devour a huge sum of energy, particularly since the final stage must land on and lift off again from the surface of the moon, under its own power. With our conventional engines, this would not have been possible for a three stage ship of relatively limited dimensions."

"Technical data!" someone shouted excitedly into the microphone.

"You will get your data," growled the general. "The full length of the ship is 275 feet—the first stage being 109.5 feet, the second 74.5 feet, and the third, the spaceship proper, 91 feet. Starting weight, with full tanks and the payload, will be about 6,850 tons. Nevertheless, the moon rocket looks hardly larger than an ordinary supply ship. The reason for this? Only the first stage runs on liquid chemical fuel. Stages two and three are, for the first time, operating with nuclear power."

That was Pounder's second bombshell. He had let it drop quite unexpectedly. Undaunted, he continued, "You will receive further data shortly. Gentlemen, the *Stardust* will blast off at three o'clock. It will land near the New-comb Crater, close to the lunar South Pole. We are interested in finding out something of the dark side of the moon; but owing to the limitations of radio communication, we must remain with one foot (so to speak) on the near side of Luna. Radio waves unfortunately require a direct line of vision in space. Our four men will nevertheless undertake extensive ground travel on the lunar surface with a new kind of exploratory vehicle. That is all, gentlemen. Further information, particularly technical data, will be released by the information officer, following the launch."

General Pounder laughed grimly as he interrupted the audio-video connection with the quick flip of a switch. The babel of voices from the loudspeaker ceased abruptly.

Now all eyes were on the chief. Pounder had spoken with such calm and confidence that one might have thought that hundreds of ships had landed on the moon before the *Stardust*. Yet no one knew better than Pounder himself that the optimism he had demonstrated was entirely unfounded.

He glanced at his watch. It was countdown hour forty-eight, 19 June.

His voice sounded somewhat less excited now as he said, "Dr. Fleet, would you please awaken the men."

At exactly one o'clock, Dr. Fleet stood before the four sleeping men. For the last fourteen hours they had been resting under the effects of psychochemical narcosis. It was the only means by which mind *and* body, particularly mind, were afforded total relaxation. A mind encumbered by worry and anticipation, even in sleep, would be most undesirable.

For a few moments, with a feeling of undefinable pity, he hesitated. Then he administered the antidote. With this, consciousness would return; with this, thought would be reborn; and with this, all those things which one had sought, with greatest effort, to ward off would return to haunt the men.

A sleepy and irritable, physically and mentally restless astronaut would be of little benefit here, as partner to soulless computer and nuclear reactor, both running at full tilt. The human mind would have to remain clear, because in the long run, it alone would have to be master of the situation.

Dr. Fleet was waiting. Beside him, with bated breath, stood the men of his medical team. Of course, there still remained the usual tests and examinations. These would take approximately an hour. The last hour, then, would belong to the systems engineers. The astronauts would be permitted to board the *Stardust* a mere ten minutes before blast-off. Once within the command center, they would have nothing to do but stretch out on their contour couches with the least possible effort, excluding any mental strain.

Once the launch had begun, however, any relaxation would be totally out of the question. Everything would follow in rapid succession. Then would begin the ultimate test, which would strain mind and body to the limits of endurance. Then would begin their torture in the narrow body of this roaring monster of molybdenum steel and synthetic fibers.

A gentle light haloed the four flat couches. Millions of pores in their foam rubber mattresses inhaled and exhaled like the alveoli of lungs. These were the last comforts for men who soon would have to endure horrendous stress.

Major Perry Rhodan, ace astronaut of the United States Space Force, opened his eyes. Instantly, almost without transition, his sleep became a state of acute wakefulness.

"You've treated me first?" he asked. It was less an inquiry than a statement. With delight Dr. Fleet observed the commander's ready reflexes. Without a doubt, Rhodan was "all there."

"Exactly as planned, young man," he confirmed softly.

Deliberately, breathing very deeply, the test pilot sat up. Someone removed the thin blanket that seemed itself to breathe. Rhodan wore a loose cut hospital gown that spared his resting body any constricting limitation.

"If I had gorgeous gams like you, Doc," said Rhodan with dry humor, "I might perhaps go along with this masquerade." There was a bright twinkle in his eyes. All the same, his lean and narrow face remained almost devoid of expression.

This mumbled curse upon the nonsense and bother of the "mummery" provoked the first grin on the lips of the men. Offering a catharsis of sorts, it had a magical effect in this somehow unreal situation.

The sound of hollow, stentorian breathing made Rhodan turn his head. Fascinated, he watched the waking-up exercises of his "problem child," who, like him, had already circumnavigated the moon. It remained still a mystery to Perry Rhodan how this chubby faced giant, this paradox with the tender skin of a newborn baby and the dishpan hands of a care worn washerwoman, could squeeze into a narrow space capsule.

Captain Clark G. Fletcher, the crew's navigator, was a specialist in astronomy and mathematics, with a secondary interest in physics. He awoke with a display of noise worthy of a mammoth.

"Has my baby arrived yet?" Fletcher's voice roared at once. The imminent blast-off was obviously of far less concern to him. "How about it, Doc? What do you hear from my wife? Have you been looking after her?"

Dr. Fleet sighed in exasperation.

"Listen, son. You have at least another three months to

wait. I can't help it if you believe your wife is an anatomical wonder. But if you ask me one more time—"

"It *could* have happened, couldn't it?" interrupted the giant with the boy's beardless face. "The index of variability for a mathematically unstable structure like the human organism is almost infinite in range. Why, all manner of— That means I'll just have to wait?"

With a wave of soft laughter, the third man on the team indicated that he too had awakened.

Lieutenant Eric Manoli, physician as well as geologist, was the least conspicuous man of the team. He was probably also the most relaxed and most emotionally stable.

He greeted them wordlessly. His glance flew to the clock. Of course, Dr. Manoli would observe the astronaut's most holy unwritten law, which stated clearly and concisely, "Thou shalt never discuss the blast-off, except when absolutely necessary. You have slept, that mind and body may rest undisturbed. Do not defeat the purpose by believing it necessary to occupy yourself immediately with the seriousness of the matter."

It was a simple formula that had proved highly effective.

"Everything all right, Eric?" inquired Rhodan. "I see by your enormous growth of beard that your whiskers have been awake all the time."

"I inherited it from my Italian ancestors," said Manoli, rubbing the black stubble that had appeared on his cheeks during the hibernation. Then he continued, "What is the matter with Reg? He sleeps the sleep of the dead, it seems."

Captain Fletcher swung around on the couch. His right hand landed with a loud slap on the well upholstered shoulders of the fourth crew member, a short, heavyset man obviously inclined toward a pot belly.

Those who knew Captain Reginald Bell would have likened him to an incredibly elastic rubber ball. His apparently plentiful adipose tissue would deceive the simple minded. Indeed, Bell had withstood the eighteen G's in the giant centrifuge far better than the short and sinewy Manoli.

"Idiot!" Bell hissed from among the foam rubber cushions. A broad expanse of face, densely populated by freckles, peered out from under the covers. Squinting in Fletcher's direction were a pair of pale blue eyes almost devoid of color.

"I've been wide awake for the last hour," Bell insisted nonchalantly. "The sedative dose was, of course, too weak for a man of my caliber."

"Why, of course," agreed Rhodan, with a straight face. Reg seemed to wither under his gaze. "I admire your consideration. You must have been breathing less than Tutankhamen, just to keep from disturbing us."

"You'll get a medal for that," Fletcher piped up. Snorting and grunting, he rolled his weighty bulk off the flat couch. "But expectant fathers and other wretches have their turn first," he added with emphasis. "I'd still like to know, what real need there is for them to examine us again."

Fletcher suddenly fell silent. With some embarrassment, he looked across at the commander. He had almost broken the unspoken edict.

Rhodan, however, acted as though he had heard nothing. Yawning with studied indifference, he said, "Begin with the baby, Doc. Our circulatory systems should probably be in perfect working order, but please keep the neutralization shots handy anyway."

Perry Rhodan began to consider his own reactions. He too felt a gnawing unrest in the deepest reaches of his unconscious mind. The senseless chatter of the men was obviously a psychological gambit, a displacement activity to relieve their anxiety.

*For heaven's sake, don't say a word about the blast-off!* It was sure to overwhelm them soon enough, Rhodan was quite certain.

Riding on the roaring gas jets of a nuclear powered, chemical fueled rocket would very likely be indistinguishable from blasting off in an ordinary ship, at least where the subsequent moments of G pressure were concerned. Yet the real pressures would make themselves felt in those depths of the mind which were almost beyond one's control.

The men were afraid. Of course they were—no one had ever denied it. But these men could overcome their fear. That was all that mattered.

Rhodan made a keen but inconspicuous observation of his men. They all seemed well enough. Clark Fletcher was perhaps a bit too restless. He thought too often of the expected baby. If Perry Rhodan could have his way, they would leave Fletcher behind this time. But the team, so carefully coordinated, could not be dismembered. An unknown astronaut could not replace Fletcher successfully, for he would not be assimilated into their Gestalt.

Rhodan had there, with resignation, accepted the unavoidable. Otherwise, he could find no grounds for negative appraisal.

## CHAPTER TWO

The contour couches were masterpieces of engineering. Hydropneumatically controlled, with autogyros that balanced out the slightest shift in weight, they could not have been more comfortable or luxurious.

When the first manned space capsule was designed, great emphasis had been placed on bedding down the astronauts in their couches while they were fully attired in weighty and cumbersome space suits. Then, as now, the men were forced by safety regulations to wear even the pressurized helmets with their transparent visors during blast-off.

Of course, small injuries sometimes occurred as the result of high G forces during acceleration. The most tragic instance had occurred when the first orbital space station was being constructed. An improperly fitted space helmet had caused a broken neck when a ship's acceleration had mounted up to 11.3 G's.

Perry Rhodan had never worn a spacesuit during blast-off. This was his special privilege, which he had also extended to his crew. The technicians, however, still considered this unnecessarily risky. With the least tear in the ship's outer shell, an explosive decompression and the consequent creation of a vacuum in the cabin were bound to result. They knew only too well how quickly blood could be brought to a boil under such conditions.

Yet Rhodan had harvested a run of good luck. His ships had never been struck by meteors or torn by engineering stresses while lifting off.

The four men were lying on their contour couches, dressed

17

only in their tight blue uniforms. The spacesuits were hanging on hooks nearby, ready for use at a moment's notice. Rhodan had spared his team a most painful additional strain and certainly the unavoidable pressure sores and bruises.

The last series of control checks was being completed. Far below them, some eighty yards away, the technicians finally withdrew, satisfied with the durability of the stabilizer fins on the first stage.

Captain Bell, electronics technician and specialist in ion reaction engines, needed more time to take stock of his instruments than Rhodan would need in checking out the autopilot ignition and the remote control guidance system.

Fletcher and Manoli were seated behind the two main couches. For the moment, they had nothing to do. The cabin was necessarily very narrow and webbed with countless cables, rubber pipes and flush instrument panels. Everything had been custom built and made to specification. Below the command center were the small living quarters, with their own kitchenette and bath. More space could not be provided the astronauts. Both these rooms lay close beneath the nose cone of the rocket.

Under the cabin and recreation area there was the storeroom, its provisions stocked with utmost care. The men could not approach the remaining section of the rocket. Isolated in the next level were the tanks of liquid hydrogen. Then, pumps and additional pipelines crowded a chamber whose heavy steel alloy walls shielded them from radioactivity. This marked the end of the "safe" zone. Beyond it, there were only the high speed plutonium reactor, needed for the production of power, and the great cavern of the combustion chamber, with all its high pressure valves and thermo-pipe conduits and cooling systems. Here the hydrogen, now volatilized, was brought to expansion.

The minute hand of the chronometer leaped forward to the next number. It was 3:01. The blast-off was scheduled for exactly 3:02.

Rhodan turned his head. He did this with difficulty, now that the foam rubber cushions of his couch had swallowed him up. "Everything okay?" he inquired.

The crew answered with smiles. They were all listening now to the monotonous voice that announced the last minute of the countdown: "Zero minus sixty seconds." For a few moments, they lavished mental ridicule upon this eerie nasal litany. They had gone through this many times, and each time it bored them.

Now, however, even that had changed. It was a nightmare to know that the nuclear reactor was only yards beneath their feet.

"Eighteen . . . seventeen . . . sixteen . . . fifteen. . . ."

Rhodan pulled the microphone closer to his mouth.

"Final report. *Stardust* to center." His voice boomed over the loudspeakers. It could be heard everywhere in Nevada Fields, even in the isolated press bunkers.

"All A-okay on board. Next report to follow after ejection of first stage."

". . . three . . . two . . . one . . . zero. . . . Ignition . . . lift-off!"

Things were as they had been each time before. They found that the hull of a spaceship was, despite all efforts at soundproofing, like a sensitive echo chamber. Their ears rang, their whole bodies vibrating like violin strings.

White flickering tongues of flame devoured the darkness of night. With split second timing, the *Stardust* began to lift off. The slow, majestic ascent was followed by a sudden jolt and a frightening spectacle, as the third stage began to wobble to and fro. This was the single most dangerous moment during the blast-off of a large rocket. The autopilot struggled against the powerful engines to stabilize the ship, which had barely started to ascend. The shouts and exclamations of the reporters were drowned out by the noise from this battle. It seemed like the end of the world. In sheer magnitude of uproar, only Hiroshima could have equaled this gigantic tumult. Not even within the soundproof bunker could men hear one another speak. Those not wearing acoustic earphones were sentenced, in this moment, to total deafness. Lips were moving, hands were fluttering, but not a word was understood. Every gesture told a tale of utmost worry and concern.

Then, at last, the *Stardust* began its flight. With the passing of these brief moments of unendurable stasis, the titan surged up suddenly, urgently, as if returning to its natural element.

Prodigious in its production of noise, the *Stardust* rose up into the blood hued sky of evening.

Moments later, the ship could be seen on camera as a fireball glowing white. Vertically, now in perfect balance, it roared skyward until only its flaming exhaust could be detected, and then as a weak pinpoint of light, which finally disappeared into a cloudless starry sky.

Only a few clicks could be heard over the intercom system. Pounder's face appeared on the video screens. He made the routine announcement. "The *Stardust* was launched at 3:02 A.M., Pacific Standard Time, according to plan. No irregularities were noted. Later, you will be able to overhear the astronauts reporting from space. The separation of stage one will follow shortly, when acceleration approaches 9.3 G's. According to our calculation, the *Stardust* will come within the range of the space station within three minutes. Afterward, you will once more be able to see the ship clearly and to follow the separation of the second stage. Now, I would like to draw your attention to the fact that no one is permitted to leave the Nevada Fields area until the *Stardust* has landed safely on the moon. This time we are planning a surprise. That is all. Thank you, gentlemen."

General Pounder finished with a smile.

"Five seconds to first stage separation," the voice of a technician droned over the loudspeakers in the control room. "No deviation from course. Everything proceeding as planned. Two . . . one . . . contact."

The electronic autopilot computers switched over with incredible precision. No one moved: no one even lifted a finger. On one side of the room were the engineers, with goggling eyes and nerves on edge, and on the other, in contrast, the newsmen waited with stoic composure.

From the loudspeakers, there issued the signal that acknowledged the completed separation. Now two separate blips were seen on the radar observation screen. Remote control took over the landing of the cast off section of the rocket, the booster stage.

The subsequent interval of recovery gave the crew of the *Stardust* eight seconds. The electronic brain was already preparing the procedure for the acceleration of the second stage.

Perry Rhodan's voice was calm but perhaps a bit choked. "Rhodan speaking. No deviation. Vibration within normal limits. Crew is ready for the ignition of stage two."

He did not have to say anything more. This was enough for the scientists and supervisors in the ground stations on Earth. The *Stardust* was racing through space.

Rhodan glanced quickly around the cabin. Reginald Bell was all right, and neither Fletcher nor Manoli seemed to have suffered from the 9.3 G's. Now it was time for the reactor to do its part in adding thrust to the second stage. Rhodan could feel the moisture in his palms. With senses as keen as an animal's, he waited; but he heard nothing out of the ordinary. For a few moments, all had become quiet.

A sudden jolt came next. This was accompanied by a howl that seemed to penetrate every single molecule of the ship and its crew. Once again, the broad hull of this vessel had become an echo chamber.

Immediately thereafter, the acceleration increased to eight G's. So far, no means had been devised to lessen the ordeal to follow.

Rhodan could feel the drugs working on his circulatory system. His body was still holding out against the stress, but breathing was an agony. Unable to move a muscle, he stared heavy-lidded at the video control panel suspended close above his head.

It seemed an eternity before the G pressures were reduced once more to the normal value of one gravity. It was a brief respite for the crew, a momentary interlude, lasting approximately seven seconds, which had been exactly calculated to take the best advantage of the efficiency of the power plant.

Rhodan croaked his customary "Everything okay!" into the microphone. His eyes responded to the bright symbols flashing by his face, but he no longer understood their meaning. Then came the second interval, for the further acceleration of stage two.

Three seconds later, they had exceeded escape velocity. Once the speed of twelve miles per second had been attained, the separation of the second stage followed so abruptly that the zero gravity it produced had the effect of a sledgehammer blow.

The men felt themselves pulled upward, and their bodies strained mightily against the broad straps of their contour couches.

For a few seconds, Rhodan lost consciousness. When he opened his eyes again, the red glow in front of his eyes had subsided. They were already well along in free flight, with speed undiminished. By that time, the *Stardust* had passed beyond the orbit of the space station and was drifting, as though suspended in a fluid medium, some 2,000 miles above the surface of Earth.

Now they had a short time to recover. Theoretically, the present velocity of the ship would suffice to free them from the attraction of Earth's gravity. Theoretically, without any additional propulsion, they could travel to any point in the universe.

But the distance was great between theory and practice. Although they had overcome her gravitational pull, Earth insisted on making her presence known by restraining the flight of the spaceship.

Furthermore, it was not enough simply to continue straight through in this trajectory. One still had to perform a great many maneuvers for which data had not yet been computed in every detail. They would have to calculate and compensate for the smallest deviation from course.

Rhodan's contour couch doubled up to form a softly upholstered chair. The instrument panel adjusted itself to a new position. Now it was hanging in front of him, rather than above his head, and he welcomed the change.

With a volley of Anglo-Saxon phrases rarely in evidence in polite society, Reginald Bell recovered. Captain Fletcher opened his eyes with a hoarse cough. There were flecks of blood at the corners of his mouth.

Rhodan shook his head. "This was tough, much tougher than before. During the last few seconds, they must have taken us as high as 15.4 G's. We were thundering through the dangerous Van Allen belt at that acceleration. . . . Fletch! What's the matter with you? What's wrong, boy?"

Clark G. Fletcher had gone pale. The ruddy glow of his chubby cheeks had faded away altogether. Had it not been for the luster of his straw-blond hair, Rhodan might not have recognized his ghastly, waxen face.

Fletcher drew his lips together with a grimace and

22

moaned, "Damn! If I'm going to pull any more stunts like that, I might as well get off right now. I still had the tip of my tongue between my teeth while we were at seven G's! What foolishness! I'm telling you, isn't that idiotic? The first thing they teach every student of the academy is, by all means, to refrain from such impulses. And *me,* of all people!"

He concluded with a shrug of his shoulders, his face drawn in pain. Rhodan looked at him questioningly from behind a masklike smile.

Bell's magnetic soles clamped onto the foil beneath their feet. Swaying from side to side, he was struggling to regain his balance. As long as the engines of the *Stardust* were silent, they were still in zero gravity. It was fascinating to watch him walk, or try to walk. With each step, he would lift his boots up with great difficulty and then let them fall heavily onto the floor. Without a word, Bell plodded heavily across the cabin to Dr. Manoli.

After a quick check of Manoli's pulse, he was nodding with relief.

"He's okay," he said briefly. "His pulse is right back again, regular as clockwork." Moving to Fletcher, he said, "Show me your tongue, Fletch. Go on, open your mouth." Glistening, livid droplets of blood rolled out. Rhodan had seen enough. This was a matter for Dr. Manoli.

The commander turned the volume regulator toward the right, and confused noises on the radio finally became clear again. Meanwhile, Dr. Manoli had revived.

Rhodan heard the low hiss of the hydropneumatic valves. Manoli's couch changed into a chair. In a moment, he was standing beside Fletcher.

The men lost time in vain debate. Manoli knew that the commander was only awaiting his professional opinion.

"It could have been worse," came his diagnosis. "Luckily, you didn't bite it through completely. I'll need ten minutes. Twelve would be better. Is that possible, Perry?"

"Fair enough. Reg, take the latest values from computer central and transfer them onto magnetic tape. I want a controlled calculation. We'll postpone everything for twelve minutes. When you're finished, let me know the result. We should be able to compensate for the loss with about four seconds of full thrust."

Some seconds later, Rhodan's face appeared on the ground station's giant video screens. Pounder, waiting nervous and restless by the microphone, breathed a sigh of relief.

"*Stardust* to Nevada Fields," Rhodan's voice rang out loud and strong and completely clear. "Captain Fletcher has sustained slight injury—bit his tongue. Manoli is stopping the bleeding. The wound can be healed quickly with plasma concentrate, if you can permit us a twelve minute delay. Over."

Pounder rose to his full height. A glance toward Professor Lehmann said everything that needed saying under the circumstances. The scientist nodded briefly in reply. It was possible. One always made allowance for such eventualities here at Nevada Fields.

The electronic brain began to work. The corrections were available instants later. These were automatically transmitted to the *Stardust* by way of special relay transmitters.

The diagram lit up in front of Reginald Bell. The smaller but highly efficient computers aboard the *Stardust* itself acknowledged receipt of the signal. A multitude of most carefully calculated previous figures was simultaneously discarded. New data raced into space in the guise of UHF radio impulses. In a moment, a grand plan was overthrown and replaced by entirely new measures.

Bell's fingertips tapped the data into the keyboard. Rhodan gave the usual routine report on altitude, radiation, temperature, cabin pressure and the health of his team.

Manoli had need of only eleven minutes. By then, Fletcher was perfectly all right again. His lacerated tongue had been carefully and almost invisibly mended.

Fletcher looked around awkwardly, his eyes full of naive embarrassment.

"This time, try your thumb, chum," said Rhodan, with a trace of a grin. "It can stand a lot more than your tongue."

Their seats tilted back again. Shortly afterward, they heard the roar of that machine whose function they still regarded with mixed emotions. They listened with an amalgam of instinctive fear, expectations of high esteem and a curiosity that gnawed at their nerves.

It was, of course, the nuclear chemical power plant,

which had performed so admirably during the operation of the second stage.

Once again, there came the rumble and the jolt. This time, however, the G's increased to only 2.1, causing neither Rhodan nor the others any particular discomfort. On fiery jets of gaseous hydrogen, the *Stardust* plunged into the vacuum of the universe.

But now that the initial difficulties of a space launch had been overcome, the real challenges of manned space-flight became apparent and would have to be mastered.

Rhodan was lulled by the nuclear powered engine's roar, which had now become an even hum. The void close below the cylindrical stern of the ship held an ice blue incandescence. There, liquid oxygen, heated by atomic power, burst forth with tremendous pressure in the combustion chamber.

The radioactive elements in the reactor would last for at least a year, but the liquid hydrogen and oxygen had to be handled with greater economy. Their supply was limited. Once the tanks were empty and there was nothing more to be released, even the most efficient power plant was condemned to total impotence.

Breathing heavily, Rhodan lay resting on his contour couch. While he submitted his short reports to the control center on Earth at carefully timed intervals, he thought fleetingly of the nuclear reactor, so wonderful and yet still so primitive.

For now, they would still require the intervention of the atomic pile, in order to achieve the necessary thrust. But if they should one day posses a *pure* nuclear reactor, a mighty engine permitting velocities close to the speed of light . . . !

Rhodan moved his lips with effort. He felt like laughing bitterly. Reginald Bell also seemed to occupy himself with similar thoughts. In a moment, he whispered heavily to Rhodan, "Heroes in fiction have it so much easier. They don't have our problems with sudden acceleration, and they never bite their own tongues! Fletch, how are you? Do you feel all right? It'll be only a few more minutes. For about five seconds, we may go up as high as 8.4 G's. Okay?"

"Okay," grunted the giant, by way of the intercom system. His breath could be heard rattling in their close headsets. "Everything A-okay. Good lord, we're on our way! Up, up and away with four men. One of these days I'll be telling my son all about it. Listening to me, his eyes will be as round and shiny as polished marbles."

Fletcher was exhausted. A rugged body and a lot of practice were needed if one wished to speak clearly under the force of two G's. These men could do it. Only Dr. Manoli ignored the opportunity. Instead, he gave an indication of his emotions with a meek smile.

Yes, they were on their way. The blast-off was practically behind them now. The cruel but unavoidable stresses were almost over and done with. What still remained was more a matter for reason and instant reflex. They watched Earth recede into the background. Earth, that swollen blue green globe with all its vast array of oceans, continents, and cloud shrouded mountains, not to mention its billions of human inhabitants.

They could easily experience feelings of godly exaltation and a lofty detachment from Earthbound existence.

Rhodan alone, his mind ever wary, did not participate in this chaos of sensations. No one saw the skeptical cast to his gray eyes. They were not there yet. Not yet had they landed, and not yet had they begun the voyage home. This enterprise was not just some relatively innocuous circumnavigation of the moon. No, here they were to face an incredibly difficult lunar landing. They were destined to be the first men ever to set foot on the moon.

## CHAPTER THREE

This time even Perry Rhodan had been cautious. The counterthrust applied throughout the braking maneuver had momentarily increased G pressures to an unnerving degree. The *Stardust* had fallen into orbit around the moon with a speed of approximately two miles per second. Only then had he given the order to put on spacesuits.

The men had carried out his instructions without comment. While the *Stardust* was being drawn into ever-narrowing orbits around Luna, in obedience to the space station's computerized remote control guidance system, they had donned the ultramodern protective suits. These garments were relatively light and yet quite monstrous looking, being fully pressurized and hermetically sealed, each with its own power pack, air conditioning, oxygen supply, and so on. The transparent helmets were even bulletproof, made from an artificial alloy as hard as steel.

Next Rhodan had insisted that they close their helmets. Only the valves on either side remained open, so that the men could still breathe the usual air of the cabin. The built-in aerostat would automatically seal the valves in an instant, should pressure drop below normal.

Thus had Rhodan done all he could to reduce to a minimum the chances of an accident.

The *Stardust* was flying with stern forward, permitting the jets to bring their thrust against the direction of flight. The trajectory of orbit was from pole to pole; consequently, when the ship sank beyond the line of sight in its path across the other side of the moon, it disappeared from within range of remote control, since radio signals from the ground stations on Earth could no longer reach the *Stardust*. Once the ship was within the shadow of the moon, therefore, the autopilot on board the rocket assumed control of their flight, which would lead, after a fifth ellipse, to a landing on the lunar surface.

The braking process continued as the fifth orbit began. On the visible face of Earth's only satellite, the sun had risen on one of the long lunar days. Six percent of the opposite hemisphere already lay in deepest darkness.

Only on the radar screen could a clear picture of the torn surface be obtained. The dark side of the moon was in all ways indistinguishable from the familiar bright side, but this had long been known. The moon held no more mystery in that respect.

Once again they emerged from the cone of darkness in the wake of the moon. Their altitude was approximately fifty-five miles, their velocity reduced by brief braking counterthrusts to a speed of 1.4 miles per second.

The autopilot announced with a shrill whistle that the powerful directional beam from the space station had locked onto the ship again, and the central computers aboard the *Stardust* received new instructions in the form of the latest calculations.

The rocket was visible on the screen as a green dot

floating along one of the prescribed lines representing the landing orbit. The end of this line was close to the lunar south pole, just beyond the Newcomb crater. A red circle indicated the landing site, a flat, apparently rock strewn surface that offered the safest place to set down the rocket.

The crew could hear the voice of the project chief as clearly as they heard the autopilot registering the guidance impulses. There were short intervals between the reports, for ultrawaves, though traveling at the speed of light, still needed some time to span the tremendous distance.

Still flying at relatively high speed, the *Stardust* arrived above the western "shore" of the Mare Nubium. Immediately ahead, the big Walter crater appeared. It was not very far from the landing site.

"Ground control, General Pounder speaking." The voice came over the loudspeaker amid the crackling of static. "You will reach the turning point in seventy-two seconds. We will time the impulse taking into consideration the distance the radio waves will have to cover. We're switching off, in the meantime, in order to avoid any disturbances. We have you clear on our radar screens. Reception is very good; hardly any interference. Primary remote control autopilot starting operations. We'll set you down safely. Begin release of your landing supports. Contact me immediately upon landing. Until you touch down on the moon, we wish you all the luck."

Rhodan pulled a lever. The four telescoping landing supports of the *Stardust* thrust out, moving away from the ship's hull at an angle of forty-five degrees. The hydraulic system extended the long tubular structures farther and farther outward. At the outermost end of each, there unfolded a flat contact disk with a surface area of four square yards.

When the critical point in orbit had been reached, the *Stardust* was still on the flight line. They had compensated for even the smallest deviations in course.

"Everything ready?" Bell's voice sounded strained. "Contact. Forward." He could hear the heavy breathing of the other men. Almost everything hinged on this moment when their future hung in the balance.

Suddenly, without prior warning, a sound shrieked out

28

of the autopilot monitor. The impulse had arrived, punctual to a split second.

The engines roared in a brief but violent counterthrust that decreased the remaining speed of the ship by another fifty percent, and subjected the men to a force of twelve G's.

When this had passed, an interval for the correction of previous calculations took place. Lungs heaving, they began to breathe again. At the next braking thrust would come the sixty degree rotation in orbit. Then the retro rockets would have to be positioned exactly perpendicular to the lunar surface.

Following these operations, the ship would hover above the point of landing and descend on its own exhaust with a speed of twelve feet per second.

Lightning quick, the various data raced through Rhodan's head. All had sounded so simple, so infallible. But now that he lay in this fragile structure, his mind seized the problems and perils with utmost piercing clarity.

The *Stardust* began its descent in a flat parabola. When the gravitational pull of the moon had grown strongly apparent, it was high time for the turnabout maneuver, when the jets from the combustion chamber would have to be turned from their horizontal position and aimed at the ground.

"Three seconds to go," called Bell in a choked voice. "Two . . . one . . . contact!"

Contact followed. With it came such an incredible screeching and howling that it seemed as though a 1,000 kilowatt broadcast station were standing beside the rocket, beaming its full energy directly at them.

The sounds broke out of the control loudspeakers in a veritable flood. Deafening noise and ultrasonic whistling assaulted the ears of the startled men. For a fraction of a second, Reginald Bell looked totally devoid of sensibility, his broad face contorted in a grimace full of pain and panic.

Rhodan had stopped short, completely immobile. When he had overcome his initial surprise, however, he reacted with astonishing swiftness. His right hand slammed down on the emergency lever. Magnetic straps closed shut to imprison the men in their seats.

No one could avoid hearing the shrill warning signal from the autopilot. The *Stardust's* electronic brain reported the disturbance. Flickering lamps gave proof that the impulse they had expected for the turnabout maneuver had not got through to them from the ground station. Even though the computer was denied the power of independent judgment, it had stated, with instantaneous reckoning, that this was cause for utmost alarm.

The diagrams were already lit up, having appeared automatically and without error. Reg glanced at them.

"Deviation!" he shouted, with a stampede of feelings. "No ignition impulse. We're falling beyond the landing site. Interference is preventing reception of the remote control signals! Where are these things coming from? They're only on our frequency. Perry!"

Rhodan abandoned any lengthy reflection. The surface of the moon, brightly illuminated by the rising sun, sped toward them. He did whatever a commander could, in such an instance.

With breathtaking speed, in an automatic reflex he switched off the main circuit built into the arm rest. The *Stardust* was thus beyond the range of the Earthbound remote control system.

An infernal caterwaul of the control instruments was cut off instantly, as if it had never existed.

A bell began to ring, and then a voice boomed through the cabin. It was the autopilot, speaking with a soulless voice prerecorded on tape.

"Central computer directing autopilot landing. Calculations are in progress. Completion. Landing initiated. Emergency signal QQRXQ has been sent with maximum intensity, via channel sixteen. Landing proceeding."

This was the message some technician had recorded on tape before the blast-off. He had neglected to mention that these cheerful plans for landing starkly ignored all safety measures.

Bringing the helpless ship down at all costs, regardless of consequences, was nothing short of an act of desperation. An impromptu resumption of the flight at this stage was impossible. The ground was already too near, the velocity of fall had increased to more than 1.2 miles per second and the necessary rotation would take too long. It was an emergency. It made no difference whether, under the flame fountains of the *Stardust*'s exhaust, there lay the charity of a flat plain or the cruel promise of a crater with its razor-edged eggshell jaws.

The engine howled. The rocket was violently whipped about by the realigned steering jets and brought abruptly into a vertical position. It fell with its face heavenward, its sharp nose pointed now into the dark and star-laden sky.

Whining gyros took over the stabilizing maneuvers. Someone shouted; no one knew who.

Rhodan no longer gave commands or issued instructions. It would have been senseless. There was nothing anyone could do for the necessary calculations and manipulations could be executed only by the computers. In such circumstances, a human brain was condemned to failure.

The men's eyes were fixed on the video screens. The exterior observation cameras disclosed the jagged walls of a crater. They were blinded by the most intense white heat below them, wherein was concentrated all the force and fury of the rocket's thrust.

Bell shouted something in the nature of a helpless croak. With the pressure of 16 G's, it was remarkable that he could still squeeze anything out of his throat.

Next they heard a roar and muffled explosions. Another jolt pressed them back into their couches. Several fittings broke loose with a loud clatter as the hull seemed to split in two. There followed, immediately afterward, a period of rattling and vibration. Yet before these ceased entirely, there suddenly came utter calm. A green lamp grew bright above Perry Rhodan. It no longer flickered but shone steadily.

The absolute silence was torn by shrill, hysterical laughter.

"Captain Fletcher!"

Rhodan's voice, though not loud, was as sharp as a knife. The cackling broke off with a piercing and unpleasant whine.

When Fletcher had again lapsed into silence, the hard lines in Rhodan's face relaxed. A mild expression appeared in the bright eyes of the ship's commander. "Easy, Fletch. It's all right."

His gaze fell once again upon the green lamp, whose light was so infinitely reassuring. Thus did the central auto-pilot computer give its wordless report. The rocket now stood on the surface, apparently hardly damaged.

Bell displayed a breathless grin. His reason seemed still unwilling to accept the facts for what they were. Dr. Manoli remained silent, as usual. In his pale face, only the coal black eyes seemed alive, and they held a question.

In a moment, Perry Rhodan would deal the men a trau-matic blow. They naturally expected some remark from him regarding the successful emergency landing, some sign that all was once again well. They waited for something, even if it was only a short sigh of relief after the agonizing ordeal of the last few minutes.

But Perry Rhodan reacted differently.

"Fletch, you'll have to determine the location and nature of this jamming station at once. You'll find the data on the magnetic tapes of the computer. Let's see how good a mathematician you are."

He had nothing more to add.

## CHAPTER FOUR

The slight, lively man with an oddly youthful face beneath a mighty bald dome was known as Allan D. Mercant. One could recognize him at once by his wreath of hair whose golden hue was interrupted so abruptly by the light silver white near his temples.

Allan D. Mercant was one of those gentle souls who, with a quiet feeling of joy, remove worms and other bugs from the garden path to avoid treading upon them. But that was the purely private aspect of Mercant's character.

As far as his profession was concerned, Mercant was the power behind the throne and a power to be reckoned with. He was identical with the almost omnipotent Chief of International Defense, who worked in closest collabora-tion with national defense and secret service organizations throughout the west. NATO had supervised the creation of the Division of International Defense, otherwise given official designation as the Security Intelligence Agency.

Mercant was thus answerable only to the high command of NATO.

When he entered the conference room, accompanied by an older gentleman, the murmur of low conversation subsided.

General Pounder, chief of Space Explorations Command, acquainted the people present with one another. This was a secret session on the sixteenth floor of the NASA building in Washington.

Allan D. Mercant began abruptly. Underneath a high vaulted forehead, his tanned and boyish face seemed friendly and exceedingly sympathetic.

He pointed to a pile of newspapers at a corner of the long conference table. "Gentlemen, we need no longer discuss the breaking of this news. I can understand, General, that you could not hold the reporters at Nevada Fields for all eternity. In any event, we have begun to receive quite a number of vocal protests, which Colonel Kaats has nevertheless been able to deal with satisfactorily."

The older man at his side nodded slowly, bemused. Kaats belonged to the Federal Bureau of Investigation, functioning also as a member of the President's special cabinet for internal security.

"Far more disquieting is the coverage in the newspapers and on television. According to their version, our *Stardust* is not only lost, but has crashed. They have, in part, given such accurate information that we can only wonder, with great concern, in how great a percentage of these reports the truth is really involved. More important still would seem to me to be the sources of these reports. We are proceeding with our investigation in the meantime. Well. . . ." Thoughtfully, Mercant looked at his watch. "The *Stardust* has been lost for more than twenty-four hours. Let's say 'lost,' because that still contains an element of hope. I am interested in your opinion of the editorials of some of our leading newspapers, wherein it is contended that an SOS from your spaceship has indeed been intercepted. They refer to the short signal QQRXQ that signifies, in the code of the Space Command, as much as attack, intentional disruption of remote control guidance systems, and initiating a crash landing. If that is the case, please let me have further details."

Mercant nodded amiably to the assembly and sat down. Wearily, General Pounder rose. His brows were knit, his face was hollow cheeked, and his voice sounded half broken. "That is correct, sir. QQRXQ can be equated with those conditions. It's a mystery to us how any reporter could get at the code. I've asked our security people to investigate—so far without any result, unfortunately. On the other hand, the reception of the SOS is less of a surprise. Several of our larger radar stations were awaiting signals from the lunar south pole area. We had also asked for the support of the great observatories. There something may have leaked through. Of course, this still does not explain how they could decipher the meaning of QQRXQ. That's all I can say."

"Let's forget about that for the moment. What has really happened to your spaceship? Do you in fact accept the possibility of willful and premeditated disturbance of your guidance signals? It was explained to me by experts that this could be accomplished only by a powerful transmitting facility situated on the moon."

Pounder lowered his head. In his eyes shone a helpless fury. "Yes, that is indeed the case. There is no other possibility, as crazy as it might sound. We've double checked all our instruments in the past twenty-four hours. Each is functioning at one hundred percent efficiency. There could be no possible failure in any phase of operation. But we've arrived at two other likely explanations."

Pounder wiped his perspiring forehead with a huge handkerchief. Heavily breathing, he continued, "Either Major Rhodan has released the wrong code signal or the radio equipment on board the *Stardust* has, as you say, been put out of action by a strong transmitter. As far as Major Rhodan is concerned, we consider it out of the question that he should have committed such a serious error. Rhodan is our top man; everybody knows that. In addition, our calculations prove beyond any doubt that at the decisive moment, the ship was pulled out of remote control. The vehicle must have been forced to land. Considering the known angle of fall, lunar gravity and the mass of the rocket, it must have touched ground some forty to fifty miles behind the polar region. It's entirely possible that we're dealing here with a harmless crash landing. Still, a total loss of the rocket must also be considered. No one *knows* what happened—we can only speculate."

Mercant's clear eyes were hooded with shadow. Colonel Kaats cleared his throat respectfully, announcing in this way that the data given agreed with the findings of internal security.

"Supposing, General," Mercant offered slowly, "just supposing that the ship's instruments really were exposed to interference. What would you conclude from that?"

"Of course, we had word from you, sir, that the Asiatic Federation had launched a lunar rocket at the same time as the *Stardust*. If this vessel arrived there earlier and if it set down in the approximate area of our landing, then this could have led to a well prepared radio disturbance of our wavelength." Pounder was now snarling like a Great Dane, his pale face flushed.

"That would be presuming that these people possessed very exact knowledge of our plans, wouldn't it?" asked Kaats skeptically.

"Naturally!" Pounder declared heatedly. "To find that out should be the job of the security services. I'm only a rocket man, Colonel. Certainly, our plans had already been made six months ago. Once again, however, I wish to stress that this radio interference could only have been the product of an installation on the moon—always provided that we *are* dealing with an attack in this form. There should be motives aplenty for this, don't you agree? We were broadcasting our directional impulses from the most powerful relay stations in the world. Even if interference had been attempted from Earth, we would have gotten through anyway. The sender *must* be up there on the moon."

Pounder sat down abruptly. He seemed exhausted.

Allan D. Mercant studied him without uttering a word. His forehead had grown furrowed. "We'll take on this case within the framework of international defense," he decided. "We'll know shortly if a regrettable error has occurred with regard to the *Stardust* or if foreign interest groups have intervened. Besides, there may very well be still other possibilities we can imagine. I'm thinking, for instance, of failure on board the rocket."

Professor Lehman thrust his narrow skull upward. He had been at a loss for words, but at last he grumbled excitedly, "Sir, the *Stardust* has not had a failure. Not a single switch could have been responsible. It would carry us too far afield at this point to indicate the overwhelming evidence for that. We only hope now that the crew will make contact with us. If the men have landed safely, then Rhodan will find a way. The receivers of our space stations are operating around the clock. If Rhodan can succeed in establishing a direct line of sight with Earth, he will be able to broadcast a signal. Until then, we'll have to wait. There is no other alternative."

"How long will it be before the sister ship of the *Stardust* is ready for launching?" inquired the chief of the security services.

"At least another two months," Pounder said with emphasis. "If my people are alive now, they will certainly have suffocated by then. Their oxygen supply is good for five weeks at most. In extreme emergency, perhaps six weeks; but that is the maximum. Sir, will you please find out what kind of mixup has occurred up there? If necessary, we may have to land an unmanned probe near the lunar south pole. It is highly uncertain whether this means of sending provisions and replacements would succeed, because the probe, after all, would first have to be found by my men. We are confronted with a desperate situation."

Allan D. Mercant abruptly closed the session. For the moment there was nothing further to say. The *Stardust* was lost and remained so. In its place was a mountain of riddles.

Before the Secretary of International Defense left the room, he said with a masklike smile, "Gentlemen, I'm very sorry . . . but the Asiatic moon rocket of which you speak exploded in the air shortly after launching."

Pounder reacted quickly. He sat up, pale, unable to utter a sound, and gaped across at Mercant.

The little man wiped his brow with the back of his hand. "I am genuinely sorry. Well, then, whether you like it or not, you'll just have to search for another explanation. No ship has taken off along with your *Stardust*. Therefore, may I ask where this stationary lunar installation is supposed to have its origin? Several things seem quite unclear to me. You will, nevertheless, be hearing from me."

Softly, he added,

"Neither do we believe that the fault lay in any error on

the part of the commanding officer of your ship. If you can prove the faultless functioning of the control mechanisms, then we're up against a hefty problem. I would like to request that you submit the facts to the scientific committee of international defense immediately. We must arrive at a convincing conclusion, and you will please try to understand."

"Rhodan could not have failed," asserted Pounder. "You don't know our men, sir. We will *prove* to you that the automatic guidance systems on board the *Stardust* were in operation. That we could ascertain in the final moments before the sudden change in angle of descent. We can even tell you, through electronic computation, with what thrust values they were working. Should that not be sufficient . . . ?"

Allan D. Mercant made his exit. Much preoccupied, he climbed into the helicopter waiting for him on the heliport on the roof of the NASA Building.

He looked up at the cloudless June sky over Washington. "We're facing very trying times, Kaats," he mumbled. "They tell me I have a certain nose for knowing that. Well, just a few moments ago my intuition spoke to me."

Kaats squinted. It was true that Mercant had this strange instinct. He could smell danger and difficulty the way a good bloodhound could sniff a scent. There were even rumors that this man possessed a uniquely developed brain with extraordinary faculties and that this was why he had become Secretary of International Defense.

CHAPTER FIVE

The rocket crew had had to wait for twenty-four hours before the radioactivity of the surface had decreased appreciably, dampened by the effect of absorbent chemicals sprinkled on the lunar soil.

When the geiger counter registered only minimal radiation, with a mark of less than thirty-five milliroentgens, Perry Rhodan had been the first man to leave the ship. It had happened quietly and without jubilation.

Searching one another's eyes, they had clasped hands

wordlessly. They were extremely conscious of being the first human beings ever to set foot on the moon.

The number four landing support had been damaged by the sudden impact of landing, they found. Otherwise, the *Stardust* had not sustained any serious damage. The ion reaction engines could not be checked out because of the still excessive radiation, but a short trial run proved them to be in the best of order. The other support structures did not seem to be broken.

The power supply still functioned flawlessly. The reactor was working at peak efficiency, and the combined air conditioning and regeneration system seemed never to have been better.

The damage to the armatures could easily be repaired. Much more serious, however, was the dislocation at the base of the telescoping tubing of landing support four. It would have to be restructured and strengthened with special equipment. Reginald Bell estimated that repairs would take at least six days. After all, molybdenum steel was an inordinately difficut metal to work with.

"We'll make it all right," he said. "It will mean sweat and effort, but we'll make it all right."

Thirty-six hours following their crash landing, they brought the pneumo-tent, an enormous sphere of synthetic fiber, out of the storage room.

The contents of a small bottle of liquid oxygen were sufficient to inflate the pliable material into a huge structure that seemed as hard as steel. The absence of exterior pressure proved to have some advantages.

Now the oblong tent stood well anchored to the rocky ground, its highly polished surface reflecting the brilliant light of the sun. All were engaged in installing the airlocks and the air conditioning system, but for the time being only the interior walls of the tent contained oxygen. This structure had been tested on Earth under the stress of simulated moon conditions. Only meteorites, and nothing else, would represent a danger.

The simplest thing had been the exact calculation of their position. Inasmuch as numerous orbital surveys had placed excellent special maps at their disposal, they had been able to work out their location with precision. The

*Stardust* had landed a scant sixty miles behind the lunar south pole. The sun was visible as a crescent, just peeping over the nearby lunar horizon.

The craters in the vicinity of their landing site and a small plateau between two huge overhanging ridges, were known and recorded. It seemed quite improbable that the rocket should have landed just here in its blind fall. It might just as easily have descended between the sharp spines of the high crater wall. Then it would probably have been curtains for them.

Earth was no longer visible. It hung in orbit far below the horizon. Therefore, no radio communication was possible. Rhodan had acknowledged these difficulties with only a boyish pout of his lips. No one else aboard the ship showed any sign of morale loss, although Fletcher had become quieter.

Rhodan had taken note of this without comment. Fletcher thought too often of his home, of his wife and the expected baby. This was cause for concern, even if not great concern. Rhodan had decided to pay special attention to the chubby-cheeked giant.

Now Rhodan stood atop one of the numerous summits of the crater wall. Within the rim, the walls fell steeply and suddenly to the flat surface, where the lunar soil was pockmarked with two smaller craters. These were typical signs of meteoric impacts to which this airless heavenly body had been exposed, without protection, for many millions of years.

He turned around slowly and cautiously, since here he weighed considerably less than on Earth, in spite of his heavy equipment. Some 400 yards below him, the pointed nose cone of the *Stardust* jutted out toward space. The solar crescent, which could barely be seen above the horizon, was shining fiercely and mercilessly. On the forward side, most fully exposed to the sun's rays, the rocks had already begun to warm up. Here near the twilight zone it was still somehow bearable.

Rhodan was not particularly disturbed by these things. He was fully aware of the dangers and difficulties, and thus he was psychologically well prepared to deal with them. Furthermore, he knew that the technical evolution of science had permitted more and more that would have seemed impossible only twenty or thirty years before.

Rhodan's spacesuit, for example, was a micro-mechanical miracle of the first rank, he pondered as he checked it over. Perhaps a thousand agile intellects had combined to construct it. One wheel had to fit into the next wheel, and one area of knowledge into others. Without a doubt, it represented a mammoth accomplishment for all mankind.

His suit was still in order. He nodded with satisfaction and directed his glance further across the vast terrain of such overwhelming, such foreboding aspect.

This area was not so torn and fragmented as other regions on the moon. Nevertheless, there was no sign of life. The stark contrast between brightest sunlight and darkest shadow painted the landscape with nightmarish contours. There was no shade, in the true sense of the word, no comforting transition between extremes of light and darkness.

Far away, no longer visible on a horizon that seemed so near, there lay the well-known outlines of the polar region. There was good reason why Perry Rhodan had ascended the lofty crater wall.

He could see no sign of any object that did not fit into the natural landscape. The *Stardust* and the pneumo-tent with its mirror-like surface were foreign bodies, obviously, but these now "belonged" in the picture.

An imperceptible smile played about his lips. Skeptically, with his characteristic detachment, he asked himself what right he had to think such thoughts. He arrived at the conclusion that here he was dealing with a certain audacity of the human mind. What man had conquered at the cost of great effort, that would he treasure and call his own. Therefore, the *Stardust* belonged with the landscape!

Rhodan chuckled to himself when he caught himself at this train of thought. Shortly thereafter, the small loudspeaker in his spherical helmet began to crackle. "What's the matter? Hey, Perry, what's going on? Have you run into trouble?"

Rhodan chuckled quietly to himself again, and his eyes narrowed as he continued his reverie.

"Perry, why don't you answer?" Reg shouted louder, having naturally overheard Rhodan's laughter through the open communications channel. "What's the matter?"

"I've taken the liberty of laughing," said Rhodan into his tiny microphone. "If you don't mind."

A short cough followed a harsh oath.

"He's standing on a moon crater all alone, and he's laughing." Reg could not help taking a dim view of it. "Who ever heard of such a thing? Fletch, he's standing up there and he's laughing."

"Well, at least *I'm* doing something," came Fletcher's grumbling reply. "For half an hour I've been trying desperately, with all ten fingers, to scratch my back. Nothing doing, though. Right where I'd like to scratch, I've got these damned oxygen tanks."

Reg was roaring. Rhodan turned the volume dial a bit toward the left. The voice of his redheaded friend could wake the dead. "Hey, Perry, what's the air like up there?" the loudspeaker croaked.

"A thunderstorm is coming up," replied Rhodan dryly.

Reg fell silent, nonplussed. Rhodan's peculiar humor always affected him this way.

"Because the air is so highly charged on the moon," he added softly.

"All right, Commander; but what good is it to know something like that?"

"That's precisely my point; but I was trying, even on the moon, to convey the information as factually and exactly as I could. From now on I will no longer depend on sound but on sight. Okay? Now, my friend, approximately how far away from you am I in the direct line of sight?"

"About 850 yards," said Dr. Manoli, amusement in his voice. "I'm seated at the radar screen now, and it has established your distance, accurate to the inch. Efficient, isn't it?"

"More than efficient," laughed Rhodan. "All right, Reg, here's something for you to do, but I want you please to make a clean and thorough job of it. Take your MPi and adapt your sights to ten times magnification. Distance 848. Fire half a magazine onto the rocky outcrop that looks like the head of a giant, about fifty yards to my left. Do you see it?"

"I see it," confirmed Reg just as briefly. "May I ask what this joke is all about?"

"I seldom make jokes when I'm dealing with serious matters. I would like to know how our rocket missiles perform in miniature, especially their force of impact and power of detonation. Begin, and pay close attention to the effect of the recoil under present gravity.

"There's no recoil whatsoever," asserted Reg. "Every shell has its own propelling force, according to the RAK principle. There can be no recoil. Quite the contrary. I've been informed in great detail on this particular point."

"Very efficient," Rhodan said sarcastically. "Now *fire* and please don't mistake me for the rock."

Reg laughed abruptly. Fletcher observed him silently as he bent to the floor and gathered up the weapon with the short stock and thick barrel. Rhodan's explicit command was that they were never to leave the *Stardust* without arms.

Reginald Bell stood in front of the half-finished pneumo-tent. To one side, hardly thirty yards away, the space-craft reared up into the lunar sky.

Very carefully, he adjusted the reflex lens on his tele-scopic sights. Magnification ten times, distance 848 yards.

Reg hesitated for a few moments. The target was far away though it seemed to leap so much nearer through the lens.

"Let's get going," came the insistent order. "What are you waiting for? Just imagine that it was this rock that destroyed our remote control guidance. Well?"

Reg swore loudly. At last he understood what Rhodan's intentions were. The experiment took on greater signifi-cance and the thought of needless tomfoolery was quickly forgotten. "For the first ten shots, with your permission, I'll fire only single projectiles," he said. "First I want to see what distance I can make with this thing."

"Very well. Begin."

Reg set the stock of the weapon against his shoulder. In the strong magnification of his sight, the rock became clearly visible. He decided that this distance, easily bridged, would be negligible for the incredibly fast missile. Consider-ing the lesser gravity of Earth's satellite and the absence of atmospheric resistance here, the path of trajectory would be an almost straight line. The lens had been constructed for just these conditions. Reg could quite as easily have fired across a distance of several miles. The probability of a direct hit would still be remarkably high.

Fletcher held his breath as Reg touched the trigger.

No sound whatsoever followed. On Earth there would have been an indescribably shrill whistling. Here the discharge took place in an eerie silence.

From the oval muzzle of the barrel, bright flames emerged and were extinguished at once. It was as if nothing had happened.

Reg was a bit startled. "Did you notice anything?" he asked breathlessly. "What the dickens . . . ? You've got to get used to this kind of marksmanship. I didn't feel a thing."

"But I did," came the dry reply. "The rock fragments flew as far as where I'm standing. The missile was here before you had bent your finger properly. Incredibly fast. The outcrop shows a hole about a foot across and just about as deep. That's really something—after all, that was solid granite. Try it now with a longer burst of fire. So far the RAK has hairtrigger accuracy."

Reg pulled the trigger all the way back. The fiery exhaust blinded his eyes, but from where Rhodan was standing, he could see a bright and whitish shining trajectory trace. This was the path of the burning solid propellants of the small missiles. Where they penetrated the heart of darkness close below the hills, a brilliant line of flames arose. Reg's magazine emptied itself before he could even adequately appreciate what was going on.

There were now only a few wretched remains of the huge rock. The stone fragments that had been blasted upward fell to the ground in exasperating slow motion.

Rhodan had been able to follow the countless explosions carefully. They had been silent and without shockwaves. Only the shower of debris and the flashing glow had indicated their occurrence.

"That will do," he said briefly. "A nice toy the armaments division has loaned us, I've got to admit. How long did you hold through, Reg?"

"Perhaps two seconds," came the astounded reply. "The magazine is empty. Good grief! Ninety shots in that moment."

"To be exact, the rate of fire is about fifty shots per second. All right, the experiment is over. I'll come down. Eric, how far along are you with dinner?"

"You can come now. I've been hard at work."

Rhodan looked around once more before sliding down.

Then his wide leaps brought him easily over any obstacles in his path. For a man who was used to the null gravity of space, the insignificance of the moon's gravitational pull offered few surprises.

Twenty minutes later he appeared at the entrance of the pneumo-tent. The construction of the air lock was completed. The air conditioning equipment had been joined to that of the greater installation on board the *Stardust*.

"Filling this tent cost us a few gallons of liquid oxygen," declared Fletcher. "Will it be worth our while to waste such a precious commodity this way? I wonder if one day we won't need it more for the control center of the *Stardust*. Our supply is limited."

Rhodan halted in front of him. Though he was tall, Fletcher still towered above him for another inch and a half.

"Fletch, you worry unnecessarily. For the repair of the landing support we will need skill and unlimited mobility. If I chose to work on the molybdenum steel myself, I couldn't be encumbered by that clumsy spacesuit and on the other hand, I wouldn't want to stand in this gaping void in the first place."

Fletcher blinked up at the dark, incredibly clear starry skies.

"I was only thinking . . ." he muttered, and a hesitant smile appeared at his lips.

"You were thinking about the journey back home, weren't you?" asked Rhodan gently. "Or of the baby or what?"

Fletcher was silent. His lips were pressed close together.

"Okay, we fully understand that. But you really ought not to think of it too often. Our plans are made. We've discussed them long enough. We will not undertake any exploratory expeditions until the *Stardust* is completely restored to working order. We cannot risk a short blast-off followed by a landing on the other side of the pole. The damaged telescoping support could not stand renewed stress. Of course, in space we could navigate for a few miles and, with a brief maneuver, come into the direct line of sight with Earth; but then, as I say, we would still have to land again. And it's entirely possible that then the *Stardust* would be so seriously damaged that we could no longer repair it with the tools we have on board. In other circumstances, I would really think twice about using the oxygen to fill the pneumo-tent. But now there are no objections to our doing so. Is that clear?" Rhodan smiled blankly.

Fletcher was still gazing up into space. "Clear, entirely clear," was his hollow reply. "But another alternative has occurred to me. Wouldn't it be better to prepare now for the return flight to Earth? We managed to have a crash landing. Okay. But why should we put ourselves out to repair that landing support? The landing on Earth will depend on the efficiency of the bearing surfaces of our wings. We'll set down with our landing gear. It will no longer matter whether the landing support is broken. We'll have a safe descent anyway."

He looked down, his eyes flickering.

Rhodan lost neither patience nor presence of mind. Only his tone of voice changed, becoming sharper to an almost imperceptible degree.

"Fletch, your proposal could of course be carried out, but it would be tantamount to desertion. Let me put it this way—we have here a mission to accomplish, and a slightly damaged landing support will not deter us from accomplishing that mission." His face again became mask-like. "Besides, I have the unpleasant suspicion that we would not be allowed to reach space unhindered. There's something here that we must get cleared up first."

Fletcher got hold of himself at once. His blue eyes begged wordlessly for forgiveness. Rég began to grin. The case seemed to have been dismissed.

"Okay, forget what I said," the heavyset man muttered, clearing his throat. "It was only a thought. After dinner we'll find out where the interfering transmitter is. I've calculated the important data; afterward I'll feed it into the computer."

"I'll be anxiously awaiting the result," said Rhodan, nodding. "Now, then, let's see what the good doctor has concocted for dinner."

An indignant snort was audible in their space helmets. Dr. Manoli began to explain, at great length, how and why the master chefs' often lauded art of cuisine was wholly identical with a simple mastery of chemical processes. It all sounded splendid, but somehow it didn't quite ring true.

At the edge of the still mildly radioactive landing area, below the engines of the *Stardust*, Rhodan stopped. Before him was suspended the wide net transport basket of the freight elevator. The long arm of the crane swung forth from the open hatch of the storage room, situated immediately beneath their cabins. Rhodan had renounced the use of the ladder along the ship's hull. They would have had to step between the widely outspread landing supports and walk dangerously close to the radioactive engines.

"For the time being, someone will have to do without the culinary delights we so eagerly expected," Rhodan announced with a grin. His eyes studied the faces of both men. "Well, Reg, will you be so kind as to take over the watch out here? I'll relieve you in about half an hour. Up there on the hill is a good place. Take a look around. We'll keep in touch via radio."

Reginald Bell was silent. Rhodan's dark voice had told him enough already. As calm as the commander seemed on the outside, within he was tortured by unrest. Before Reg left, his weapon at readiness, he said slowly, "One more question. Are you still thinking of that report according to which a manned moonship is supposed to have been launched by the Asians?"

"You've hit on it," agreed Rhodan. His eyebrows rose upward. "It's quite possible that someone wanted to make certain that we crashed; and they wanted to see it happen at close range. In my opinion, the interfering transmitter must be near the polar region. So keep your eyes peeled. Our automatic frequency direction finder is systematically probing all possible wavelengths. If we hear something out of place, things will start moving very quickly around here." He looked around, wearing an expression of ostentatious boredom.

Further up, in the cabin of the *Stardust*, Dr. Manoli began to feel a chill. He suddenly felt very uncomfortable. He was among those men who would endure the risk and labor, defying any challenge, in the interest of Science. But it would be quite a different matter if this led to surprising complications. For such as this, Manoli was not well equipped. Plagued by heavy thoughts, he listened to the hum of the crane motors as Rhodan and Fletcher came up in the basket.

On the video screen Reg's image, becoming smaller and smaller, was still to be seen. Finally, however, it disappeared into the deep darkness of a sun shaded overhang.

In a moment a whistling sound issued from the air locks. The equalization of atmospheric pressure had been completed. When they entered, the most Manoli could manage was a forced smile.

"Hello," he said weakly. "We've heard nothing from the direction finder. Nothing at all, except your conversation."

Rhodan peeled off the space suit. Fletcher's face was covered with perspiration. With joyful gurgling he rubbed his itching back against the wall.

"Ah!—oh!" he sighed. "That's like heaven on Earth."

"On Earth they'll think we're lost," Manoli interjected gently.

Fletcher's cooing stopped.

"Yes," agreed a nonchalant Rhodan. "That they will, but not for very much longer, I give you my word. Right after dinner we'll begin repair of the landing support."

Manoli thought of his wife, and Fletcher of his baby. No one talked about it, but everyone knew it. Here was a situation that demanded a firm hand and an iron will to keep things under control. Rhodan possessed both these characteristics.

## CHAPTER SIX

They were all alone on a strange world, without air, without water, and without life. . . .

The thin molverdin skin of the low slung full track tank could undoubtedly have withstood fire from heavy cannon. Yet it afforded them no feeling of safety and security.

Beyond the sheets of steel began the void—the absolute vacuum of space, with all its dangers, known and unknown. It was, however, not so much the constant threat of death that strained the nerves of these men; it was more the forlorn, incredibly alien landscape, more the blazing crescent of the white shining sun, and the high rising crater walls interspaced with barren planes torn by deep ravines. It was caused by the bizarre ridge and summit of mountain chains that had never been gnawed by the jaws of weather.

Even the most desolate wasteland on Earth would have seemed familiar and welcoming compared with this.

All this exerted a psychological pressure not to be under-estimated. These were the dangers to mind and soul that one had to accept somehow. One either rose above them and adjusted to them with stoic unconcern or perished. There was no remedy for the insidious corrosive influence of these surroundings.

In view of these considerations, Rhodan had left Clark G. Fletcher and Dr. Eric Manoli behind in the spaceship. At least two men had to remain at all times in the *Stardust*, and the commanding officer did not believe that either Fletcher or Manoli had the necessary powers of endurance.

Fletcher had been given explicit instructions, in writing, to start the *Stardust* and to bring it into the remote control area should Rhodan not return within eighteen days.

Captain Fletcher had nodded silently. He was quite capable of launching the fully automated rocket. It would be relatively simple to pilot it into space and follow through with the necessary procedures.

They had required only five days to repair the broken landing support. Only another twenty-four hours had been needed to set up and equip the lunar tank.

After an extended period of sleep under the effects of hypnonarcosis, Rhodan and Reginald Bell had departed. The full track vehicle had been tested under the most rigor-ous conditions. Failure was inconceivable. Each and every part had been checked again and again by a multitude of highly specialized technicians.

The tank was an unarmed overland transport vehicle with a spacious four man cabin. Its transparent silicon steel dome could be darkened according to need. For the time being, the small loading platform behind the pres-surized dome contained only the necessary provisions and spare parts. Rhodan was unwilling to carry out any of the many orders for exploration and research during this expe-dition.

Here the major issue was survival, and that meant estab-lishing contact with Earth relay stations. The tank's trans-mitter could operate, at maximum capacity, with a power of twelve kilowatts, which should enable them to communicate with Earth.

By now, they had been on their way for the last twenty-four hours. Only five of these had been sacrificed for sleep. Then, with screeching E-motors, Perry had forced the vehicle across the next swell in the ground.

The solar crescent had rounded considerably as they neared the pole, where Earth would come into their direct line of sight.

They still wore their spacesuits but had pushed their helmets back onto their shoulders. The pressurized dome of the vehicle was just as safe as the control center on board the *Stardust*. The hull of special artificial alloys could be damaged only by brute force.

With eyes shaded, Reginald Bell looked ahead. He did not like the looks of the high mountain summits. Again he studied their special maps.

"The Leibnitz Mountains, no doubt," he said under his breath. "Stop a moment, will you?"

Rhodan drew the lever back to zero. The high whine of both E-motors in the front wheels faded into quiet as beneath the heavy radiation shield, the reactor lowered the rate of nuclear fission to a minimum.

Rhodan wiped the sweat from his brow. Without a word he began to polish the dark lenses of his sunglasses. The ultraviolet radiation had become very unpleasant.

Meanwhile, he was looking across to the mountains. The tip of his tongue moved across his lips, which were broken and chapped.

"Roughly five more miles, not any farther. You can be very much mistaken here when you guess at distances. Before us lies the Husemann Crater, which is not visible from Earth. Another ten miles or so should bring us to the other side of the pole, but not if we follow this course. We must turn to the left and move eastward. Otherwise, we'll come into the Leibnitz mountain range, and that would be distinctly unpleasant."

Reg's dirty index finger pointed to the map. Beneath his day old beard, his broad face looked haggard and puffy. The drive had become torture. Rhodan had been racing like a wildman. If they had played on a straight path, they would have reached the polar region long ago; but again and again they had had to circumnavigate countless obstacles. On the map their recorded route looked like the scrawl of an imbecile.

Rhodan cleared his throat. Without a word he passed the water bottle to Reg.

"Okay, we'll turn here. Leibnitz will be a problem. I don't want to get into those ravines. We're approaching the eastern ridge now. The main mountain range stretches farther to the west. We'll get through all right."

Reg drank several huge swallows. As Rhodan began to cover the hull of the tank with additional highly reflective screens, a burdensome silence was evident in the cabin. The sun was too much for them. Soon it would become a problem even to dissipate the heat.

Finally Reg said somberly, "Something's bound to happen. My neck is itching. Something is bound to happen. Here, take a look at that."

He again tapped on the map with his forefinger. The new course passed through the circle that Fletcher the mathematician had drawn earlier.

"Yes, I know," said Rhodan broadly. A masklike grin hovered about his face.

Agape, Reg stared at him. His lips were dry and cracked in many places. "We ought to drive in a huge detour around . . . that certain place . . . and first make certain that our broadcast to Earth arrives without fail. Then we can see our way further. How about it?"

For a few moments Rhodan gazed out into the void. When he finally turned to face the other man, Reginald Bell saw a face heavily engraved with lines. Rhodan's eyes sparkled like molten steel.

"Problems are made to be solved. Whether we want to or not, we must attack this affair. It would be of little help to us to delay the outcome with lame excuses. I prefer a quick operation, so we'll take the shortest path. Very much will still depend on which party is faster. The other side must also be suffering from the conditions of space, perhaps even more than we are."

"We sure are some heroes!" said a disgruntled Reg. "Okay. From now on I'll take care of the infrared prober. But with the faintest signal, you'll have to drive like the devil himself."

As if unconsciously, his hand felt his weapon. Now they were wearing heavy, fully automatic weapons that worked on the same principle as the larger machine guns.

Rhodan thrust forward a lever, and the tank started with whining E-motors. After they had driven around the crater wall, they reached a wide even stretch full of small rocks. Dust was whirled up behind the racing chains. Oddly motionless, individual particles of dust remained floating above the ground until at last they began to descend so slowly that it seemed it would take forever. Nothing could have more clearly illustrated the absence of wind and the reduced gravity.

When another six hours had passed, the sun became fully visible. Now they proceeded very quickly. After they had passed the critical point without any particular incident, they drove over the borderline into the direct line of sight. In a moment the great crescent of the Earth loomed up large. It was almost full and easily recognizable. Radio communication was certainly possible, although Earth was still quite low above the northern horizon.

Rhodan cast a brief glance to his right. They had become very sparing with words during these last few hours.

Reg grinned, all the while whistling shrilly and quite off-key. Rhodan forced the vehicle up a steep incline. The chains dug into the ground, and the laboring roar of the motors rose louder. Arriving at the top, they stood on a small rocky plateau. At their right, a dark ridge wall towered high into the void. But far ahead of them hung the illumined orb of Earth. They had made it. They said little at this point. Lines of exhaustion were deeply imbedded in their faces. The necessary manipulations followed quickly, perhaps a bit too hastily. Both had the vague notion that it was high time for action.

Rhodan brought out the parabolic direction finder, and Reg connected the reactor, full strength, to the transmitter. Rhodan adjusted the antenna, and Earth was soon suspended in the crosshairs of their sights. Hesitating, with a clumsy movement, Rhodan turned the seat around. In front of him the needles of the control dials were jerking. The instruments were in perfect working order. He moved the microphone closer to his mouth. With some ceremony, he tuned in the automatic frequency selector.

51

"Ready?" Reg asked roughly. He stood hunched over in the cabin, the heavy RAK automatic ready in his hand.

Rhodan nodded. The normal static blanket of space was audible on the loudspeakers of the receiver. In no way could this be compared to the hellish crackling and whistling of the controlled interference that had caused them to crash.

As a tired smile played about Rhodan's lips, he switched over to BROADCAST and spoke with muted voice into the microphone.

"Major Perry Rhodan, commanding officer of the *Stardust* expedition, calling ground control, Nevada Fields. Please reply. Major Perry Rhodan, commanding officer of the *Stardust* expe—"

It came as suddenly as lightning out of a clear sky. A sudden shimmering reinforced itself into a stark green glow that limned their upturned faces in the ghastly hue.

Directly above them, the antenna began to glow with a greenish fluorescent fire of such intensity that Rhodan buried his agonized eyes in his hands with a moan.

It happened with astounding swiftness and, moreover, in complete silence. Above the squat lunar full track tank hung a broad hemisphere of pulsing flame. In comparison, the sun faded into a dimly lit body. Their surroundings became indistinct.

Before Reg could utter his horrifed cry of warning, a crackling sound began to emanate from the radio. A bright spark of electricity bolted out of the plastic wall covering and acrid acid vapors rose from the box. Small flames played about the smoking insulation.

Rhodan's kick came just in time, interrupting the connection to the reactor conduit. Reg hardly realized that Rhodan's hand was smashing against his helmet. Only when he was able to fill his wheezing lungs with a welcome breath of oxygen did he realize he had been screaming.

Perry Rhodan sat motionless in his seat. The incident seemed to have passed over him without effect. The enigmatic glow had vanished just as suddenly as it had appeared. Nothing further was to be seen, not the slightest flicker.

Only the completely molten antenna and the smoldering radio were witness to an event that lay beyond ready comprehension. Reg moved awkwardly about in the cabin. Wildly he searched for a tangible opponent, his weapon drawn and threatening; but nowhere was such a form to be found.

The sharp hissing of the dry foam fire extinguisher made him turn again abruptly. Rhodan sprayed the gutted radio with a face bespeaking such indifference that Captain Bell began to swear. He swore intently and quite loudly, though his lips were hardly moving in his puffed up, deathly pale face.

The fire was out. The air conditioning drew out the noxious vapors as fresh oxygen streamed into the cabin. The affair had cost them a few more gallons of precious breathing air.

Rhodan removed his helmet. Slowly, entirely devoid of expression, he gazed upward. Then his voice sounded. It vibrated rather like a resonant mandolin string. "Finished. Finished completely. That's what they were waiting for."

"Good Lord, what was that?" whispered Reg. He sank back into his seat, fully exhausted. "What was it?"

"A particularly funny way of interfering with our broadcast, but don't ask me how they've done it. I'm innocent; I have no idea; I don't have the faintest notion of an idea. I only know that the glow appeared all of a sudden just as our transmitter first began to operate. That means they were lying in wait for us with a fully automatic direction finder. The mechanism switched on at once. And that's all I know."

Reg slowly swallowed a capsule of concentrate. His eyes had grown narrow. The capable engineer in him, that part of his brain wherein was stored a wealth of expertise in electronics, awakened.

"Otherwise, you're feeling all right, aren't you?" he inquired. "I've always thought of you as a clear headed, exemplary pupil of the Space Academy."

"And you don't any longer?" asked Rhodan, with a line of bitterness showing around his lips.

"Not at the moment. You were just now talking like Superman in the funnies. What do you mean by 'fully automatic direction finder'? Do you realize what you've said? Man, we were working with a sharply defined directional beam. The antenna was pointed toward empty space. How could they locate such impulses so quickly? Perhaps you have an explanation for that greenish glow? Can you imagine what great energies they were working with?"

"You'd better not ask, or I'll have to give you an answer that sounds absolutely crazy."

"We were lying under a bell-shaped dome," Reg insisted obstinately. "I saw it clearly. A ray of green light darted out of it toward the bottom, and that was the end of our antenna. Perry, I tell you, nothing like that exists. Otherwise, I could understand everything, really everything. I might even have accepted the idea of controlled bolts of lightning; but here my brain stops working."

Rhodan did not move from his rigid posture. His eyes alone stirred, and violently.

"Well, then, we were dreaming, were we? In your place I would have said simply that my reason had reached its limit. Someone heard my broadcast at once, and someone just as swiftly went into action. How he did that is of only secondary interest to me, since I can make neither heads nor tails of this, even with my technical background. Much more important, it seems to me, is that this 'someone' intends to make us prisoners on the moon. I'll bet my head that the *Stardust* couldn't take off even one mile into space. Don't ask; I just feel it. No, I *know* it. What remains to be done now?"

Reginald Bell changed color even more. Now completely pale, he looked hard at his commanding officer, whose bright eyes had darkened considerably. "You're the most cold blooded guy I've ever seen," he gulped. "You have nothing else to say?"

"Insoluble problems range too far outside the boundaries of our consideration. We should not waste our breath on them."

Reg cleared his throat. Color seemed to return to his cheeks. "Okay. Let's hide our head in the sand," he laughed bitterly. His glance searched the landscape. It seemed unchanged, desolate and lonely. "Still, I don't understand anything any more. If it didn't seem crazy to me I would talk about a force field. But how could it be constructed practically out of the blue? No poles, nothing at all. Who wants to get rid of us here?"

"Perhaps the rocket from the Asiatic Federation landed

a few hours before us. They might have new inventions on board. How about that greenish glow?" Rhodan observed his friend's reaction closely.

Reg grinned. His heavy hands were dangling across his knees like unwanted appendages.

"Let's drop this pointless discussion," conceded Reg. "You don't believe that yourself, old man. I've now arrived at a point where, in the final analysis, nothing matters to me any more. I'll swallow a rusty nail if the Chinese have invented something of the sort. That was an overpowering display. What are you planning now?"

Rhodan smiled with uncommon geniality. Such a broad grin meant, for Reg, alert procedure number one. He knew the tall man with the lean face.

"Let's drive there and have a look and, if possible, pull the trigger a tenth of a second faster than our opponents. I can no longer see any other possibility. If we remain where we are, we'll suffocate in a matter of weeks, and if we try to leave, we'll surely be shot down."

"Negotiate?" asked Reg doubtfully.

"Oh? With pleasure, even. I only wonder if we can negotiate with these people. Events seem to indicate the contrary. Why wouldn't they let us begin transmission? Who would be threatened by it? Everybody on Earth must know by now that the *Stardust* has landed on the moon. It seems senseless to interrupt our communications so drastically. What's at the bottom of all this? This affair seems like the game of a madman. It seems simply irrational. Even if they tried to kill us, I could still see some sense or purpose to it; but they don't seem to have considered that at all. Why haven't they?"

Again Reg began to whistle shrilly. "Well, after all, they *are* killing us slowly," he pointed out. "And *very* slowly indeed. Once our oxygen has been used up. . . ."

He fell silent, but his brow showed evidence of concern. Briefly he added, "All right, Commander. I'll chart our new course on the map. Let's make short work of it. In eight hours we can be there."

"First, let's get some sleep, for exactly eight hours. Then we'll shave neatly and make ourselves presentable. I don't want to give the impression that we're savages."

Reg stared through the transparent dome of the tank,

quite speechless. Finally he was able to collect his wits. "Shave?" he groaned. "Did you say *shave?*"

"Unlike ourselves, the Asiatics will have no such heavy growth of beard," declared Rhodan with a strange smile. "They might not appreciate it."

Reginald Bell suddenly felt a chill. What did his commanding officer have in mind?

## CHAPTER SEVEN

Less than twenty miles from the pole, toward the dark side of the moon, the infrared sensors had come to life. A body radiating heat in excess of the norm was in the vicinity. The source lay exactly within that limited area which Captain Fletcher had estimated as the probable location of the interfering transmitter.

They had left the tank and continued on foot along the edge of the huge crater, a mighty edifice never visible from Earth. The ring of mountains rose to a height of more than 1,800 feet. Then, after about half an hour's climb, they had passed the last obstacle. They were still at the foot of the crater wall but now somewhat farther north.

The portable direction finder had given more and more indication that they were nearing their goal. They were shortly to find the other rocket.

Then Reginald Bell's collapse had come.

He was crouching and then kneeling on the ground, his hands thrust out before him. His incoherent babbling was picked up by the microphone and broadcast from his helmet transmitter.

Perry Rhodan did not utter a sound. Instinctively he had taken cover but now he was struggling for his self-control with all his might. The sight alone had delivered the *coup de grace* to the frayed nerves of these men.

"No, no . . . not that! Not that!" Reg began to moan over the speaker. The same words followed in singsong rhythm, again and again.

Rhodan sat up with a jolt. His fists, once clenched relaxed. More roughly than necessary, he pulled his friend behind the cover of a big rock. Reg rallied from his state of shock. Trembling, he riveted his eyes on Rhodan. The helmet visor clouded over from his heavily perspiring face. Rhodan switched on the small ventilator within the helmet. Reg sorely needed it.

"Calm yourself. Don't lose your nerve. Take it easy, for heaven's sake. Don't talk. If they turn that green glow on our antenna, all will be lost. Get a grip on yourself."

Rhodan took refuge in the utterance of stereotyped phrases. They might have sounded monotonous in their constant repetition, but for this very reason, merely through the lulling effect of the words, they became effective. Rhodan had thought himself mentally prepared for it, but the sudden confrontation with the truth had bowled him over. They were no longer alone. They had never *been* alone.

This realization upset him and dealt a telling blow to his equilibrium. He felt as if he were facing a tremendously tall, unscalable wall. Reg's sobbing helped him fo get his feelings under control again.

Perry Rhodan needed a few more minutes. Then again his face assumed a firm expression. The wild pumping of his heart decreased. His glassy eyes regained their sober glow. Only his hard grip around Reg's upper arm remained steadfastly the same.

He decided his friend would need longer to regain his grip. This was probably the greatest shock Captain Reginald Bell had ever suffered.

Cautiously Rhodan raised his helmet above the rocky outcrop. His gaze devoured the titanic structure that lay before him. His last doubts had disappeared. No, this was no longer a dream. Before him lay the vast and tangible reality.

He was silent until Reg began to speak once again. Rhodan no longer intended to forbid radio communications. It was almost a certainty that it would have been quite senseless.

"You knew that all along, didn't you? You've known it for hours already!" Reg's hoarse whispering came over the loudspeaker. "That's why you wanted me to shave. What gave you the idea, Perry?"

"Don't get upset, old boy," Rhodan replied. "It won't do you any good. This spaceship was never built in Asia. In fact, it is probably untouched by Earthly hands. I suspected something of the sort when the green glow came.

Nothing human could produce such a field of energy. No one of our race could have interrupted our broadcast by such means. Control yourself, old boy. We must bear it. We have no other alternative."

Reg sat up erect. No longer was there a dull cast to his eyes. Now he too was looking eagerly ahead.

"They've made a crash landing," he said after a little while. "They've grazed half the crater wall, with a force such as one can hardly imagine. Who are they? What do they look like? Where do they come from? And. . . ." Reg set his jaw, before completing his sentence with a somber undertone of sudden suspicion. "And what do they want here?"

This question roused Rhodan completely out of his momentary stupor. He regained his cool composure. His lips were drawn up in a faint smirk as he said, "That we will soon find out. Now an apparently senseless action begins to make sense. Of course they had to interrupt our communication. Obviously they're not at all anxious for Earth to learn of their presence here. They evidently assumed that we had already noticed them, that we had seen this gigantic thing here shortly before our landing. Now the affair makes sense."

Of course it made sense. Suddenly Rhodan looked at the structure through different eyes. Though his brain still signaled danger with the rapid fire of nerve impulses, he regarded the foreign ship this time with the sober eyes of a scientist.

No irregularity could be detected in the smooth surface of the spherical giant. There was not a single protuberance and no visible opening. At the height of the equator line, however, there seemed the impression of a ring-like bulge.

The ship stood motionless at the edge of the splintered crater wall. Although it was quite clear that it had broken through the ring, it seemed to bear no scars from the encounter.

The whole structure was resting on short supports rather like pillars. These were arranged in a circle and had obviously emerged from the lower quarter of the sphere. That was all the two could see. In the bright light of the sun, the material of the mighty hull was shimmering in a pale copper glow. In order to see the upper part of the spheroid structure, they had to tilt their heads all the way back. From behind the concealment of the crater wall, they had come very near the ship.

By now Reginald Bell had also got hold of himself again. His voice, rough and measured as ever, was proof enough of that. "A perfect sphere. The ideal structure for a giant spaceship, provided one has the correspondingly great propulsions system. Good heavens, that thing measures some 500 yards across. At least 500! It's almost higher than the crater wall. It's enough to drive you out of your mind. How could they launch such a mass into space? I'm only beginning to have some notion of what kind of engines they must have on board. I'd better not even think about it or I'll feel only two feet tall."

More softly, in a slightly choked voice, he added, "And there we were, so proud of our success! We've reached the moon with such a tiny thing. Ha! With such a pitiful little spaceship, and we could just barely make the absurd and insignificant leap to the moon. Beyond us lies the galaxy, and of course, first there is still our own solar system. Do you have any idea what we proud little men are in comparison to those beings over there?"

"If you're about to compare us to monkeys I'm going to explode!" said Rhodan icily.

Reg grinned sheepishly. "Something of the sort was just on the tip of my tongue. You're really a very proud human being, aren't you?"

"I'm proud of my humanity, proud of our race, proud of our rapid development, and proud of our future. We've conquered this little moon, and someday we shall also conquer the stars. This improbable spaceship has not at all proved yet that its occupants are more intelligent than we. It might be nothing but the heritage of 10,000 industrious generations, something that simply fell into their lap. Ignorance is by no means the same as stupidity. You should take into account whether the ignorant person has been given the opportunity for learning, and even if he has had that opportunity, it would still depend on the degree of wisdom possessed by the caretakers of knowledge. One cannot assimilate more knowledge than is supplied by one's teachers. We human beings are a young and hardy race. Our brains are like sponges. There is a lot that can still be absorbed by them, I give you my word! So don't ever let me hear you say that you suddenly seem to yourself like a kind of monkey."

Rhodan had really grown furious. He seemed to have forgotten that an alien spacecraft, with all its cargo of menace and mysteries, stood before them.

Reg laughed, then tentatively placed his hand on his holstered automatic.

"Leave that alone," warned Rhodan. "We can't solve our problems with that. We must resign ourselves to knowing that we are not the only intelligent forms of life in the universe. For me that comes as no surprise. People of our breed should already have given thought to such a possibility. Any man who gets out into space *must* have considered it at least once, if only in reverie. So now, stop that. The situation is quite unlike our first estimate of it."

"I'd feel much more secure if this were a lousy rocket from the Asiatic Federation," whispered Reg. Then, more urgently, "And what happens now? Fortunately, *you're* in command. A burning curiosity is slowly rising within me."

"I've noticed that for quite a while already," Rhodan said with grim emphasis. "It is almost beyond comprehension—it looks as if these creatures are really not out to get us. And there's still more."

He gazed over at the splintered ridge again. "A reasonable commander would never have landed in such a manner, would he? *I* certainly wouldn't. If you raze nearly half the wall of a crater during your landing it is to be presumed that this was not a matter of choice. It almost looks to me as if these unknowns had crashed. That makes them *almost human,* doesn't it?"

Rhodan grinned. "Something isn't quite right over there. Since I'm supposed to be such a good loser, I'll see to it that we get a closer look at things." He rose to his full height. A sarcastic smile hung from his lips.

"Are you crazy?" hissed Reg. "Get down! Don't be a fool!"

"Not at all a fool. Consider our situation. We can't get away from here any more. By the time General Pounder sends another rocket up here we will have been long since dead. And the fate of the next crew will be identical to our own. There is nothing further to consider. Perhaps the deeper meaning of my words will penetrate even your thick skull."

Besides, truth be told, Rhodan was consumed by curiosity. It was the original human instinct, invincible, eternally restless, urgently asking, "What lies *beyond?*"

Suddenly Rhodan's eyes widened. Someone had laughed. It was only a momentary, almost inaudible sound. But someone had laughed!

Reg drew himself up, his weapon in readiness. His face had again become contorted. "Did you hear that too?" he whispered breathlessly. "There's somebody on our wavelength, dammit!"

"What did you expect?" Rhodan's voice sounded very cool over the speaker. "And why do you think I was performing this play with all this extensive dialogue. Of course they're listening in! The fact that they chose not to destroy our miserable helmet transmitters is a sign of their intelligence. They know very well we can't get through to Earth with them. The logic is simply overwhelming. Let's go."

Reg remained standing, motionless. His weapon dangled loose in his hands. Drawling with a chill undertone, he said, "Well then go if you want to. I'm not at all interested in running into the clutches of sentient cuttlefish or similar monstrosities. I'm staying right here."

Rhodan's face hardened. "You've been reading too much space opera my friend. Living creatures a la octopi will never construct spaceships, even if, against all probability, they should become intelligent. Don't confuse your fantasy with well founded fact. These are realities, neither more nor less. There are an adequate number of respected intellects on Earth who consider it quite probable that some form of intelligent extraterrestrial life does exist; but they do not imagine them to be monsters at all. So don't talk any more nonsense. Just come along. Shall I insist once again that we have no other way out?"

"Perhaps we still do," mumbled Reg, still greatly disturbed. "I simply don't like the idea of running into that ship like some helpless, bleating sheep. That is strictly contrary to my instinct. Get it?"

"Of course. I always understand reasonable arguments, and the human fear of the unknown is probably the most reasonable reaction that the creator implanted in us. That is all very well. But under certain circumstances we must also be capable of overcoming the dictates of instinct. You can follow me if you like. I shall give you no further orders in this affair."

Rhodan turned. With broad, even steps, he emerged from behind cover. In his word and deed, reason had won the upper hand. He knew that he had the "choice" of a single alternative. Therefore, Major Perry Rhodan drew the consequences.

Rhodan's machine gun dangled on a strap over his right shoulder. His hands hung loosely at his sides. Rhodan was not about to turn this encounter—the first encounter of a human being with an alien intelligence—into a debate conducted with bullets. It would have been an unseemly and reprehensible welcome, unworthy of a man of his clear and tolerant outlook.

He felt a certain emptiness well up within him. The nearer he came to the gigantic structure, the more he felt the unendurable sadness of this confrontation. The strangers had obviously seized the initiative. Still, they had acted only indirectly. Rhodan was led inevitably to the conclusion that the radio interference had probably been more a precautionary measure than an omen of imminent destruction. This thought calmed him. He trusted to the benevolence of these no doubt lofty souls for whom he could very well make allowances.

He had been quite mistaken in his estimate of the distance. The gigantic vessel was much farther away than he had believed. The crater walls vaulted upward, mightier and mightier. They loomed ominous, oppressive. When he had gone still several hundred additional yards in the blinding sunlight, he could no longer see the spaceship in its entirety. It had a diameter certainly in excess of 1,500 feet.

It was supported on massive pillars ending in flat plate-like structures. He smiled weakly when he noticed this resemblance to the *Stardust*'s construction. The aliens must have thought processes similar to those of man, he decided, for there were evidently some common denominators in their technical and scientific vocabularies.

He suddenly became aware of Reg's rapid breathing over

the speaker in his helmet. Immediately afterward, the shadow of his friend appeared.

Reginald Bell accompanied him without another word. He uttered not a single further sound. Silently Rhodan nodded to him, an awkward gesture because of the bulk of the pressurized helmet. Reg grinned back feebly. With all his self-control, he could not disguise the glow in his eyes.

Their steps became slower and slower as they approached. Above them rose the incomprehensible sphere. The sun lit up only that part of the ground which lay underneath the towering mass, and where a heavy darkness began, Rhodan stopped completely. He looked up until he had bent his upper torso all the way back.

His eyes seized upon the wide gaping opening at the lower edge of the equatorial bulge he had previously noted. Now it was a mighty ring more than seventy yards in diameter.

"If they were to blast off now, we would be atomized," he said blandly. His hand motioned upward. "These are probably the jet exhausts, if our propulsion systems are at all related. This glazed ground surface around the ship must have boiled once in white heat. Hmm. I estimate the initial payload of this craft, under Earthly gravity, to be about two million tons. How does one launch such a tremendous mass?"

"I would suggest a firecracker," offered Reg. Within his chest a dull fury demanded release. Obviously no one seemed to be paying any attention to them. He could hear again the inner voice that made mention of monkeys. Reg could not overcome that feeling, try as he might; he did not possess the remarkable self-confidence of his friend, so he took refuge in his rather offbeat sense of humor. This was, in effect, his last resort when his reason could carry him no further.

Rhodan maintained his composure. It was his guess that within the ship, discussion was in progress. Probably the unknown entities were also grappling with this perplexing situation. They would of course know that they could do away with both these human beings with little effort. One push of a button, very likely, would suffice for that.

Rhodan considered this very fact to be a point in their

favor. If the strangers were not in possession of an entirely alien ethic—if they were familiar with the concept of tolerance—then they simply could not do a thing. Their only choice was between continued silence or the communication of some sign of life. Therefore, Major Rhodan armed himself only with patience.

Reg reacted quite differently. After a few moments, he said loudly and ironically, "Below your ship stand two horrible monsters with thirst in their throats and hunger in their bellies. Hello, there! My name is Reginald Bell. You were kind enough to force us into making a crash landing. Now we're coming to present you with the bill."

He stopped talking. Under different circumstances Rhodan would have laughed, but now his throat began to dry out. Reg's uncompromising behavior did not seem wholly appropriate to the time, the place and the nature of the event.

They spoke no more. Now, however, Rhodan too felt tempted to clutch his weapon. Quite a while ago Reg had got a firm hold on his RAK automatic, while Rhodan had continued his restraint. Rhodan's disapproving glance elicited only a grim shrug of the shoulders from Captain Bell.

The blinding light came just as suddenly as had the greenish glow a few hours before. Rhodan was startled. Quite against his will, drawn as if by a magnet, the automatic weapon slipped down into the crook of his arm. He muttered a blunt oath. Raging inside, he pushed the weapon back onto his shoulder.

A wide opening appeared in the hull of the sphere. The bright light was issuing forth from within. This had taken place, like any process on the moon, in complete silence. Rhodan had never before missed the sound conducting property of atmosphere as much as he did now.

Something was thrust out of the opening. When its base had touched the ground, it unraveled into a flat, broad band. That was all. Nothing else happened.

With measured tread, Rhodan stepped up to this weakly fluorescent band. Close in front of it he stopped.

"An invitation," he said softly. "A welcome mat. No steps. Hmm. The hatch is still a good ninety feet above us. The *Stardust* could fit comfortably into the space in between."

"Probably a little IQ test, likely as not." Reg snorted

nervously, meanwhile looking upward. Not a living soul was to be seen.

Rhodan stepped onto the slanted surface. It rose up to the hatch at an angle of at least forty-five degrees. When he felt himself being borne aloft, he instinctively stretched out his arms, wishing to balance himself, before he realized that here there was no question of falling. Nevertheless, his shoes did not touch the band, but hovered a few millimeters above the fluorescent material. He was carried as gently along as if he had been standing on a moving escalator.

Reg was cursing. He could not detach his hands from an imaginary support. On all fours, he followed Rhodan.

Once they had arrived at a large anteroom, the conveyor belt deposited them safely inside. This was the origin of the bright light. Again they heard nothing as the air locks closed behind them.

They were inside the alien ship.

"No one would ever believe this," said Reg in a low voice. "Not a living soul, and I doubt if we'll ever be able to talk to a human being again. What do you plan to do?"

"Negotiate. Use my head. What else? The situation no longer appears fantastic, if one looks at it objectively. It's nothing but a matter of instinct. Try to silence your fears for the time being."

They became aware of the hissing sound of penetrating air. At this point it was impossible to tell whether human beings could breathe this mixture of gases. Rhodan realized that they were indeed undergoing a test. Had he opened his helmet now, trusting to good luck, his rash action would undoubtedly have been considered a demerit. He could not know what kind of gas they had blown into this room. He therefore kept silent until the interior air locks opened.

They found themselves in a high, wide arched passageway, ending at a fluorescent shaft. They went ahead. There was no longer anything else they could do. The ship seemed devoid of life. It was an unreal dream-like situation. Reg was certain that he could not stand this stress much longer than another five minutes. Then he would simply lose his nerve. He felt like ranting and raving or running amok. If only he could have *done* something!

The clear voice, in the flawless enunciation of an English teacher, came next.

"You may open your protective suits now," it said. "You will find the air suitable for breathing."

Rhodan let his breath out with a "Whew!" Without uttering another sound, he removed his helmet.

## CHAPTER EIGHT

Khrest was his name. His race apparently knew no distinction between first name and surname. He was a humanoid. He had two upper and two lower limbs, a compact torso, and a large head, all combined in a fashion most human beings would recognize. Though frail in appearance, with a fragile bone structure, he was at least one head taller than Perry Rhodan. To judge from his color, he might have belonged to some velvet skinned Polynesian tribe. This illusion was shattered, however, by the contrast of his white hair and the reddish, almost albinoid pigmentation of his eyes.

From beneath a high vaulted forehead, those eyes emerged to impress one with their almost hypnotic effect. He wore the ethereal expression of a very old and very wise man whose skin had remained firm and youthful in spite of his years.

His outward resemblance to man was quite remarkable; yet he radiated something alien, something unreal. Undoubtedly, the real differences would lie in areas invisible to the naked eye. Rhodan guessed that it might be an unusual organic structure or a metabolism wholly unknown on Earth or something else along these lines. Nevertheless, Khrest was an oxygen breather.

The heat was almost intolerable in the chamber where Rhodan stood, illuminated by an exceedingly bright blue light that probably bordered on ultraviolet.

The mode of illumination and the oppressive room temperature indicated that this creature had come from a planet with a hot and brilliant blue dwarf sun. This was all Rhodan could ascertain, for the time being.

No, there was something more. He had noticed it at once. Khrest looked weak and emaciated, like a person deathly ill. His movements seemed almost helpless. Rhodan thought back to the cropped off mountain top and wondered if there was any connection between that and the apparent weakness of this alien.

There were two others in the room. Both were male. Rhodan squinted as he surveyed the scene. This was his first encounter with such lethargy. These people were so obviously apathetic, indifferent and generally lifeless that even a poor observer would immediately have been struck by it.

Compared to the others, Khrest seemed, for all his weakness, lively and energetic. It was extraordinary how little stir their arrival had created. When Rhodan and Bell, strange and otherworldly visitors to the aliens, had entered the room, none of them had even turned their heads. They acted as though Rhodan and Bell simply did not exist.

They lay listless on their mattresses and stared up at oval video screens above their heads. They seemed transfixed. Rhodan could find no significance in the instruments to which they gave their rapt attention. He could discern only a kaleidoscope of colors, appearing and vanishing, flickering across the screen. Abstract geometrical patterns were formed in enormous variety. Additionally, he could hear a high whine and whistling.

Rhodan began to feel uncomfortable. Something was not quite right in this otherwise immaculate spacecraft. There was an almost palpable atmosphere of sickness and decay, as though he had stepped into some asylum by accident. The ship itself was spotless, but Rhodan had the feeling that cobwebs and mildew would be more appropriate.

Khrest addressed one of the other aliens. He elicited a charming smile, but after the merest pittance of a reply, the other alien returned once more to his video screen.

Astounded, Bell stood there gaping. That changed abruptly, however, when *she* entered. Rhodan felt a sudden chill. It was easy to see why. With her whole manner, she seemed to generate coldness, insensitivity and arrogance. Indeed, she deigned to give them only a sideward glance and then proceeded to ignore both Bell and Rhodan.

She was as tall as Rhodan and had the luminous red hued eyes of her race. On Earth, she would have been declared a singular beauty. Nevertheless, this thought quickly lost itself amid others, as Rhodan's instinct issued a warning. This woman, who so coolly regarded him, was dangerous, and dangerous because it was obvious that she would not face the facts. In her eyes, he and Bell were neither more nor less than some form of creeping prehistoric sea slime, devoid of intelligence and burdened with lips that uttered naught but gibberish.

This realization hit Rhodan with painful impact. He had never before been the object of such scorn, such nose-in-the-air contempt.

He changed color and clenched his fists. The woman wore a tight fitting suitlike garment with red fluorescent symbols on the breast. Rhodan was only later to learn that they represented insignia of rank. He felt much more at ease with Khrest, whose boyish face and easy aristocratic manners could enchant as well as impress. With a fluent mastery of English, Khrest introduced the young woman as Thora.

Rhodan thus found himself welcomed by attitudes he could not reconcile. The clash of opposites and paradox was everywhere to be found. Within a spacecraft whose very presence testified to the existence of alien creatures far superior to man, he was ignored by incredible lethargy. On the one hand he was greeted with utmost courtesy, on the other, confronted with icy rejection. These were the strangest moments of his life. To Bell, it was like dancing on a powder keg. It suddenly struck him that they had not been asked to surrender their weapons. This, too, was more than peculiar.

Khrest studied them for a long while, so openly and obviously that it seemed not in the least offensive or intimidating.

Thus far, Rhodan had hardly said a word. He simply stood tall and straight in the center of this room, which was silent and spotless and without furniture, surrounded on all sides by a multiplicity of video screens, instrument panels and the like.

Khrest leaned back on his cot. Behind a weak smile, he was breathing heavily. Then Rhodan recognized, for the first time, a look of genuine concern on the face of the young woman Thora.

She called out sharply to the other two aliens. One

of them rose halfway up from his mattress, then returned with an idiot smile to his surreal pleasures.

Rhodan knew that now was the time for action. Bell could stand the tension no longer. One needed only to look at his face—shock white, with a rigid jester's grin—to know that.

The veiled expression was now gone from Khrest's dark encircled eyes. He seemed to sense that his guests had had quite enough of this affair. Rarely had Rhodan observed such curiosity in the eyes of another. Khrest seemed only to lie in wait of that word which would bring him salvation.

What role did he play aboard this ship? Did this woman wield any power? In what capacity did she serve?

Thora turned swiftly as Rhodan came a few steps closer, his helmet dangling on its hinges. Like a threat, her hand flew to her belt with a blur of color. Rhodan countered her glance. Hers was an expression of utmost disgust, but his own communicated such cool unconcern that she was more startled than repelled. Bell's plaster cast of a smile relaxed. His eyes narrowed. He knew Rhodan, and he knew that Rhodan had just switched over. They could either discuss this in a sensible manner, or they would have to settle for a split-second duel to their mutual disadvantage.

Rhodan brushed past Thora. She recoiled as though she had been touched by some venomous scorpion.

Khrest watched tensely. When Rhodan stood close beside him, he closed his eyes. Reg had never heard his commanding officer speak so softly.

"Sir, I know you can understand me. How and why this is so is of no importance to me at the moment. Nor does the current situation concern me greatly. My name is Perry Rhodan. I am a major in the United States Space Force and the commanding officer of the terrestrial spaceship *Stardust*. You have forced me to make an emergency landing. However, we need not discuss this just now."

"If you take another step, you are going to die!" rang Thora's voice, half retching with unrestrained rage.

Rhodan's nerves jarred at the sound of this dark voice. He slowly turned his head and displayed his famous grin.

Apparently, this woman had also switched over. For a moment, it seemed she was enveloped in a silken halo;

or that was the way it seemed to Rhodan. A mixture of shock and surprise swam in her eyes. Slowly Rhodan began to understand. She was obviously possessed of such a superiority complex and such interplanetary chauvinism that she regarded his very proximity to Khrest as a kind of blasphemy. Rhodan revised his initial estimate of the reasons behind her all too apparent contempt. Here, she was the rational being and he was the scion of a fine old Stone Age family. *That* was it. At last he understood the situation completely.

Khrest seemed to have guessed what was going on in Rhodan's mind.

"I am sorry," he said weakly. "It was not in my power to circumvent these difficulties. You see, we were not prepared for your arrival. According to my information, the third planet of this solar system is supposed to have been an undeveloped world inhabited by primitive mammals. There was no mention of. . . . Well, things seem to have changed a great deal since our last exploratory flight. We had no desire for a confrontation between our races."

Thora intervened. "Leave at once! You have violated the laws of the Imperium. I am forbidden contact with creatures below developmental stage C." Her face was on fire. "Leave immediately!"

Rhodan's hopes collapsed like a house of cards. "Creatures," that is what they were, in the aliens' eyes. A helpless fury welled up within him.

"Then why have you let us enter your ship at all?" he asked sharply. "Why? What do you mean by it?"

"It was at my suggestion," said Khrest. "You will not understand this at once. Your race is still in its infancy. Because of my disease, I am permitted certain privileges by the Law. There are special provisions for these circumstances. We may take up contact with inferior forms of life as soon as our existence becomes—"

"I understand," Rhodan interrupted. "I understand completely. Sir, you are in need of our help."

Thora snorted at the absurdity of such a statement. Nevertheless, she seemed once more to be worried.

"You are very young and spirited," murmured Khrest. "Is it thus with all of your race?"

70

Rhodan was moving his lips. Khrest could be sure of that much.

"Have you no doctors on board? Why can't you be helped?"

"There is no cure," returned Thora tersely. "Now, will you go? You have humiliated me quite enough. Khrest has seen you. My patience is at an end. I am commanding this spacecraft."

"Huh?" was all that Reg could find to say. Following this, he sank slowly into a stupor of amazement. He had had quite a different conception of the first encounter between alien intelligences. All this seemed too fantastic, too much like a Gilbert and Sullivan operetta.

In reply, Rhodan removed his helmet. His eyes were burning. Henceforth, he would simply ignore her. Khrest grew even more attentive. His gaze was an inquiry and an analysis.

"You are refusing?" he whispered faintly. His astonishment knew no bounds. "Do you not know to whom you speak?"

Rhodan was rude. He replied, with sarcasm, "Yes, indeed I do. Yet, through no fault of my own, I can claim a high IQ, although your commanding officer would prefer to think otherwise. It is therefore obvious to me that I have a ship full of either mental or physical invalids on my hands. If I consider your scientific advancement, I can find no reason why your sickness should not have been treated by now. Your people just don't seem to give a damn. You and your commander are probably the only sane individuals aboard. I have a feeling that all of you are only the decadent descendants of a formerly highly developed civilization. You have my sympathies, but just take a good look at those two men over there. On Earth, they'd be sent to a sanitarium for treatment."

Rhodan turned abruptly. He brandished his weapon, now menacing, his finger on the pushbutton trigger.

Thora paled, but in an instant there were two whirring metal monsters at her side. The only robots Rhodan knew were the bulky machines and electronic computers of Earth. These, however, were huge automatons in human form, with ingeniously equipped appendages for tools and weapons. They were just, suddenly, *there*. Empty eye sockets in bullet-shaped heads defied him. The barrels of un-known weapons, emerging *en masse* from metallic holsters, were aimed at him.

"Stop this nonsense!" Rhodan's voice was high and shrill. "Let's use the *intelligent* way and discuss our differences. You yourself know that I've spoken the truth. If it bothers you that these conclusions come from a 'savage,' then you should never have let us come aboard."

His finger lay ready on the trigger. Reginald Bell had already taken cover behind a couch.

Thora's face was now ugly in a paroxysm of rage, as she gazed, quite pale, at Rhodan's weapon. "How dare you?" she shrieked. Her fists were clenched and her fingers drawn in angered spasm. "How dare you speak such heresies in a vessel of the great Imperium! How *dare* you! Unless you leave immediately, I shall have you annihilated on the spot!"

"Agreed. I'll go along with that. Then you will let us leave without any interference? Will you let the *Stardust* blast off again? This is only the Earth's satellite. We can't live here."

"I cannot permit that. I cannot allow you to spread the word of our presence here among the inhabitants of the third planet."

"Very well. So you think it's perfectly all right to let us suffocate here, or what? We haven't the technical know-how you seem to have inherited from your illustrious an-cestors. We can't produce oxygen from stones, nor food from dust. We've only just begun the conquest of space."

Rhodan would have thought impossible the response that followed in the wake of his statement. This stranger Khrest, previously so decidedly tranquil, uttered a wild cry. Once the very antithesis of strength, he seemed now to have forgotten all weakness.

"What did you say? You have just begun with *what?*"

"With the conquest of space," Rhodan repeated, matter of factly. "Does the thought disturb you? We shall go our way, and someday we too shall possess great ships like your own, but much sooner than you would ever believe possible."

"Wait!" moaned Khrest. "Please."

Nonplussed, Rhodan paused. The RAK automatic was

lowered. In that moment, there ensured such a heated discussion between the bedridden alien and his feminine superior that he felt his presence there quite superfluous. Rhodan joined Bell on the sidelines.

"The most idiotic situation of a lifetime," Bell whispered hastily. "What's going on? It looks like a battle to the death. I'm not at all happy with those robots watching over us. Shouldn't we get out of here while there's still time? What do you think?" His questions followed in rapid fire succession. He had waited too long with curiosity unquenched.

Rhodan observed the proceedings closely, trying to interpret what was going on, and in a low tone of voice he said, "It would seem to me that our fate is being decided. Certainly, he has some authority, or she wouldn't yield so much ground to him. What a woman! It still escapes me how they can speak and understand our language so well. What do they mean by 'the great Imperium'? It sounds to me as if mankind has lived for thousands of years alongside the most astounding events and been wholly ignorant all along of what was going on. That's a frightening thought. Obviously, these are not the only intelligent creatures in the universe. There are tremendous possibilities here.

"Pull yourself together, old man. We're staying. This is a great game, even if it does seem ridiculous. These people must think in concepts far beyond our comprehension. They are accustomed to things whose mere mention would cause our statesmen on Earth to break out in uncontrolled weeping. Don't let them notice your surprise. We must speak up while we have a chance. Here we are the representatives of mankind, and I would like very much to see mankind at last united, strong and mighty. Do you understand that?"

"Of course I do," Bell replied. "But I'd also like to come out of this adventure alive."

"I have an idea that Khrest is reaching a decision now. Look at that! Thora's growing more and more meek and nervous by the minute. Something is happening. I can feel it. Just watch."

Thora seemed to be beside herself. Her eyes, which so fascinated Rhodan, had become the color of bronze. Khrest added something that sounded hard and decisive. In response she assumed an angular pose that impressed Rhodan as a respectful salute with which she honored her superior.

He caught her enigmatic glance. She was pale and plainly disappointed. With no further ado, she turned and left the room, accompanied by the two hulking robot servants.

Then they were alone with Khrest. The two wraith-like forms, reclining glassy eyed on their cots, did not count.

Exhausted, Khrest had sunk back onto his couch. A feeble gesture of his hand urged Rhodan to step forward. He bent over the alien with a feeling of honest compassion. Only then, at close range, did he first realize that he had before him, in reality, a very old man. His ageless complexion was a mask behind which many tales were left untold.

"Sir, I have an outstanding physician on my ship," Rhodan insisted. "You must be examined and treated. You have not convinced me that you can find any help here. How long have you been on the moon?"

Khrest recovered somewhat. The sharp lines of exhaustion were now less pronounced. "We have been here for what you would call four months." He hardly seemed to breathe. "It was an accident, an involuntary crash landing. However, we have made use of the opportunity to learn the predominant language of your planet. Improbable as it may seem to you, our brains are utterly unlike your own. We have photographic memories and the power of total recall. Of course, we were eavesdropping on your conversation. It was very simple. We have been monitoring your broadcasts for weeks, and from what we have heard, we were fortunate in not having landed on the third planet itself. You are about to commit a horrible transgression against the laws of life."

"Atomic war—yes," muttered Rhodan sadly. "It grieves me to have to admit it. The crisis is almost at the boiling point; but rest assured that mankind really doesn't want this war."

"But it will lead to it all the same. Our conclusion was, therefore, to regard your species as a still primitive form of life. I have now changed my opinion. You are young, curious and ambitious, with very receptive, lively minds. After careful consideration, I have officially classified you under developmental stage D. It is my prerogative to make

74

such a decision. I have given Thora the command to enter this revision of your planet's status in the memory banks of our positronic brain. I am the scientific leader of this expedition, or that is what I imagine you would call me. Thora is responsible only for the effective operation of this ship. Can you understand this? Are there similar differences in your terrestrial chain of command?"

Rhodan confirmed that there were.

"Your words have had direct influence on the classification system of the Imperium. Living creatures who have already undertaken the conquest of space may be upgraded by an authorized scientist. This I have done. Consequently Thora's objections have become invalid and irrelevant. We may therefore take up contact with your species."

He smiled weakly, silent triumph shining in his eyes. Rhodan understood.

"Sir, you need our help," Rhodan repeated. "Let me fetch our physician. Something must be done."

"In time. First, listen to me. I do not believe that you can help me. Though we may resemble one another in appearance, I should nevertheless have a basically different body chemistry. Our organic structures may also vary. At any rate, in the judgment of the Imperium, you have met the basic requirements. You are intelligent and, in your behavior, recall the lives of our ancestors, and you have successfully applied the newly discovered source of energy toward constructive goals. I refer, of course, to atomic power. Thus far, you have still not committed the cardinal error of using nuclear power in order to bring about the extinction of a major proportion of your species. I am, as I have said, one of the leading scientists in the service of the Imperium. I am also one of the few whose motivation and strength of will still remain strong. Are you surprised at Thora's position?"

Bell glanced uneasily at the other aliens. They lay unmoving, as before, while they watched the peculiar programs flickering across their video screens. The kaleidoscope of geometrical designs seemed to have changed but little, but now a torrent of sparkling sounds could be heard.

"Is that the reason?" Rhodan asked. "Degeneration?"

"Your conclusions are correct. My race would be several million years old, in your reckoning of time. Once we were even as yourselves—hardy, inquisitive, adventurous. Then a few thousand years ago, we noticed the onset of progressive decay. The galactic empire was splintered, subject races rose up against our might, and the great Imperium, which had endured for millennia, was shaken to its foundations. Unlike other alien intelligence in the universe, we were rulers known for our benevolence. Now, it is all at an end. The Imperium is in decline. We are struggling for dominance, but to no avail. Dozens of highly evolved races clash in devastating wars conducted throughout the galaxy. But you would not know this. Your solar system lies far removed from these events, in an insignificant branch of the Milky Way."

"And what," interjected Reg, "are you doing about all this?"

The old man spoke sadly. "Nothing. Nothing any more. We have weakened and surrendered our will. Yet I am, like Thora, born into the ruling dynasty on Arkon. Ah, yes. Arkon is a world nearly 3,700 light-years from Earth."

Rhodan had turned pale. The magnitude of the figure struck him like a hammer blow. "That means you've mastered faster-than-light space travel!"

"Certainly. It has been thus for hundreds of your centuries. We knew Earth some thousand years ago, at the time of our last visit. It was during that period when degeneration began to set in among the Arkonides. Exploratory flights ceased, and our spacecraft remained inoperative at their bases. A view widely held is that one cannot escape the laws of nature. Still, we are planning and dreaming, and in our minds we have laid the theoretical foundations for the renaissance of empire. However, this is where our efforts end. We lack the energy and application necessary to realize our design. We are beginning to overlook things of immense importance. With each day, the empire declines more and more. The ruling class on Arkon itself has fallen into decay. We seek only beauty and a peaceful life and indulge ourselves with the luxury of passive pleasures. We are resigning, we are yielding. We are spent with age. We have simply been used up, and . . ." Khrest stared at them. "And heretofore we have found no race with the promise and potential that once was ours. You would seem to be the exception. You see why I have upgraded you. It is not only my right but my duty."

Once again, the scientist in Rhodan awakened. There were limitless questions to be answered and mysteries to be solved. "You say you've been here for four months. Why haven't you taken off again?"

Khrest nodded slowly. His glance grew more intense and searching.

"That could only be the question of a creature who takes inexhaustible energy to be his birthright. You would not ask if you could see life through our eyes. Why have we not done this? Our engines failed us, forcing us to resort to an emergency landing on your moon. We are no longer occupied with the problem of our ship's upkeep. There is only minor damage, but we do not have the spare parts with us. We simply did not think of it. That is why we are stranded here. We wait and wait, and nothing happens. My illness prevents me from doing the necessary work myself. We are in urgent need of certain fluidic micromodules. I do not believe they can be found in your world."

"Then we'll *make* 'em!" interjected Bell. "Show us how it's done, and we'll get them for you. Don't underestimate us, sir. We'll put the best brains on Earth to work on the problem. If necessary, we'll pluck the stars out of the skies, if only you tell us what's needed. There are colossal industries back home. We can do anything. I said anything!"

Khrest was aroused by these optimistic words. "I believe you," he whispered excitedly. "You must now convince Thora. The women of our race have been less affected than the males by our general debilitation. Therefore, many of our important positions are held by women. This has been happening for centuries. Prior to that, women knew only the duties of the household. Thora will prove shrewd in any bargain, I assure you. You are the right man for the task, Major Rhodan. She is afraid of you, which I find quite remarkable."

Rhodan gulped. So that was it. Bell was grinning. Nevertheless, the situation had not become any clearer.

"You should not be surprised that I am able to converse in terms you understand." Khrest continued. "It has always been my business to negotiate with the inhabitants of other worlds. I easily adapt myself to the conceptual perspectives of alien races. That is why we were not surprised by your appearance. In fact, we always count on such a possibility as a matter of course. You are solemn, sorely vexed, overwhelmed. You did not know that you were not alone in the universe. I could cite many similar instances. The sudden arrival of superior beings always comes as a shock. You have already overcome that shock, I see.

"What are those people over there doing?" inquired Rhodan. The strange music had changed once more and now resembled an urgent whispering.

Khrest turned his head painfully. "They are engaged in the usual simulator game. It has contributed much to the collapse of will and spirit among my people. Billions of Arkonides stand vigil by those screens daily while games are created by different masters of the medium. Highly complex. It is the audio-visual representation of elements in the subjective psyche. My people would waste their lives in this fashion. The situation is gradually worsening. For example, there are only fifty persons on board. Rarely do I get to see them, but when I do, they are seated, trance-like, before the *fictif* screens. Our degeneration is not to be found in the realm of normal attitudes or ethics but rather in a total relaxation and surrender of will. We have become indifferent to everything. For us, nothing remains exciting, nothing stimulating. Nothing evokes any response in us. The work of a new *fictif* artist takes precedence over all else. They are preoccupied, you see, with experiencing the latest creation as quickly as possible. I suppose we have always been too peaceful, too civilized. We seldom engaged in war. We were able to conquer the galaxy through the mere fact of our superior science and technology. No one dared defy us, in war or in revolt. No, it would not be a colonial system, as you use the word. It should not be regarded as such. The attending circumstances were—and are—not so simple. It will not be possible for you to understand this in a matter of moments."

"So they've just let you lie here and suffer and weaken for four months—is that what they did?" Speaking these words, Rhodan was uncommonly emotional. "Without doing anything whatsoever, without even making any attempt to find a remedy! It should have been simplicity itself for your people."

"It would have been simple if only someone were willing to apply himself to the task. The medical supplies aboard ship are ordinarily quite sufficient, but I have contracted an illness unknown in our world. Numerous tests and analyses will be necessary. These may require time, effort and intensive work, however, and will therefore not be done. Among the crew are important artists who are constantly creating new *fictif* works. Our robot crew is attending to the maintenance of the ship. Your emergency landing, Major Rhodan, was also supervised by the automatons. Intricate safety circuits—you might say 'safety valves'—were involved. Upon learning that we were not permitted to communicate with you, the positronic brain took action accordingly. It was very simple."

"Very simple," muttered Rhodan. He was appalled. "You regard as 'elementary' things that are to us almost beyond imagination. By the way, what do you mean by positronic? We have our own electronic brains, computers, but a positron has an extremely fleeting existence."

Khrest laughed. His expression suggested the tolerance with which an adult might view the antics of a two year old. Bell bit his tongue to keep a curse from escaping his lips.

"You'll understand, one day. We are simply unable to take off again. May I ask for your help?"

In an instant, Rhodan once more became the commander of the *Stardust* and, not least of all, a human being. Gone was his boundless astonishment. He was thinking again with the steely precision of a machine.

"Sir, I know from our latest intelligence reports that the outbreak of war between the Western world and the Eastern bloc is almost inevitable. Neither can I explain in only a few words, why this war can be avoided with only the very greatest effort. As the causes, conflicting ideologies are at the bottom of it. You may not be aware of this, sir, but that's the way it is on Earth. Now I have a simple question for you—"

Khrest sighed deeply. "The 'simple' question," he repeated. "So you say. I have not heard such a phrase since my youth. We no longer ask such questions, I'm afraid. Please, tell me—what is it that you want?"

"Do you have at your disposal means powerful enough

79

to prevent a disastrous confrontation with nuclear weapons? If so, what do you have?"

"What manner of nuclear weapons?" asked Khrest with interest.

"Two kinds, sir. Nuclear reaction by means of fission and fusion."

"Ah, yes. We are familiar with the primitive technique of fission. Fission processes may be counteracted by a complete absorption of the free neutrons. In the absence of neutrons, as you call these particles, it is impossible."

"Yes, yes, of course. We know that too. But we have nothing by which to achieve that effect. And what is it, then, with the fusion weapons, the hydrogen bombs?"

"Also an obsolete procedure, which we have long since abandoned. The antineutron screen is not effective in the case of nuclear fusion."

"Indeed. But as yet, sir, we know of only the so called hot modes of reaction. That means that thermonuclear fission must be used to bring the hydrogen loads to reaction in our heavier bombs. If the fissionable material serving as detonator malfunctions, it will never go so far as the fusion of light nuclei. Am I not correct?"

"You are a scientist? Very good. Provided you are still, as you say, working with the more primitive technique of fission, I can assure you of a total failure of these weapons. We need but a small device for that."

Rhodan trembled. "For the whole Earth?" he asked.

"After all, it is only a small planet. Do not forget that we are emissaries of a galactic empire. We will succeed."

Rhodan swallowed hard. He did not dare look into Bell's wide open eyes. The catalog of all these technical miracles was making him dizzy. The alien spoke of these Earth shaking machines in the same way as a boy back home would speak of last week's football game.

"Then it would make sense to take you to Earth and have you undergo the proper diagnosis and treatment there. But first you must be examined by Dr. Manoli. He'll be able to find out what is really wrong with you. As a diagnostician, he has no peer. Could you perhaps supply him with information on the nature of your physiology and metabolism? I assume he'll find this necessary."

"I'm driving off in the tank," Bell declared, now restless.

"Good Lord! If I don't get back in time, Fletcher's going to blast off without us! Then all hell will break loose."

"You need not drive to your vessel," whispered Khrest. "Speak to Thora. You do not know of what we are capable, Major Rhodan."

Mentally, Rhodan readily agreed.


## CHAPTER NINE

Captain Clark G. Fletcher was trembling convulsively. He had completely gone to pieces as he stood looking around in the dome of the gigantic alien spacecraft. What Rhodan and Bell had swallowed, he would have to digest gradually, in small doses.

Thora fixed him with her iron gaze. Dr. Eric Manoli had long since disappeared. He had pounced upon Khrest with all the mercurial enthusiasm of the explorer, in the true sense of the word. There were still others in the command center. Khrest had described them as being among the more active members of his race, but they offered a pathetic sight.

Rhodan suspected that they were longing with every fiber of the minimal will to watch the next *fictif* program. Though wearing the uniform of the "Great Empire," they seemed to think only of their simulator screens.

This, then, was a portrait of the descendants of a once mighty stellar race. One could hardly imagine that, once upon a time, beyond memory of man or mother Earth, their ancestors had founded a galactic federation reaching across a broad path of the universe. Khrest had assured them that the Arkonide expansion had taken place with a minimum of conflict. Rhodan, however, had his doubts on that score.

He could not conceive of how such a colonization could have occurred, save by blood, sweat and tears. Still, that was long since past. He stood before what were very nearly the last remains of this once great people whose technological and scientific heritage now lay gathering dust. Just the thought of the so-called rescue operation made Rhodan's head swim.

Thora had been alone in the command center, surrounded with the most astonishing array of mechanisms. Rhodan had not counted the robots, although in the final analysis, it was they who had done the job.

Fletcher had almost lost his mind when the *Stardust* was seized by a "mysterious force." He shuddered at the thought of it.

"It was horrible," he had declared with a gurgle. "The solitude had already become almost unbearable. Eric and I took turns standing guard. We were always anticipating the sudden appearance of an Asiatic scout probe. But more than that, we were worrying about you and the message you were supposed to send. Then, all of a sudden, there was this jolt. Something lifted the ship off the ground, as though it were little more than a feather. Panic stricken, I pushed the ignition button. I shifted from autopilot into manual control, full speed ahead; but it was no use! On the contrary, the reactor suddenly stopped working, and we were left without any power at all. So the *Stardust* was carried over the craters at maddening speeds. An instant later, we got a look at the giant sphere. They landed us so gently that we hardly knew it. I was overjoyed when I saw Reg's face. You haven't got any more surprises in store for us, have you?"

Thora had then interjected a brief explanation of the phenomenon. It had been "merely" a rather ordinary transport field for the movement of solid bodies. It was quite common on Arkon.

She had chosen her words carefully, but she had been unable to hide their sting. She had still not forgotten. It would probably be a great while before she could forgive them. For her, *Homo sapiens* was, as before, a primitive creature with whom one might collaborate only in view of the crisis at hand. This alone she had been able to accept, nothing else.

They stood in a small anteroom, awaiting Dr. Manoli. He had been given enough visual material to provide him with some idea of the Arkonide anatomy, inside and out. In any event, Rhodan was certain of this much—he had tackled a problem unique and extraordinary in the history of medicine. Many questions would arise. It was too much to ask of any doctor in the world, that he be able to treat a wholly alien organism with no more than intuition to go on. Such could be a branch of learning in its own right, quite apart from any estimation of damages that might ensue from medication and therapy.

It would simply have to be a game of chance, played with high odds, with the alien's life at stake. No one could say how he would react to the terrestrial medications.

Nevertheless, Dr. Manoli was a man worthy of the highest esteem. One could trust implicitly in his verdict. If immediate help was not forthcoming, then the best minds on Earth would just have to be consulted. Rhodan was prepared to set all the pharmaceutical industries of the world on their heels, working at breakneck speed, if this were necessary. This stranger must be saved, no matter how; and the devil take the hindmost.

Dr. Manoli had already been gone for about ten hours. Lacking his medical background, none of the others could help him. Thora grew restless. She seemed to divine that she was standing on the threshold of a decisive turning point in her life. The ambivalence of her position on the chances for man's development was still more oppressive.

Rhodan observed her worriedly. She made every effort to conceal her anxiety beneath biting sarcasm and haughty condescension. At the same time, she felt that this tall man with the twinkle in his eyes was seeing right through her.

It would have been so much simpler for Thora if these alien intelligences had not so much resembled the people of her own race. That confused her and depressed her, all unconsciously. It presented her with a most distressing situation. She could have dealt very easily with creatures of monstrous appearance, but *here . . . !* She felt the obstinacy of Rhodan's will. He wanted to be recognized. He also wanted to be regarded as a fellow rational being, as an equal! So casually had he permitted himself the liberty of comparing himself to her, the Arkonide!

That brought her to the edge of eruption. She knew suddenly that the human race held a position unparalleled anywhere else in the universe. Never before had she encountered such candor or such insolence and belligerence. She was accustomed to submission. It was natural for her to expect an unconditional surrender to her immeasurable superiority. But this . . . *man* . . . seemed not in the least intimidated by her. With his impertinent grin, he had irritated her to the boiling point. Then, to add insult to injury, he had treated her like some silly creature!

Thora was quite beside herself.

She sat up erect when Rhodan again approached her. Her furious glance produced only a friendly nod in reply. Could he not feel the power of her presence, or had he simply chosen to ignore it? Obviously, it was the latter. She found this frightening.

"I've got another simple question for you, ma'am," said Rhodan. "Or rather, I'm wondering about a certain pragmatic issue. . . . Tell me, is there such a thing in your world as 'money,' or means of payment, or standards of exchange? You see, one offers it in purchase of certain goods, and—"

Sardonically she declared, "With a galactic trade between more than 1,000 inhabited planets, we could hardly avoid such a thing."

"Very well, then," he laughed, unmoved. "I shall have to take Khrest back to Earth. We have neither the required medications nor the needed diagnostic instruments on board the *Stardust*. An operation might even be necessary. What can you offer us in return? If only banknotes, letters of credits, or something of the sort, we're not interested. We wouldn't know what to do with them. So what do you have? How about your precious stones, crystals, artificial elements or other such materials?"

"We have with us the customary items of exchange for worlds in developmental stages C and D. These are tooling machines with automated control units and their own power supplies, guaranteed for some eighty of your solar years. These may be applied to all branches of industry. In addition, I can offer various micromechanical devices, such as portable spectrometers for the detection of elements, an antigravity apparatus for one man flight, and—"

"Stop, stop!" moaned Fletcher. "This is too much for me. You're going to turn everything topsy-turvy on Earth. They'll be killing each other off just to get a chance at your magic machines."

"That is *your* affair. We are merchants. We deal in only those things which we consider harmless, even in the hands of primitives such as yourselves."

"And what," asked Rhodan, "do you have for 'genuine'

rational beings? Never mind, you don't have to answer that. I can just imagine. Then will you please see to it that the *Stardust* is equipped accordingly. Pack everything that will be needed by Khrest, plus . . ." He paused, with a sharp glance at her as he continued. "Plus, don't forget the *other* instruments. They might come to be of great importance. You do remember our conversation, don't you?"

She examined him slowly. Was it respect that he found, newborn, in her eyes?

"You are risking your life, do you realize that? Your reasoning meets with my approval, nonetheless. It seems better for all concerned. After all, who knows what brute response will come from such low— I mean—"

"Don't hesitate," Rhodan smiled. "Finish what you were saying. It doesn't bother me at all. I shall be tolerant; I shall regard you as one who is simply not responsible for her actions. Just forget it. Please start loading the cargo aboard the *Stardust* immediately. You may throw out whatever remains in the storage room of the ship. We won't need it. The payload should not exceed sixty tons, all told. I have a very difficult landing operation ahead of me. Or perhaps, if you would reconsider . . . why not let us have one of your auxiliary vessels? With one of those, we could be back on Earth in an hour."

She corrected him. "Within five minutes. I'm afraid not, however. This is the limit of my hospitality. Nothing, except Khrest and some few instruments, may ever find its way to Earth. I simply cannot permit it. I have my orders."

"Khrest has rated us one stage higher on the developmental scale, don't you recall?"

"And lucky for you. Otherwise, these negotiations could not have proceeded even this far. Nevertheless, I am not permitted to send a minicraft into your atmosphere. The positronic brain would never assent to such a move, and there is no way to overrride its decision. The computer's circuitry cannot be tampered with. Please understand that this was not the enterprise we foresaw when we left Arkon."

"What was?" Rhodan asked this with mounting discomfort.

"Once again I regret. . . . Suffice it to say that we did not land here by choice. Our destination lies elsewhere. Light-years from here, in fact."

At just this moment, Dr. Manoli appeared, looking pale and weary. His manner was brusque; he fended off their attentions.

"Spare me your questions. It was more than strenuous. I find that they are not as different from us as I had feared at first. A rather novel arrangement of their inner organs, and the skeleton is also of a singular nature. Yet they do have the same blood composition as we. It was this fact, I suppose—the hunch that their blood was like ours—that aroused my diagnostic suspicions that first minute I saw him. We are dealing here with a case of leukemia. I've exhausted all the possibilities of our shipboard laboratory but the blood tests have proved this beyond all doubt. Two years ago, after many unsuccessful attempts at conquering this seemingly incurable disease, an anti-leukemia serum was finally developed. Now, I only hope that it will be effective in Khrest's case. Even though the Arkonides are physiologically similar to ourselves, we must not overlook the possibility that the serum could still have disastrous effects. This must be kept in mind. Yes, I am certain —it is leukemia."

Rhodan was again perplexed. Thora showed signs of being highly distraught as she inquired into the nature and cause of this anomaly. By now, she had dropped her pose of prideful superiority.

"Let's get on with it," said Rhodan firmly. "Don't ask questions. We've got to start loading up right away. Our time is running out. Your crew and their dream worlds can go to hell, for all I care. What a waste! I can't understand such 'supermen' whiling away their lives with the pleasures of lunatics."

Thora seemed to weigh it in her mind before answering at last with a face devoid of feeling. "You wished to know what we were looking for in this sector of space. I will tell you. We are seeking to preserve the lives of our last great minds. We have not yet succeeded in escaping death and decay. We have had partial successes, but nothing more. My instructions were to proceed to a planet that is known to us from previous exploratory missions. The inhabitants of this planet hold the secret of biological cell preservation, which must be equated with a prolongation of life. Not only is Khrest our most important personage, he does not suffer from our general debilitation. Save him, please. Do everything in your power. Everything possible, everything imaginable. I will give you any support you may require, Major Rhodan, and that means a great deal. Do *everything*. If you should encounter opposition, you may call me by way of this device. Your advice will be acted upon. It must be apparent that the combined strength of all your terrestrial forces is but a ridiculous nothing that I could sweep away, with simply a twist of a dial, for all time. A single one of my energy cannons would suffice to change any of your larger continents into a boiling sea of lava within a fraction of a second. With this ship alone, I could destroy your entire solar system. Just remember this. Call me, please, before it is too late."

She left without another word. Captain Fletcher turned as pale as a ghost.

"If I've never believed in anything before," he whispered roughly, "I believe this; I accept all this completely, 100 per cent without reservations. But good God, what have we gotten into? Where is all this going to lead? Things will be chaos in Washington! They'll never believe this."

"On the other hand, they might not be that surprised." Bell interjected this with such emphasis that Fletcher started.

"What do you mean?"

"Oh, nothing." Bell stared with a vacant expression at his commanding officer, and after Fletcher had gone to check on the exhausted Dr. Manoli, he once again queried him.

"Perry, what have you got up your sleeve? Something doesn't seem quite right here. Have you made some kind of deal with Thora?"

"Perhaps I offered her my hand in marriage," was Rhodan's dry reply. He now had the serpent's eye stare of a merciless conqueror. Or at least that was Captain Bell's impression. "You don't mind, do you?"

"No." Bell asked no more questions. He had abruptly fallen silent when robots filed into the room. According to carefully made plans, the *Stardust* was being equipped from the gigantic arsenals of the alien space sphere. These mechanisms would weigh 60.3 tons under Earth gravity.

Rhodan went to Khrest. With an encouraging smile, he said, "Sir, we're ready to start. Unfortunately, Thora still refuses to put the space vehicle at my disposal. Isn't there anything that would change her mind? I'll have to subject you to enormous stresses in the *Stardust*. We know no means of counteracting natural inertia. Thus we must submit to high G forces during acceleration."

"I have no influence over Thora's decisions, but you will not have to suffer under these conditions. A small null-gravity adaptor will be brought on board. You will not feel a thing."

Once more, Rhodan was swallowing hard. He realized that he would simply have to get used to the miraculous. The Arkonides obviously made use of techniques that still seemed, for human scientists, to beckon remotely from the limbo of insoluble problems.

## CHAPTER TEN

"They've made it! They've made it!"

General Pounder, chief of the Space Exploration Command and of Nevada Fields, uttered these same words over and over again. He stared with rapt attention at the gigantic radar screen.

After a flight of fourteen hours, the *Stardust* had entered the upper layers of Earth's atmosphere. She had then begun the third orbital braking approach.

While still out in space, her high velocity of free fall had been throttled to three miles per second. The efficiency of the new nuclear chemical power plant had not been overestimated. It had enabled them to perform maneuvers ordinarily denied to a ship using chemical fuel.

The ship had been turned around close above the first molecules of air. The autopilot functioned with precision and reliability. Another failure seemed highly unlikely.

Major Rhodan's explanation for the cause of his long silence had sounded somewhat peculiar. According to his account, given via radio just a few minutes previously, some trouble had occurred in the circuits of the reactor; but he could make further details available only after they had landed safely.

Moments earlier, the *Stardust* had again come within range of the relay stations in Alaska and Greenland. Its altitude was then only 110 miles and its velocity somewhat less than 5,000 miles per hour.

Pounder turned around angrily. The little man had announced himself by clearing his throat.

Allan D. Mercant, head of the NATO security organizations, could not be persuaded to remove himself from the control center. He knew very well that his presence there was a disturbing factor, but this did not bother him.

He had shown up suddenly three hours before. His companions had silently departed, and shortly thereafter the armored tanks of the U.S. Fifth Reserve Division had arrived. Never before had Nevada Fields been so thoroughly quarantined.

Next came heavy transport vehicles with special crews. The FBI (internal security section) had provided their best people. With an enormous array of men and ammunition, they were waiting for the landing of the *Stardust*.

General Pounder had been furious. Allan D. Mercant smiled as affably as ever.

"I'm sorry, General. You brought the avalanche down on your own head. Now I would like to know what really happened up there. The report from the commander of your ship sounded rather off, you must admit."

"But there was no need to mobilize an emergency division of 10,000 men just for that!" Pounder had sputtered in a rage.

The Defense Secretary could only offer his regrets. He had deemed it necessary. For a moment Pounder thought of warning his four astronauts by radio.

But when a number of conservatively dressed men began to appear in the control center, he had to abandon any such thought.

Pounder could find no explanation for this. The technicians and scientists were nervous, and the chief of military security at Nevada Fields had been temporarily put out of action.

"Now what do you want?" snarled Pounder. "Can't you see that the *Stardust* is landing according to plan?"

"No longer," Mercant said with emphasis. The friendly smile was gone now. "Deviation. You can see for yourself. What is that supposed to mean, General?"

Pounder whirled about. Just then there came the alarming report from the remote control autopilot computer. A bright light lit up, and the loud hum died down.

"Contact interrupted," droned the mechanical voice. "Manual control assumes command of vehicle."

"Has Rhodan lost his mind?" Pounder roared, shaken to his roots. With a few great leaps, he bounded over to the microphone. The video screen was blank. There too Rhodan had broken the connection.

"Rhodan, General Pounder speaking! What is the meaning of this? Why have you discontinued remote control guidance? Rhodan! Where are you, Rhodan?"

There was no reply. The general grew pale. Helpless, he stared at the security intelligence chief, who walked slowly toward him. Allan D. Mercant had lost every trace of good humor, and fury shimmered in his blue eyes.

"You see?" he said coldly. "I had a premonition. There's something amiss here. Send out an alert to air defense. Unless Rhodan changes course at once I will have them open fire. Inform him that at this present altitude, he is in range of our new ground to air missiles."

In the same instant, however, an emergency signal from the *Stardust* squeaked from the receiver. It was a conventional SOS without any attempt at code. The SOS signals came through again and again. The first signs of panic appeared in the Nevada Fields control center. Men looked agape at each other. Why had Rhodan sent the universal distress signal? There were so many other ways to inform them of an emergency situation. Why had he chosen the SOS, and why on the international frequency?

Allan D. Mercant went into action. With a few terse commands, he activated the continental warning system.

The men of air defense, who had been on standby alert for weeks, ran now to their battle stations. At that moment the *Stardust* was continuing its flight over the Taimyr Peninsula in northern Siberia.

Once again the *Stardust* changed course. Continuously broadcasting an SOS, Rhodan turned south. He flew across Siberia.

In the headquarters of the Eastern Defense high command, the command to fire—already given—was canceled at the last moment. They had recognized that they were dealing with only the harmless American moonship. A hand withdrew from the red button. It had been very close to sending 7,000 atomic ICBMs into the sky.

This overflight had caused an international crisis and almost triggered a nuclear holocaust. Marshal Petronsky stared silently at the screens of his infrared stations. In its mad descent, the *Stardust* flew south over the Siberian steppes. Computers were calculating the probable point of landing from moment to moment. If the American vessel kept to the same course and held its velocity of fall, it would come down in the vicinity of the Sino-Mongolian border, somewhere in the middle of the central Gobi. Marshal Petronsky could have shot down the ship with no particular difficulty. Yet, being a practical man, he abandoned such a course of action.

The giant transmitters at his headquarters were set to work instead. He personally directed the operation.

The commanding officer of the Twenty-second Siberian Army Corps received detailed instructions. Those obtained by the division's commanders a few minutes later were still more explicit. The Eighty-sixth fully motorized border patrol in particular, then assigned to the area of the Obotuin-Chure and Goshun salt lake, were given orders to start marching.

The Fourth Mongolian Airborne Division, under the command of Lieutenant General Chudak, was put on emergency alert.

With this, Marshal Petronsky had done everything possible to guarantee capture of the American moon rocket—provided it still touched down within the Mongolian border.

If, on the other hand, the ship should land *outside* the border, in the territory of the Asiatic Federation, serious problems would undoubtedly arise. The marshal requested and received an immediate line to Moscow.

Concluding his discussion, he stated briefly, "It is to be assumed that serious failures have occurred within the ship's control system. The *Stardust* is presumably under manual control and piloted by an astronaut of the American Space Force. Our evaluation of radar data confirms this. I have abandoned the idea of dispatching high altitude jet fighters. I suggest we wait until the *Stardust* has landed and then, and only then, proceed with those measures which seem to be in order. I request special jurisdiction in this area."

Petronsky was granted his authority. But he had not counted on Major Perry Rhodan.

Immediately upon reentry into the Earth's atmosphere, the rocket had proceeded in the proven manner to the aerodynamically effective glider flight. The mighty delta wings had taken over the weight. As the air envelope became denser, the rudders proved more and more effective. The high velocity lost itself through increasing air friction. Landing in this manner, it became necessary only to slowly and progressively decrease speed. The outside temperature rose to 870 degrees Centigrade, particularly on the moon rocket's surfaces and its nose cone.

The automatic transmitters were continuously broadcasting "SOS" over the international emergency frequency. Rhodan had taken for granted that this would accomplish exactly what it did—there was no thought, in any of the capitals of the world, of bringing the *Stardust* under fire. Of course, all the Eastern powers were intensely interested in examining the *Stardust* at close range. For this, however, they would need a ship that remained intact. A pile of radioactive debris would be of no use to anyone.

Perry Rhodan landed the rocket in northern China, on a rocky plain near Lake Goshun. Although a salt lake, the Goshun was fed by the fresh water river Morin-Gol. This was in the middle of the vast central Gobi, scarcely south of the Mongolian border, just 102 degrees east and 38 degrees north.

Rhodan landed the *Stardust* as though it were a regular aircraft. The huge tires, designed specifically for this purpose, touched ground perfectly. A few moments later, the nose cone of the ship that had at last returned home pointed like some signpost at the nearby banks of the Morin-Gol.

The high whine of the auxiliary landing engines became silent. Rhodan detached his hand from the steering lever, suddenly aware that it was painfully cramped. Once the *Stardust* had overcome the first dangerous moments of reentry and landing approach, it was easy to land the ship like some heavy air freighter. Earth had one benefit the moon had probably always lacked—namely, a supporting air envelope.

With a quick movement, Rhodan had freed himself from the upright contour couch. His hand sprang so quickly to the open holster of his automatic that Captain Fletcher could not even begin to act.

Fletcher stared as though frozen into the barrel of the exceedingly dangerous RAK automatic weapon.

Bell remained unmoving in his seat, and Dr. Manoli did not venture to lift a finger. Khrest, occupying the fifth couch, made plain a lively interest in the proceedings. Fletcher had raved with a madman's senseless fury since their deviation from course. Try as he might, he had been unable to free himself from his seat, for Rhodan had locked the automatic fastening mechanism. Now, with a last rash effort, Fletcher tried to reach the weapon shelves built into the wall behind his couch.

"Forget it, Fletch," Rhodan cautioned. "Just hold on. We're back home again. If I were you, I wouldn't try anything else."

Fletcher stared at him. He was shock white, with trembling lips. "Home!" he repeated loudly. "Did you say 'home'?" He laughed furiously. His face was misshapen with maniacal rage. "Damn you, traitor! You've landed the ship in the middle of Asia! You must have had it planned all along; otherwise, you wouldn't have flown straight to this barren waste. You charted our course long ago. So that's it! You want to hand the *Stardust* over to the Chinese. Since when did you hatch such a treacherous plot? What reward will the ace astronaut of the United States Space Force receive for a job well done? How much—"

Rhodan interrupted him. "Shut up, Fletcher! Right now!" He had turned pale. A flicker of warning sparkled in his gray eyes. "Fletch, you can leave any time you want. No one will prevent you from leaving. You will see your baby, and Eric will have quite a lot to tell his grandchildren. But whatever you say, I never want to hear you suggest that I am a deserter or a traitor."

"And why *did* you land here?" Bell interjected calmly. He showed a frozen grin and narrowed eyes. Captain Bell was still himself in doubt. After all, one could not ignore the weapon in Rhodan's hand.

"I'd like you all to listen to me for a moment," began

Rhodan. "I am not a man who has ever done anything without good reason, and this time it is no different."

"Oh, no!" Fletcher moaned in desperation. He tugged with all his might at the magnetic bonds that held him fast in his seat. "You've deceived us! You've forced us to play along with your game. We were helpless!"

"Of course." Rhodan nodded with a straight face. Khrest smiled. He knew Rhodan's plans, just as Thora before him had been informed about them.

"You must understand by now that the *Stardust* has become only a worthless toy. Even if it should fall into Chinese hands, it would be hardly more than a joke. For on the moon there is a ship, and in that ship are people who, from this day forward, are the only important ones. It is they alone who have the power to prevent our world's total annihilation through nuclear war. From now on, the *Stardust* plays only a subordinate role. For the time being it makes no difference that in Moscow and Peking, as in Washington, they still believe her to be the greatest miracle of all time. This view is merely the result of sheer ignorance of the true situation. If our leaders had any idea of what we found on the moon, they would, with a wave of the hand, write off the rocket as entirely negligible. What matters exclusively is that mind we've brought to Earth with us. From now on, only Khrest counts, for he is heir to an immeasurably superior science. With him, mastery of the last secrets of Nature has come to Earth. Concealed in his photographic memory are things that will permit our space travel to leap across more than five millennia of painful development.

"You must understand that it is no longer a question of the *Stardust*. The problem now is Khrest, and the alien intelligences of the galaxy. The problem now is the union of all mankind—*all* human beings, irrespective of race or faith or ideology. The eternally misguided and misinformed will awaken, and men of goodwill may at last breathe a deep sigh of relief. It would have been the greatest mistake of all time to permit any one nation to capture Khrest.

Fletcher, who seemed more than amazed, shut his gaping jaws. He looked around helplessly.

"By now, Nevada Fields should be cordoned off by special security forces. Our people are hardly such fools. They could easily see that we must have experienced something out of the ordinary on the moon. The Eastern bloc, on the other hand, is still of the opinion that they are dealing with only an emergency landing. I have no intention of surrendering Khrest—the representative of an age old civilization and the unchallenged master of a superior science—into the merciless hands of some security organization.

"Let's be honest. Had we landed in the proper manner, Khrest would already have been taken into custody. Naturally, they would have *had* to do this. They would have placed him in isolation and interrogated him. They would have been extremely kind, considerate and polite; but still, he would already have been a prisoner. Khrest himself posed this condition—that he be permitted to act freely and without hindrance. He represents a *third power* on Earth. He is ill and needs our help. I consider it my duty, therefore, to guard him from all these embarrassments. He has the right to insist on freedom, even if he is an alien intelligence. Besides, he expects fair treatment, regardless of where we land. Any nation on Earth would be licking its chops if they could get a crack at his staggering knowledge. Every power would be embarking upon a feverish endeavor to win his ability for its own advantage. You cannot convince me that such a one sided concentration of power would be in the best interests of all mankind. His arrival in the United States would have led inescapably to catastrophic consequences. The Asiatic Federation would feel itself under threat. They would insist that they be allowed to share his knowledge. One ultimatum would only provoke another. It would lead ultimately to a worldwide crisis. That is precisely what I wish to avoid.

"I am a human being, and I would prefer to act in a human fashion. In other words, decently. No one is going to squeeze Khrest like a lemon and then declare, with a regretful shrug of the shoulders, that it was absolutely necessary for this or that reason. If he wants to give something of his knowledge to humanity, he should do so out of his own free will, without coercion. We will all profit from it. Foremost, however, by this freedom of action and movement for Khrest, we have won the guarantee that there will be no World War III. I now assume you will understand why the *Stardust* has become wholly insignificant. I have landed in this desolate area so that Khrest might have a chance to mount his special instruments before the inevitable armed opposition arrives. I have nothing further to add."

"You might loosen my straps," said Bell calmly. His brow furrowed, he turned to the alien. "I'll help him. No doubt you realize we'll be having some fireworks around here within an hour."

"Let them start shooting! Someday, here on this very spot will arise a metropolis. Here will be built hyper-light spacecraft; and here the seeds of one humanity will be sown. What have you decided, Reg?"

The heavyset man laughed. He did it without ease, but the worry had left him. "I think I know people pretty well," he said slowly. "They mean well, but all the same, they look out for their own advantage. I believe it better that Khrest remain uncommitted. That's about all I can say."

"Dr. Manoli?"

The medic raised his head. The color had returned to his cheeks.

"Your conduct is not without its logic. If Khrest can guarantee that his knowledge will be used only for the benefit of all men, I have no objections. On the other hand, it would be a crime if he should prefer one certain bloc."

"Rest assured," whispered the alien, "that I have no such plans. My only request is that you respect my wishes and assure that I be safe from incarceration by any of the entities you refer to as 'states.' This would leave me with incalculable difficulties. Major Perry Rhodan has chosen to land here at my request."

"How do you plan to defend yourself?" shouted Fletcher, quite beside himself. "I think this is nothing but a dirty trick. I think—"

"Fletch, if we had landed at Nevada Fields, by now we would already be in protective custody. There would simply have been no other alternative for our people. Uninten-tionally, or even under duress (or so they would tell us), we might have let slip some word about our experiences. This way, we act with motives that are, I think, honest and honorable."

"But I'm an officer of the space force, and I—"

"So was I. But now, in the face of these events, I am only a human being who wants to see all mankind become great and powerful—and united. Do you believe this to be a crime? Individual nations are of no importance here. All that matters now is the planet Earth. And from now on, it behooves us to think on a cosmic scale. Are you incapable of understanding how utterly childish our Earthbound differences are, within the framework of the great Imperium? Can you not see that we must become unified as quickly as possible. An alien intelligence would refer only to the third planet of the solar system; but never would he speak of this or that nation. From a cosmic point of view, we are only inhabitants of Earth, and never Americans, Russians, Chinese, or Germans. We are standing on the threshold of a new age. We will just have to get used to that. Once more I stress—under no circumstances must Khrest fall into the hands of any single power. We're staying where we are."

Bell stood up slowly. With a pained expression, as though offended, he murmured, "You could have told me that before now, while we were still on the moon. I knew something was up. Okay, let's get a move on. Khrest, you'll have to pull yourself together. When the first troops arrive, we'll be in need of real protection. All the flowery language in the world, about the desired unity of mankind and our future significance in the galaxy, et cetera, et cetera, ad nauseam, won't be able to fend off a single bullet. The warlords of the Asiatic Federation would split their sides with laughter, and then, of course, off you'd go to the interrogation room. All right, then. Let's go."

"I shall remain on board," declared Dr. Manoli quietly, "until the necessary medications have arrived. It is my duty as a physician and as a human being to help a sick person. All the more so, in this particular case. It would be a great error to act so precipitately so soon after our first encounter with an alien being. You are right, of course. We must no longer concern ourselves with the question of profit to any one nation."

Sitting in his chair quite rigidly, Captain Fletcher was silent. Khrest rose painfully.

Rhodan put his weapon away and said, "Fletch, we mean well. We have the best of intentions. My God, we're no criminals! Could it ever be wrong to risk everything for the sake of humanity? I think not. Once again, we are at the dawn of a new era. We must be careful to do the right thing; we must be aware of our responsibilities. No one will ever lay a hand on Khrest. Take my word for it."

Rhodan threw open the heavy bulkheads of the air lock. The fresh air of planet Earth streamed into the cabin. It was hot and dry, just right for Khrest's lungs.

Rhodan stepped outside. So far, nothing could be seen of the army, but it would not be much longer before they arrived. Rhodan could just imagine what frenzied activity there must be now in the various command posts. And they did not even know what had been brought to Earth with the *Stardust*.

No one had any idea of their power yet, but it would not be long.

Even while Rhodan's gaze measured the immense task that lay before him, something began to take shape in his mind's eye. In images still remote and nebulous, he saw gigantic interplanetary vessels race into the skies and heard the hum of their faster than light engines; and he knew, proudly, that these were built by human hands.

He saw a global government. He glimpsed a world of peace and prosperity, a world that had earned galactic recognition. It was, of course, merely a vision but he had grasped it with all his senses. For a moment, it was real to Perry Rhodan.

As a mysterious engine began to whir in the storeroom of the *Stardust*, the Third Power began its mission on Earth. Perry Rhodan stood smiling up at the blue sky. Then, slowly, he detached the insignia of rank from the epaulets of his uniform.

# THE THIRD POWER

## CHAPTER ONE

The silence was deceptive.

The mirrorlike surface of the Koshun salt lake in northern China was unbroken by movement. Still as death, the lake lay sprawled across the wide desert. Not the slightest breeze could be felt, and the atmosphere was oppressively hot and dry. The glimmering air was buoyed above the heated stones and lost itself in the blue of a cloudless sky. Far away on the horizon rose a ridge of low mountains, from which had come the river that fed the salt lake.

The river was the only thing that stirred in this part of the Gobi Desert. Heavy and sluggish the river flowed, neither wide nor deep but never becoming completely dry.

Vegetation could not have grown on this stony ground, and animal life would not have found food amongst the flat rocks. Nothing was alive; yet the silence was deceptive.

A slender structure of glittering silver stood close beside the banks of the river. It did not fit into the picture of this lonely wilderness, for it was an interplanetary craft more than ninety feet long whose aerodynamically designed hull and delta wings were in stark contrast to an environment so inimical to human life.

The *Stardust*, the first terrestrial spaceship ever to land on the moon, had returned to Earth and landed in the Gobi Desert. The whole world already knew this, but only a few would begin to suspect that it had been not an emergency landing but an intentional maneuver.

In the hull of the vehicle, a rectangular opening appeared. A man came into view in the opening. His gaze swept along the river, across to the mountains and then to the lake, where it remained. Captain Reginald Bell, test pilot for the U.S. Space Explorations Command and engineer of the *Stardust,* drew in the air with eager breath, although it was anything but refreshing. The captain was short and heavyset. He wore the tightfitting blue uniform of the newly created Space Navy and held his cap under his right arm.

His eyes, which seemed almost devoid of color, bore a faint glimmer of hope as he turned and called into the interior of the spaceship. "You think it's possible to take a bath in that puddle over there?"

Someone emerged from the dark corridor and stepped up beside Reg. He wore the same uniform but without epaulets. He seemed to be about thirty-five years old, tall and lean, and above a face with hard gray blue eyes there fell short blond hair. This was Major Perry Rhodan, commander of the *Stardust* and leader of the first lunar expedition.

"Of course it's possible," he said in answer to Reg's question, "but the water is warm and hardly inviting. Besides, it's far too salty for my taste."

"Oh, I always liked highly seasoned food," declared Reg in a very serious tone. "I could even drink the whole lake, if necessary."

"You'd really be in for a surprise. The waters of the Atlantic would taste like sickening sweet lemonade compared with that over there."

Reg squinted up at the sun, which was nearly at its zenith. "I hope I'll have a chance to find out, because they won't be leaving us in peace much longer. I hope Khrest has thought of something in the meantime."

Khrest was the scientific leader of an extraterrestrial expedition that had had to crash-land on the moon. His race, which had been master of a large part of the Milky Way for many thousands of years, had degenerated through the centuries. Now he and his people were suffering from leukemia. His blood had begun to deteriorate. He was hopelessly lost if the human race would not choose to help him. Therefore, he had agreed to come to Earth with the *Stardust;* but so far no one had any idea of the great secret that had accompanied the spaceship back to Earth.

"The protective umbrella will be sufficient for the time

being. Khrest has assured me that nothing can penetrate it, not even a hydrogen bomb. One twist of a lever and we'll lie under a transparent dome of energy against which our whole world could rage in vain."

"That sets my mind at ease." Reg nodded. "The Chinese won't keep us waiting very long before they arrive. They probably think that we fell into their big sandbox here just by accident and that we're only waiting to be picked up by them. Wouldn't they give their eye teeth to get hold of the *Stardust!*"

"And their right arms as well, if they only knew what kind of passenger we have with us," Perry assured him. "I only know from some hints what powerful means the Arkonides possess, but it's already quite clear to me that Khrest all by himself is capable of keeping the world at bay. In any event, you can rest assured that pretty soon a lot of people will be very annoyed with us."

A shadow darted across Reg's broad face. "I'm afraid our own people will be among them. Couldn't we explain to them, at least, why we didn't return to Nevada Fields?"

Perry shook his head. "Don't you know General Pounder by now? Don't you think he—to say nothing of the national security and international defense people—would be most interested in our extraterrestrial guest? And don't forget Mercant . . ."

Allan D. Mercant, Secretary of the NATO Division of International Defense, had only the higher commands of NATO above him. Additionally, Mercant was head of the special department known by the official designation of International Intelligence Agency. There was no country that did not unknowingly play host to some of Mercant's agents.

Reg sighed deeply. "I can understand Fletch wanting to return home. At heart he probably understands that you've done what's right, but he can't help thinking of his young wife and the baby she's expecting. I really don't know if we can keep him here for any length of time."

"He can leave if he wants to," Perry said, to Reg's surprise.

Reg gulped. "Leave? Where to?" With his short, stubby fingers he pointed toward the desert. "To go *there?* Do you *want* him to get lost in that desert?"

"It won't be lonely here very much longer." Perry glanced at his watch. "I'm only surprised that no reconnaissance plane has shown up before now."

He nodded briefly toward Reg and returned to the interior of the craft. In the rather crowded messhall, Dr. Eric Manoli, the ship's physician, was tending to Khrest, who lay stretched out on a narrow bunk. Clark G. Fletcher stood at the hatch and, his lips tightly pressed together, looked out into the desert.

"Well," said Perry, as Manoli looked up, "how is he getting along?"

Khrest answered before the physician could reply. "I am well, thank you, Mr. Rhodan. I feel a bit weak, but that is all. The air of your planet does me a great deal of good. Do you really believe you can help me?"

Dr. Manoli began to discuss Khrest's condition. "Leukemia is a disproportionate increase in the number of white blood cells. The oxygen carrying red blood cells are consequently pushed out of the way. One suffocates, so to speak, even though he may breathe fully throughout his lungs— for what good are lungs filled with oxygen when there are no red blood corpuscles to transport the oxygen to the organs that require it? At first, fatigue manifests itself. The sick man becomes progressively weaker. The physical deterioration is followed by a gradual wasting away of the mind. Just recently has a means to conquer leukemia been discovered. It was an Australian research scientist who developed the antileukemia serum."

"Of course we'll be able to help you, Khrest," Perry concluded. "But we can do this only if there is mutual trust. I am interested in your inventions, in your technical advancement and—let's be honest—your weaponry. In exchange for this information, I can offer you recovery and complete regeneration. It's a business proposition, if you like."

"Your honesty is refreshing. Thus did our race behave some thousand years ago; but nowadays too many of us are weary of such forthrightness. I almost believe we could learn something from you."

Perry thought of the Arkonides who, far away on the surface of the moon, reclined on their couches and sought to while away the hours by watching three dimensional abstract images on screens with six planes. By this occupation they convinced themselves that they did not suffer from boredom. Their emotional inertia did not permit them even to attempt a repair of their gigantic spacecraft. Many millennia of computerized government and untiring robot servants had made the Arkonides aesthetes whose only *raison d'etre* was to lie on their backs and dream with open eyes.

"A renewal of blood is known to us also as the best precaution against degeneration and genetic decay," the major said.

Khrest sat up on the bunk. He leaned his back against the wall, and one could see that he was at least a head taller than Perry. Externally, he seemed to differ but little from a human being. His only extraordinary features were his almost white hair, albinoid eyes, and unusually high forehead. Invisible to the naked eye, an extra brain, unknown in any earthly creature, was situated atop the normal mantle of the cortex. This hypercranium possessed a photographic memory and an intricately developed memory bank. That Khrest had a protective breastplate instead of ribs surrounding his heart and lungs was also unknown to any of the four crewmen. Khrest, for all his unique anatomy, was the last descendant of the ruling dynasty of Arkon, home planet of his race. Being a scientist, he interpreted Perry's remark concerning a "renewal of blood" perhaps too literally.

"Of course, such an intermixture of blood would show positive results. But fraternization with the members of a primitive . . ." He paused, then tactfully rephrased his statement. ". . . not yet completely developed race would stand in defiance of our law."

"I have no intention of marrying Thora." Perry smiled a bit dryly. Reg, who had just entered the doorway, broke out unabashedly into a bleat of laughter that seemed incongruous coming from his bulky body. Manoli carefully took his patient's pulse. Fletcher showed no reaction.

For a fleeting moment Perry felt himself transported back to the immense spherical spacecraft of the Arkonides on the moon. In his mind he saw Thora, commanding officer of the expedition whose task was to search for the planet of eternal life. She was a tall and singularly beautiful woman with light, almost white blond hair and large eyes glowing golden red.

A woman? Perhaps, judging by her outer appearance; but that was all. In reality, she was a creature cold and calculating, with crystal clear reasoning ability and the highest intellect. Her attitude toward "the lower forms of life," *Homo sapiens* among them, was ruled by an incredible prejudice. Only her logical mind had permitted her to conclude a compromise with Rhodan. She knew that no other alternative had remained, unless she wanted to spend the rest of her life on the moon.

Khrest slowly shook his head. "I admire your imagination; yet I believe we should abandon these useless words and think rather of what should be done. You promised me help."

"And you shall get help," Perry assured him. He turned to face Reg. "Forget about that bath. Take care of the news first—try to tune in to the most important broadcasts. We must know what's happening in the world now."

"Nobody's going to inform us officially if they plan an action against us. I'd rather speak directly to Pounder."

"Nothing but silence at the beginning, Reg. Let them rack their brains for the reason we don't answer. I must get them good and ready for what I intend to do."

Perry paid no further attention to him. He knew Reg, and he knew he could depend on him. "Eric, you take care of Khrest and do nothing else but that. Fletch, I'd appreciate it if you could get us some food. Later on we probably won't have time for that. Meanwhile, I'll worry about the strategic end of things. What kind of weapons has Thora sent along, Khrest?"

The Arkonide was still sitting on the bunk, his hands folded in his lap. "To begin with, the force field, which should be the most important. It serves only for defense, but it should not fail to leave a certain impression on potential aggressors. Further, we have three hand weapons called psychoradiators. Their strength can be regulated. At maximum intensity they can paralyze a human being at a distance of up to one and a third miles, but they can never kill; at lesser intensity the victim's conscious awareness is so weakened that it will be quite easy, even for you, to dominate him. Moreover, one may give posthypnotic commands, which must be carried out at all costs, even when the person affected no longer remains within the radius of these psychorays. Connected with these is an artificially induced amnesia. He is simply unable to remember a thing."

"That seems like it might be useful." Perry nodded. "What else have we got?"

"Only the broadcasting set, with which we can reach Thora at any time. You are probably aware that these special waves will penetrate even the mass of the moon. That is necessary because our ship is on the other side of your satellite."

"Hmm," Perry muttered pensively. Krest understood.

"Do not worry. The energy vault and the psychoradiator will do for the time being. In the event of further difficulty, Thora will intervene."

"What about the G force neutralizer, the thing you brought along to nullify the interior effects of our acceleration when we were blasting off in the *Stardust*?"

"I almost forgot about it. It cannot really be considered a weapon. Its range is enormous, more than six miles, straight ahead as well as in a circle. You may free an expanse of about six miles in length or a circle of twelve miles in diameter from the Earth's gravity. The neutralizer is at the center of the circle—in our case, the *Stardust*."

"Excellent," said Perry. "That should be quite enough." He went to the door.

Clark G. Fletcher, the pudgy faced giant with the gentle touch, turned away from viewing the desert and stared defiantly at Perry. But when his glance met the steel hard gaze of his commanding officer, he nodded hesitantly.

"Okay, Perry, we'll talk of other things later on."

Reg caught Perry at the exit hatch. "There's some interference with our radio reception. Perry, I can't pick up the United States. There must be some extremely powerful broadcasting station very near us. This guy speaks English with an accent and says we shouldn't do anything, since the rescue action is already underway."

"Rescue action!" Perry exclaimed. "What a pleasant expression for what the Chinese no doubt have in mind for us. Tell them that we don't need any help."

Reg did not reply. He looked past Perry. Far away,

beyond the river, close to the chain of mountains, a cloud of dust rose slowly toward the sky and settled over the desert like a slightly dirty blanket. What seemed to be tiny dots were approaching the salt lake.

Perry followed the direction of his friend's gaze.

"Ha! Here we are. Here they come; there's a helicopter."

The slender body of the helicopter was shining brand-new in the bright sunlight, its whirring rotors hardly distinguishable from the natural vibration of the heated air. The sand below the helicopter was whirled up by its descent as it landed about 300 feet from the *Stardust*.

"Reg, you will remain here. Take one of the hand radiators and wait until I give you a signal. Maximum intensity. I'm going out to meet them."

"But—!"

"No buts. They want us alive. There's no danger."

Reg disappeared, returning some five seconds later. In his hand he clutched a silvery rod with a multifaceted lens at one end. A small red button on its side could be moved up and down a slide or pushed in wherever needed.

Perry nodded briefly and descended the ladder, walking toward the helicopter's landing site. Two men in the uniform of the army of the Asiatic Federation had disembarked from the vehicle. They studied him curiously as he approached.

The pilot of the helicopter remained in the cabin, his hands nervously clasping the stock of a heavy machine gun.

Perry smiled as though he were feeling sorry for them. Wouldn't they be surprised!

The two officers came forward. They spoke English with hardly any trace of accent. "We are so pleased that you made a safe landing!" said one of the officers, the one with the gold bars. "I am Marshal Roon, commander in chief of the land based forces of our People's Republic, and this is Major Buta'an."

"Perry Rhodan," said Perry, inclining his head slightly. "What brings you here, if I may ask?"

Both officers were so nonplussed that they were incapable of uttering a single sound. They exchanged hasty glances and eyed the space pilot who they thought was in need of help.

Perry smiled obligingly. "It's very nice of you to try to help us, but it's really quite useless. I'd give the same answer to an officer of the American or the Soviet army, if that puts your mind at ease."

"I don't quite understand what you mean," Roon admitted, smoothing out the wrinkles that had accumulated in his trousers from sitting so long in the helicopter. "You made an emergency landing, did you not? You need our help. Or can you start under your own power?"

"And if that were the case?"

"Inasmuch as you have already trespassed on our territory, we would have to forbid that."

Perry smiled. "Well, now you're getting to the heart of the matter. You're really less concerned with helping us than with claiming us for salvage. Very well thought out. But we have not landed here to become your prisoners."

Roon felt ready to lose his temper, but a warning glance from the major was sufficient to calm him, and he regained his composure at once. The major seemed to have some strange influence over the leader of the army.

"Who said anything of the sort, that we might wish to limit your freedom of movement? But of course, we will have to examine your rocket, to make certain no photographs were taken over Asiatic Federation territory."

"We have even photographed the whole Earth from the moon. Do you want to forbid that, too? Doesn't *your* moon rocket take any pictures?"

The two shared a quick glance.

"Our moon rocket was destroyed shortly after take-off, through sabotage. Or haven't you heard?"

Perry was honestly shaken. He had always considered the conquest of space to be the task of mankind as a whole. He knew that the barriers between nations would fall only when the far greater barriers of space forced them to. For him there existed no differences of race and nationality; for him there were only human beings—Earthmen. Even to his enemy, if he had one, he would not have begrudged a successful flight to the moon. Thus it was a heartfelt sentiment when, on impulse, he stepped toward the marshal and offered his hand.

"I'm very sorry, but I had no idea. Saboteurs?"

Roon overlooked the hand extended to him. "It can't be explained any other way. Our most capable scientists made an inspection of the rocket before takeoff and could find nothing wrong with it. Yet at an altitude of about sixty miles, the ship disintegrated completely."

"There are a thousand possible causes for such a failure," stated Perry, and slowly let his hand drop. "You have no evidence of sabotage."

"A hireling of the Western Bloc had concealed himself on board the ship and tampered with the reactor."

"Rubbish," Perry said sharply. "You can't excuse your own failure with such rationalization." He was quite annoyed with the insulting suspicions of the Asiatics. He noted that Roon was not Chinese but had possibly come from India or Indonesia. "No one from our side would have the least interest in preventing your flight to the moon; but there's no sense in talking about it any more. What do you want from us?"

For the first time the major addressed Perry. "Did you land here voluntarily?" he wanted to know.

The question was directly to the point. Perry decided to answer in the same straightforward fashion. "Yes. We could just as well have landed in the Sahara or in the United States."

"And what made you land here, of all places?"

"We have our reasons. In the future, I must ask you to regard this domain as the frontier of a neutral power, even though it be situated in your sovereign territory. You don't need the desert; therefore, this won't cause you any economic inconveniences. We assure you that we shall respect your borders and make no intervention in your internal affairs. We shall even undertake direct negotiations with your government, if necessary. As for you, Marshal Roon, I'd like to recommend the recall of those troops already on their way here to seize an American moon rocket as a booty. Is that clear?"

Major Buta'an had stepped back, his right hand on the stock of his pistol. His lips were firmly drawn together. Something was flickering in his eyes.

Marshal Roon, on the other hand, was much more in control of himself. He smiled with disarming courtesy. "You are joking, Mr. Rhodan! It is our lawful right to inspect any and all aircraft that land in our territory. In case there should be no cause for suspicion, we will release it as soon as possible. That so-called neutral power I will over-look as a bad joke."

"That's up to you. I've given you fair warning. And now, goodbye. I'm sure we'll be running into each other again, on some other occasion."

"Just a moment." Major Buta'an had raised his weapon and aimed it at Perry. It was a large caliber pistol that used high explosive shells—a bit old-fashioned, but still effective, especially at such short range.

Perry folded his arms over his chest. He could sense now, at about eighty yards behind him, Reg was itching to try out the ray gun. He would surely have done so long before now, had Perry not remained in the direct line of fire.

"Yes?"

"You are a spy, Mr. Rhodan. Your moonship is nothing but an outpost for the Americans, who landed you here on purpose. A military base, if you wish. At first we hoped that we could be lenient with you, because we believed you were in difficulty. But we have seen through you. We know what your designs are, and we shall—"

"Don't make any promises you won't be able to keep," Perry warned. "The Americans are just as surprised as you are that we landed in this place. They're just as ignorant of our intentions. We would send them off, just the same, if *they* tried to approach us. Is that finally clear? All right, then. Permit me to return to the rocket. I'll tell you once again, Marshal—withdraw your troops. Otherwise, I cannot be held responsible for anything that might happen."

He nodded briefly to both officers, casting a glance of warning at the pilot with the machine gun. He turned and walked slowly back to the *Stardust*, where Reg was standing in the hatch, the silver rod playing undecidedly in his hands. One could almost feel Reg's relief when his commanding officer stepped out of the line of fire.

"Shouldn't we get them?" he called to Perry. "The one with the golden trousers is certainly a general. I'd implant the suggestion that he is a doorman in a circus and then send him back. Wouldn't that be fun?"

Perry had reached the bottom of the ladder. He turned round.

Marshal Roon and Major Buta'an (Perry could have bet

that the major belonged to the counterespionage authority)
both stood quiet, waiting and indecisive. Buta'an still held
the weapon in his hand.

"I've nothing against some fun," Perry admitted, when
he stood next to Reg in the hatch. "Go get the neutralizer."

Reg disappeared at once and seconds later reappeared
with a small rectangular metal box that looked so unobtru-
sive but could nevertheless work wonders. This box must
have a tremendous capacity for storing large amounts of
energy in a very small space. Gravity neutralizer, Khrest
had called it. What was hidden in this single phrase? The
dream of many generations.

Perry set up the apparatus and slowly pulled forward
the lever that activated the directional ray.

On the desert, Major Buta'an hesitantly thrust his weapon back into the holster on his belt. "Marshal, how can
you permit a spy to give us orders? I consider this irrespon-
sible! I shall have to inform my superiors of your conduct."

"Go right ahead," Roon agreed. He looked with half
closed eyes toward the *Stardust*. "I believe I have acted
correctly. There may be more to this affair than either of
us imagines. You think that this landed spacecraft is a
camouflaged act of aggression by the peoples of the Western
Bloc? The installation of an official military base, is that
what you want to believe? Not a bad idea. It might even
be true. But we just don't know for sure. Perhaps this
Rhodan is not so crazy as he seems. Sometimes I wonder
if they haven't found something extraordinary on the moon,
something that gives them a great deal of power."

He stopped short. Something was not quite right. Suddenly he felt light and giddy, as if he had been drinking
too much—drinking far too much. The bad thing, however, was that he seemed to be losing his balance in the
same instant. It was as though he grew taller and taller
and was still growing far beyond proportion.

Dammit, if only the major would notice.

But Buta'an was too occupied by his own troubles to
. . . watch out for the marshal. A careless movement had
made him lose the ground beneath his feet. He was rising slowly upward like a balloon, upward toward the

110

xpanse of blue sky. At the same time, he was turning over ke a trampoline jumper in slow motion.

Roon had not budged. He stood as before on the hot nds of the Gobi, mouth agape, looking up at Buta'an ho cursed, stuttered, and implored his ancestors for help. ut apparently neither oath nor ancestor could help; he ept ascending.

"Pilot!" screamed the marshal suddenly, and abruptly rned around.

If only he hadn't done that! His rotating motion could not e arrested, and in a spiral-like movement Roon was lifted cyward, following the chief agent of the Asiatic Federation ecurity Service.

By now the pilot could stand it no longer. He held ist to the back of his seat, as was customary, until he ached the narrow exit. For a long moment, mouth and es wide-open, he gazed up toward both his superiors as ey floated by near him, rising ever upward. Then he astily whipped out his machine gun.

His first shot swept him out of the cabin. The helicopter coiled sideways a few inches above the ground. Involuntar- y, the barrel of his weapon dropped down, but the startled ilot had depressed the lever for continuous firing. Like a cket, his speed increasing with every shot, he sped into e cloudless desert sky. Even when the magazine of his in had been emptied, he still continued his ascent.

It was an incredible, eerie picture, and in broad daylight. hree men were floating through the air, and a helicopter vered obliquely and hardly balanced between the rocks ke a ship stranded in the current on the ocean floor.

Perry looked up into Reg's radiant face. "Well, what do u think of that?"

"Just great! A unique circus act. This general or marshal llow hangs so well up there in the air. They're scared stiff, bet. But now what? You aren't going to let those guys arve up there, are you?"

Perry slapped his palm to his forehead. "No, not that! ell me, can you fly a helicopter?"

Reg nodded, quite surprised. "Of course. Why?"

"Later. Now we'll let those 3 kites land, very gently. hat's the way. Push the lever back a little. Half a G; that rould do it. . . . No, I'm afraid they're falling too fast.

A quarter gravity, so they'll get at least a few bruises a
souvenirs and won't believe it was nothing but a dream
Yes, that's fine!"

In the meantime, Marshal Roon had reached the groun
again. Completely beside himself, he looked all around a
if in hopes of discovering the invisible giant who had lifte
him up. Buta'an landed a bit less gently on a rock, som
thirty feet to one side. His painful expression told every
thing. The pilot was in danger of falling farthest. Fortunate
ly, he had drifted over far enough so that now he fell hea
over heels into the river; and because he was under only
quarter of Earth's gravity, he was swimming about like
cork—which undoubtedly contributed to his confusion. H
had dropped his machine gun quite some time ago.

Perry shouted as loud as he could. "Marshal Roon, ca
you hear me?"

The marshal raised his fist and shook it menacingly
"You'll pay bitterly for that! What on Earth was that, som
form of antigravity?"

"For a general, that's pretty smart," Reg roared in hig
spirit, and slapped his thighs. He seemed highly amuse
by the whole affair.

"Unless you order your troops to turn around, you're i
store for quite a lot of such surprises," Perry said. "In ou
arsenal are weapons beyond even your wildest dreams."

Perhaps he should have kept silent, but he wanted t
ensure that the others would behave more cautiously.

His revelation, however, achieved just the opposite effec
"Weapons, that's it," mumbled Roon, glancing quickly to
ward the younger chief of security. His glance said, No
we see how much your office and your information ar
worth! Nothing whatsoever! I don't know a thing abou
new American weapons capable of nullifying gravity.

"Well, what is it?" Reg bellowed gesticulating wildl
"Has this little trip through the air left you speechless?"

Roon said something to the pilot, who had reached th
shore and rejoined the two. Perry had pushed the lever o
the neutralizer completely back, and normal gravity wa
restored.

"Just a moment," Perry called out in warning when h
saw the pilot move toward the helicopter. "The aircraft r
mains here. It landed without permission on the territor

of our newly proclaimed power. The helicopter is hereby confiscated."

The marshal turned red. This was visible even at such a distance.

"Looks good on him," commented Reg. "I particularly like the contrast with his gold uniform."

"How dare you!" roared Roon, quite beside himself. "I'll—"

He did not say what he would do. Major Buta'an whispered something to him.

"You'll be hearing from me," Roon added quickly. He then turned, signaled the major and the pilot over to him and marched off toward the distant mountains.

Meanwhile, the cloud of dust had come much closer. Perry breathed a sigh of relief. "Well, that was our first encounter with the Asiatic Federation. I'm not so eagerly anticipating the second. I'm afraid we'll have to switch on our force field. Since its radius of activity is about a mile and a quarter, the river, part of the lakeshore, and the helicopter are included. Well, that will be our new territory. The smallest domain on Earth but also the most powerful."

"And what do you intend to do with the helicopter?"

"Silly question! We have to get away from here somehow, don't we, in order to get spare parts and the drugs for Khrest? Or had you intended walking through the Gobi Desert?"

Reg's face lost much of its healthy glow. "Me? How come me? Must I—?"

Perry nodded deliberately. "One of us will have to, so why not you? I can't rely on anyone as much as I can on you."

Reg's hair, which had seemed at this point to be standing on end, returned to its unruffled state. He made a grand gesture that seemed to embrace everything. "Hmm. Yes, of course. You're right, as always. When is this to be?"

"As soon as the world has calmed down," Perry replied. He took the neutralizer and returned inside the *Stardust*.

Reg followed slowly. With an expert glance he studied the helicopter, which lay askew, put the psychoradiator in his pocket with a regretful shrug of his shoulders, and closed the hatch.

In the command center they met Fletcher, who said, "Dinner is ready. What happened?"

Perry explained everything to him in a few words.

"And you believe you can be successful? I've told you already that I'm not going along with it. I want to go home. I want to see my wife again. In three months she'll be having a baby."

"Everything will be finished by then, Fletch. You've got to be reasonable. Look here, we've known each other quite a long time. I'm certainly not doing anything without reason, and I'll explain to you once more just why we had to land *here* and not in Nevada Fields."

"You can't convince me."

"The peace on Earth we have for the time being is wholly illusory. With the least provocation, every deadly missile in our automated arsenals will fire in all directions and completely destroy our world. Should this state of affairs endure forever, now that we have the chance to intervene and bring about changes? The Western Bloc and the Asiatic Federation oppose one another. The Eastern Bloc, with Moscow, plays only a subordinate role since the Chinese have risen to become the greater power. We are now in a position where we can tip the scales; we are now standing between both giants, and we are backed by the incredible technology of the Arkonides. The might of the Arkonides in the hands of one nation would mean the end of all freedom, even if that one nation were the United States. You will come to understand."

"Do you realize that you are a traitor?"

A poignant expression played across Perry's face. "Many will call me that, because they will not understand. But I am not a traitor. I am simply no longer an American, but a Terran. Do you understand that, at least?"

"Perhaps. But is that all of it?" Fletcher swallowed hard. "You could just as easily have landed in Nevada Fields."

"Not at all. We will be forced to defend ourselves here as well as there, and I'd much rather fight the Asiatics than our own people. No, I could become soft, someone could persuade me . . . That could never happen here, because I know what's in store for me if I should give in. Khrest means unlimited power, Fletch. It is in his hands, and therefore in ours, to prevent the outbreak of war. If the great powers recognize that they are threatened by a might greater than their own, they will quickly forget their own conflicts. This might even lead to a unification, to one accord."

"That's a Utopia, nothing more."

"Let's wait and see for ourselves. There's a grain of truth in the modern myth in which the flying saucers arrive and bring peace to the world. Khrest is helping us only because we have assured him a cure and personal freedom. He would not have that freedom if we surrender—no matter to whom—because the others would then feel threatened, and quite justifiably so. This would eventually unleash the last of all wars. But *now* they will be careful."

Fletcher made a weary gesture. "You'll let me go if I wish?"

"Reg will take you along when he leaves to get the medicine and the spare parts. The helicopter is waiting outside."

That was all, for the moment.

With a twist of the lever Perry activated the force field. The *Stardust* was now surrounded by an invisible but impenetrable bell one and one-quarter miles high and extending just as far in all directions. From an aerial perspective, one would see, far below in the desert beside the lake, nothing but a small wreck incapable of flight.

In reality, however, the spacecraft was the germ cell of a new dominion whose boundaries, though presently no more than 9.4 miles in circumference, would one day be measured in thousands of light-years.


## CHAPTER TWO

The mere sight of General Pounder reminded one of a bulldozer. His square build bespoke incredible energy and strength of will. As head of the United States Space Explorations Command, he was known to fear nothing, and his courage was undaunted neither by Washington nor the Pentagon. He was in equal measure feared and loved by all his staff, for they knew they could come to him with their problems at any time. Nevertheless, his biting humor so rarely came to the surface that some fools were convinced the general would one day be devoured by his own acid.

Now he sat in the office of his headquarters, behind an immense desk almost completely covered with all manner of communications devices. In between were heaps of official documents and dossiers. Across from him sat a man of almost insignificant appearance.

The other man was the complete opposite of General Pounder. A spare, thin wreath of blond hair encircled his mirrorlike bald dome, and white hair at his temples lent him a peaceful appearance. Despite the few remaining hairs and the temples of gray, this man appeared incredibly young and as harmless as he seemed youthful. In his eyes shone a mild and tolerant light.

And yet, Allan D. Mercant was anything but mild, anything but tolerant, when there arose any question of his duties as International Defense Secretary for the whole of the Western Bloc. One could hardly imagine a more obstinate and unwavering sentinel.

"You have a great deal of confidence in Major Rhodan and his men," Mercant said gently, then pointed to the map of the world that covered one wall of the room. "The *Stardust* landed in the Gobi Desert, and you still believe it to be pure chance?"

"The ship gave the international signal of distress before transmission ended. Its power must have failed."

"And why didn't Rhodan land with the help of remote control, which surely would have brought his rocket into the Nevada Fields landing area? Why did he assume command himself? Will you explain that to me?"

General Pounder shook his head helplessly. "This is exactly what I can't do; but it is still no justification for making prisoners of myself and all my staff. You've surrounded all of Nevada Fields with your people."

"Just a precautionary measure, nothing more," said Mercant, smiling calmly. "There is an old saying, if you expect the worst, you won't be disappointed."

"Let us suppose that Rhodan made the decision himself to land in the Gobi Desert and therefore has very definite plans," Pounder said.

"I'll gladly believe that," Mercant remarked with sarcasm.

"A plan or an intention that is in no respect directed against us," the general continued. "If you're suggesting, perhaps, that he wants to hand over the *Stardust* to the Asiatics, you are entirely mistaken."

"And what other intention do you suppose he could have?"

"That I don't know," Pounder admitted, "but I do know Major Rhodan. He is reliable and above suspicion."

"A human being is an uncertain factor in any equation, General. No one can look into the heart of another. Wealth and power—or at least the chance for these two—can confuse even the most loyal mind."

General Pounder seemed to sit a bit larger behind his desk. "Do you mean to say with all this that Rhodan might have become . . . mentally disturbed?"

"Not at all, General! No one who strives for wealth and power can be wholly insane. *He is nothing but a traitor!*"

In one swift movement, Pounder rose from his chair, bent his massive body over the desk and thrust his fist under the man's nose. "Stop that now! Even if you are Allan D. Mercant, I won't have my people insulted by you! Rhodan is *not* a traitor. It was an emergency landing for the *Stardust*. And please, before you continue like this, will you kindly offer proof to the contrary? By the way, Washington has already entered into negotiations with the government of the Asiatic Federation."

"Interesting," was Mercant's comment as he pushed aside the fist with a careless elegance that disarmed Pounder. "Is it also possible to know of the result?"

"Nothing so far," confessed Pounder. "I'm still awaiting word directly from my staff in Washington."

"Then I'll tell you what the report will say. Quote, 'The government of the Asiatic Federation of course regrets the incident and promises to do everything possible to rescue the stranded space pilots. The wreck of the *Stardust*, if not already burned, will be released for return.' Shortly thereafter there will be a second announcement saying that the *Stardust* was totally destroyed on impact and that only the unrecognizable remains of the crew could be found. And then silence will descend over the whole affair, and no one will ever talk about it again. In reality, however, all will have been quite different."

"If I had your imagination I'd be writing novels." Pounder seemed to envy the man across from his desk. "Nevertheless, let's hear how it could have been—according to your opinion. How could it have been 'in reality'?"

"The Asiatics will dismantle the *Stardust* and evaluate for themselves the result of the moonflight. Rhodan and his men will receive their promised reward upon surrender of all their newly gained knowledge. Perhaps a villa in Tibet or perhaps even only a bullet in the brain."

Pounder sank back into his chair. "You are not only no longer normal, but a victim of your profession as well," was his diagnosis. "Rhodan certainly knows that he was guaranteed a good life with us, that we would have given him *two* estates if he had only expressed such a desire. Nor are there any ideological motives. The only remaining alternative is an emergency landing. That is my opinion. Rhodan will resume communications with us as soon as he is in a position to do so, just wait and see."

Mercant brushed his hand across his bald head. "I'd much rather rely on the information of my agents. Major Perkins will hardly leave us in the lurch."

"Perkins? Wasn't that the man who uncovered the plot against the NATOM installation in Australia and then finished off the leaders?"

"That's the man. Just a few hours ago I sent him to Peking to take matters in hand for himself."

"And you believe—"

"Under an alias, with the proper papers. Lucky for us that we have good commercial relations with the Asiatic Federation."

Just at that moment the visiphone buzzed. Pounder delayed his intended reply and pressed a button. The small screen lit up, and a face appeared.

"A line from Washington for General Pounder and Mr. Mercant," came the announcement.

"Both present." General Pounder gasped for breath. "Are you sure that both parties are wanted?"

"Washington expressly desires that I make the connection when, and only when, both gentlemen can be reached."

"Then make the connection. Mr. Mercant is in my office. Hurry up."

"Just a moment, sir. Wait just a moment, please."

Pounder looked at Mercant. "What do you have to do with Washington?" He seemed surprised.

"Quite a lot." Mercant smiled innocently as he moved to where he would see the visiphone. "There is, for instance, my immediate superior—the President."

Pounder swallowed and stared into the screen.

The face of the operator had disappeared, and another face became visible. It was the White House Press Secretary. "General Pounder?"

"Speaking." The general nodded briefly. Mercant bent slightly forward to include himself within the range of the camera. "Mercant is also present."

"Thank you. The reply from the Peking government has arrived. This reply is of such a strange nature that we have decided to undertake nothing further without first consulting you. Is your recorder running?"

Pounder pressed a button concealed beneath the rim of his desk. "It is now."

"Well, then, please listen. Our request to Peking was as follows:

'Washington to Peking. Would like immediate permission to send a board of inquiry to inspect the wreckage of the lunar rocket *Stardust*, which has crash-landed in your territory. Inasmuch as this is an exploratory vessel, no diplomatic obstacles should stand in the way. We expect your consent.'

"The reply was just received. Here it is:

'Peking to Washington. *Consent refused.* The government of the Asiatic Federation considers the intended establishment of a Western base in our territory to be in blatant defiance of all previous agreements. There can be no doubt that this was not the crash landing of an alleged moon rocket. The crew has rejected a rescue unit and deployed a new device which renders human beings weightless. Unless your government issues a command for this military base to surrender itself, undamaged, at once, it will be destroyed by the division of our army that has surrounded it. We will give you two hours.'

"Well, these are the two communiques. What do you have to say to that, General Pounder?"

The whole face of the Director of the Space Explorations Center lit up with radiant excitement. "Thank heaven the *Stardust* managed to land undamaged! Damn good luck! Rhodan and his men are alive. And we've reached the moon. We were the first to land on the moon. Magnificent!"

"Very gratifying," commented the Press Secretary, "but at the moment I'm far more interested in your opinion with regard to the Asiatic communique. What does it mean, a weapon that nullifies gravity? Was there equipment on board the *Stardust* of which we have not been informed?"

"Nonsense. Nullification of gravity! We have conducted experiments in that area, but they remain unsuccessful. The Asiatics are trying to bluff you. They only want to let the *Stardust* vanish, that's all."

Mercant interrupted. "Do you have any confirmation that the moonship landed without damage?"

"None," replied the Press Secretary. "If we did, it would probably have been through your office, Mercant. We've informed Peking that we are unfortunately not in communication with the *Stardust* and that we therefore cannot intervene. The ridiculous assertion that the lunar rocket is an American military base has been sharply denied. So far we have received no reply. . . . Wait a moment! Peking is calling right now. Hold on, please. I'll arrange for you to listen in."

The face of the Press Secretary disappeared from sight, and although the screen remained blank, Pounder and Mercant could understand every word spoken in the room some 2,500 miles away. Unintentionally, they became witnesses to the beginning of a development that could very well mean the end of the world, unless some miracle happened.

"Washington speaking. We are waiting, Peking. Over."

"Peking speaking. You have not complied with our request. Your base in the Gobi Desert has likewise refused to permit an inspection, whereupon a division under the direct command of Mashal Roon was given the order to destroy it. Although you are undoubtedly very well informed about what happened, we still wish to describe briefly the events that followed.

"Our tanks advanced and about one and a half miles

120

from the landing site encountered an invisible obstacle. Following the perimeter of this transparent wall, we found that it extended in a circle around the *Stardust*, enclosing an area a bit in excess of seven square miles. A certain Rhodan refers to this circle as the 'territorial boundaries of a new and neutral power.' Our tanks withdrew and opened fire on the base. Our shells detonated far from their goal, as if the invisible wall also extended upward, enclosing the grounded rocket like a protective bell. Our scientific advisors are of the opinion that the base is surrounded by a force field. Thus, the base may be unconquerable. We wish to point out, first of all, that we consider the presence of the *Stardust* a threat to world peace and that inevitable consequences must follow unless appropriate action is taken. Should this base not be eliminated, or should it not surrender to us, within the next twenty-four hours, we shall regard all diplomatic relations between the Asiatic Federation and the United States as dissolved. We await your reply. No further communications will follow."

Pounder looked at Mercant. His complexion seemed less healthy than it had been hardly ten minutes ago. Even the Defense Secretary had exchanged his bland smile for a few lines of worry.

"Force field?" he murmured. "We know nothing of this. I must say, Pounder, your scientists really know how to keep quiet about something."

"Don't talk such nonsense, Mercant. I know as much about a force field as you yourself. The Asiatics are calling a bluff, that's all. They've been looking for an excuse to get rid of their nuclear warheads, and now they've found one."

Mercant leaned forward. "Are you telling me that you don't know anything about this 'bell of energy' around the *Stardust* and that you also don't know anything about a new device to counteract Earth's gravity?"

"Nonsense, both of them! Nothing of the kind exists. I've already told you that the Asiatics are bluffing."

"Hello?" The Press Secretary had come on again and interrupted their conversation. "You've listened in, haven't you?"

"Of course," confirmed General Pounder. "That is absolutely the greatest nonsense that I have ever heard, and I would suggest—"

"General, even greater nonsense can result from this. Namely, war. We must prevent this under all circumstances. Please try, at all costs, to contact the *Stardust*—Mercant can assist you—and then find out what they meant by the force field. Lehmann will certainly know what to do. We'll be expecting your reply before expiration of the ultimatum given us by the Asiatic Federation."

"Will do," snarled Pounder, who had absolutely no idea how he could accomplish this. "I'll get in touch with you in time."

The screen grew dark.

Mercant sighed. "If Major Perkins doesn't send us some word pretty soon, we'll really be in a bad spot. Now, I suggest we get in touch with Lehmann. Is that all right?"

Pounder barked a number of commands into one of his phones. Moments later a tall older man entered the office. This was Professor Lehmann, Director of the California Academy of Space Technology and supervisor of the scientific project Moonshot. There was admittedly no expert greater than he in his field. Indeed, in an occasional candid moment General Pounder could even be persuaded to confess that Lehmann was the spiritual father of the *Stardust*.

With a somewhat astonished expression, the professor addressed the two men. "You wanted to see me?"

Pounder nodded. "You've probably met the bloodhound Mercant. A formal introduction will be unnecessary. I'd like to save myself a long story, so just listen to what has happened." He manipulated controls under the desk until sound emerged, followed by a buzz, with further noise ensuing. "The tape," Pounder explained, as if demonstrating a new invention. "Occasionally it saves a lot of trouble."

While Professor Lehmann was, by means of the recorded exchange, informed of what had occurred, Mercant sat innocently in his chair, already lining up his mental chessmen and working out future plays. If Perkins succeeded in making contact with Rhodan—provided, of course, that the latter was still in the Gobi Desert and had not yet become a pawn of the Asiatics, as he presumed—then the whole affair must soon be explained. There were several possibilities:

The *Stardust* had landed on purpose in the territory of the Asiatic Federation. That meant that Rhodan was a traitor. But it was equally possible that she had been forced to crashland and was now being dismantled by the Asiatics, who only pretended to have encountered opposition. This—and Mercant was convinced of it—was nothing but a preparation for a subsequent broadcast that would say the defenses of the *Stardust* had suddenly collapsed and the ship had been destroyed in the process.

Then there was a third possibility . . . but this was too fantastic for serious consideration. Despite his love for animals (he had once been observed to pull a worm off the hook of a most surprised fisherman and carefully place the worm in the earth) Mercant was a terribly sober and pragmatic person. His life consisted solely of facts, reports, and regulations—never of suppositions.

And yet—

He did not have an opportunity to finish his thought. The episode on the recorder had concluded. General Pounder jutted out his chin and looked at Lehmann. "Well, Professor, what's your reaction to that? Do *you* believe Major Rhodan is a traitor?"

"Traitor? Who came up with that crazy notion?"

Pounder glanced at Mercant with a significant expression. "That was merely a rhetorical question, Professor. I am much more curious to learn your opinion of this force field concept and—and the other thing."

"Nullification of gravity, is that what you mean? Both are nothing short of fantasy, impossible with the means presently at our disposal. The Asiatics have concocted a fine fairy tale there, in order to find a suitable pretext for keeping the *Stardust*. I'll wager that tomorrow we discover the ship has been destroyed and therefore cannot be returned to us."

Mercant nodded in agreement. "Very well done. A splendid analysis. If I'm going to retire, I'll recommend that you become my successor."

"Not interested. I'd rather fly along to Mars. Well, at least we know that the landing of the *Stardust* occurred without any serious damage. The ship is safe; otherwise, this smokescreen maneuver would be uncalled for. If we could only find out the cause of it all, our questions would no longer remain unanswered. If only we had a good intelligence agency, we'd have no problem."

This apparently innocent remark found its mark. Mercant turned red. In an instant his mild expression collapsed. A steel hard expression arose in his eyes. Without bothering any longer with the grimacing General Pounder, he rose to his feet.

"The last word hasn't been said. You'll be surprised," he threw at Lehmann. "You'll be surprised how well our intelligence agencies are operating. General, please call me the minute you hear from Washington. Goodbye, gentlemen." He slammed the door behind him.

Professor Lehmann, quite surprised, looked at Pounder. "What's the matter with him? Since when is Mercant so sensitive?"

"You've hurt his professional pride." Pounder grinned, obviously very pleased. "Serves him right. Why does he have to treat everyone who isn't a fellow bloodhound like half human beings? Well, now we are undisturbed. Tell me, Professor, what's your honest opinion? We agree that Major Rhodan is above suspicion, do we not? What really did happen in the Gobi Desert?"

Lehmann bent forward. "Perhaps we should phrase our question differently and ask, What really happened on the moon?"

Pounder stared at him, incapable of reply.

In Peking Major Perkins had left the stratoliner and proceeded to a first class hotel. Within a few moments of his arrival he had already received from a contact the address of a reputable firm in the employ of the Asiatic Federation government. He sought out the manager, and a meeting was arranged.

Agent Perkin's papers were in the name of Alfons Hochheimer, mining engineer. According to the passport he had lived in the Asiatic Federation for more than ten years and had worked several times for the official government agencies in the exploitation of mineral resources.

In the reception room of the business firm—equipped, Perkins noted, with the most modern conveniences—a Chinese in European clothing approached him, an inscrutable smile playing about his lips.

"Mr. Hochheimer, I presume? My name is Yen-Fu. What can I do for you?"

"I understand that you participate in the development of economically uninteresting areas," replied Perkins. "Working for other enterprises, I have already had occasion to explore many parts of the Gobi Desert with radar sounding. I know a place where uranium might be found, if one digs deeply enough."

Yen-Fu smiled more intensely. "Gobi? Uranium? I believe you are in error. There is no uranium in the Gobi Desert. We have sent several expeditions there already, but no success could be achieved in that respect."

Now it was Perkins who smiled in an inscrutable fashion. "Your people did not have access to my research instruments, Mr. Yen-Fu. Have you ever heard of the radar sensor of Professor Gottfried Spielmann?"

The Chinese shook his head. "To be honest, no."

Perkins was not at all surprised—he had just invented the name. "How unfortunate! Spielmann is one of the most impressive figures on the scientific scene in the Western world. Thanks to his invention, the United States and her allies have located the great uranium deposits along the Amazon River. I myself have one of his latest models."

Despite his continued smile, some mistrust became evident in the face of the Chinese. "Are you not American?"

"No, I am German, but I've been residing in the Asiatic Federation for ten years. Here, my papers. I hope they will establish my loyalty."

Yen-Fu examined the exquisitely skillful forgeries with great care but could detect no irregularities. Hesitating slightly, he returned them. "And do you know where in the desert uranium can be found?"

Perkins nodded. "Enough to supply twenty power stations for a hundred years. Of course," he added with a sly smile, "one can also do other things with it."

"Wait a moment. Please."

Perkins waited but not for long. Soon he was speaking with the president of the firm, then with official representatives of the government, and finally with the pilot of the plane that was to bring this *ad hoc* commission into the supposed uranium area.

"This radar sensor, do you have it with you?" inquired Yen-Fu with interest. "Is it possible to read the results directly on it?"

Perkins thought of the cleverly constructed metal box that contained no more than a battery and some cables inside and a few dials and several buttons outside. He nodded.

"But of course! Do you think I would come to you without the necessary equipment? When shall we start?"

"In one hour, if you like. We are still expecting confirmation from the proper authorities."

*If only everything goes well,* Perkins thought, although no one could do anything to him. His papers were probably more authentic than those of the Chinese. Nevertheless . . .

In the little cafe across the street, Perkins quickly drank a bottle of lemonade and gave a few coins to a beggar who, in a loud, high voice, lamented his misery and bewailed having to feed seven small children.

The man in rags thanked him for the coins with many bows and in between the many bows suddenly whispered, "O father of justice, heavenly paragon of human pity, thanks be to you for your kindness! (Hey, fellow, don't you recognize your old friends any more?) My children will offer up prayers to our ancestors for you. (Why did Mercant have to send you of all people?) May the goddess of fertility bless you, my lord, for having given such riches to an undeserving beggar! (By the way, the government official on the plane is one of our men. Go easy on him.) Permit me to kiss your feet."

Perkins briefly winked at the beggar, then turned away with a gesture of displeasure. He tossed a coin on the table and left the cafe.

It was a jaunty little jet. Aboard, besides the pilot, were a representative of the government, a chief engineer, and Perkins. The small cabin showed evidence of some luxury and thus indicated that it also served in a private capacity. Interchangeable skid runners and pontoons enabled it to land on uneven ground or on water.

The jet engine roared, but the noise almost entirely lost itself in flight.

Peking sank below them. The jet flew straight westward. Fertile valleys receded quickly into the east. The first mountain ranges appeared, then brown arid deserts.

The government official bent forward and tapped the shoulder of the engineer, who was sitting next to Perkins. "Where is this region located, Lan-Yu?"

"East of Suchou, near the Koshun salt lake, near where the American moon rocket is supposed to have crashlanded."

"Do you know something about it?" The words escaped the government representative quite against his will.

"I've heard about it." The engineer tried to evade the issue. "Just rumors." Then he looked around and grinned. "Or is there truth to that rumor?"

"Of course not! Nothing but idle rumors, what else?"

They had been in flight for some ninety minutes when the pilot opened the tiny door of the cabin and said, "The flight center in Peking has just given us orders to turn around at once. We are forbidden to fly over the area between Ordos, Shan-si, the Nan-shan mountains, and Ninghsia. The Koshun salt lake lies exactly in this area. No reason was given."

Lan-Yu looked at the government official, who nervously chewed at his lower lip. "What does that mean? You received permission from the authorities to accompany us on this flight. You should have known in advance."

"Just keep on flying and turn off the radio," the representative of the government ordered the pilot. "Don't pay any attention to the order from the flight center."

"But I have to receive the weather forecasts, and I must announce my position every five minutes."

Perkins caught a glance from the government's representative. He nodded imperceptibly and put his hand in his pocket.

"Turn the radio off completely," the government man repeated. "I urgently advise you to follow my instructions to the letter from now on; otherwise, you will have to suffer the consequences. I represent the government, just remember that. Land at the Koshun salt lake. How long before we land?"

The pilot hesitated, then looked for a moment at his instruments. "Ten minutes."

"I'll be up front in eight minutes, and I'll supervise the landing operations. Until then, no change of course. Do you follow me?"

"You will be responsible for this," said the pilot, and disappeared.

Engineer Lan-Yu had followed the conversation without comment. His smile had faltered, and his narrow eyes had become narrower still. He noticed that Perkins, alias Alfons Hochheimer, was still keeping his hand in his pocket.

"Why do you not follow the instructions of our government?" Lan-Yu asked slowly. "I would not like for us to run into any difficulty. I am certain that this has to do with the foreign spaceship."

"You can bet your bottom dollar on it," he was assured by the government official. "But rest assured I know exactly what I'm doing."

"I couldn't care less," admitted Lan-Yu, "as long as we find the uranium." His glance hovered over the impressive metal box that lay on the free seat next to Perkins. This metal box had been able to convince even the president of his firm when he had seen it. "I really hope we find the location."

Five minutes later the pilot announced, "An air force jet is ahead of us. They are urging us to turn around."

"How can you know that if you have no radio contact?"

"Warning shots," the pilot replied. Apparently he knew no fear.

Thirty miles.

"Switch on the radio. I'm coming up front."

The government representative turned to Perkins with a meaningful gesture, then disappeared into the narrow pilot's cabin and closed the door behind him.

Perkins pulled an automatic out of his pocket and pointed it at Lan-Yu. "Do you happen to have any weapons on you?"

The engineer was so startled that he gasped. His eyes became as round as buttons as he stared into the black muzzle of the gun and shook his head.

"What do you want from me?" he stammered.

"Just keep still and keep your mouth shut. If you pretend you don't exist, you might come out of this adventure safe and sound. But if not . . ."

An impressive silence made the alternative all too obvious.

"But . . . you *can't* all by yourself."

"I am not alone. And now, don't say anything more. We're going to land now."

The jet began its descent. In the meantime the military escort had turned around. Unhindered, the jet passed the air barriers of the Asiatic Federation, swept low above several tank units, and suddenly sighted, farther off by the river Morin-Gol, the *Stardust*.

The lunar rocket was standing forlorn and deserted. No life was evident in its vicinity. High above, in the clear sky, a tiny dot could be seen, circling round like a bird of prey. The circle became narrower, and it seemed as if the predator would at any moment pounce upon its victim.

Neither Perkins nor his co-agent had the least inkling that this tiny dot in the sky was an atom bomber of the Asiatic Federation air force in search of its target.

"Where do you want me to land?" asked the pilot.

The government representative, one of the most capable men in the International Intelligence Agency, pointed below them.

"Close by the moonship, in the desert. Make sure the plane comes to a halt not more than a hundred yards from the *Stardust*. Is that clear?"

The pilot nodded in agreement. He began to bank, preparing for landing. The jet was gliding at an angle toward the desert. Its altitude was only a few hundred yards. The distance to what they believed to be the wreck of the *Stardust* decreased rapidly. Only three more miles . . . two more miles . . .

Meanwhile, high above them, an H-bomb was falling. The tiny speck in the sky stopped circling and flew off in a straight line. With different velocities and from different directions, two objects approached the *Stardust*.

But it happened in the same instant.

Perkins had gone into the pilot's cabin after he had tied Lan-Yu into his seat. The jet had just touched down and was skidding across the ragged earth with breathtaking speed. They were still more than two miles away from the

*Stardust,* when suddenly, about two miles above the space-craft, a second sun rose.

Three pairs of eyes were blinded by the immediate presence of a white hot mushroom cloud whose glowing gases began to flow down along the outlines of an invisible bell.

They were alive only long enough to feel the impact when the jet came to a sudden halt as it slammed into the force field.

And then there was nothing.


## CHAPTER THREE


"Perry, Pounder is on the line! And he's all upset."

Perry Rhodan nodded to Khrest, with whom he had just been talking. "If you'll excuse me, Khrest, I don't want to leave anything undone."

"On the line" was obviously an understatement. The connection via Echo satellite was flawless. Pounder's face was clearly visible on the view screen, as if he were looking in through a window. The Asiatics no longer interfered with the reception—a sign, perhaps, that they were becoming quite confused.

Reg bowed deeply and made a grand gesture toward the screen. "And may I introduce to you . . . the general!"

Perry pushed him aside. "General Pounder, reporting with my crew, back from the moonflight. All are well. The *Stardust* is no longer flightworthy because of technical troubles. Your orders have been executed. The scientific results of our expedition will be forwarded to Professor Lehmann."

The general gasped. His gasp was fully audible halfway around the world. "Rhodan, have you lost your mind? Will you explain why you landed the *Stardust* in the Gobi Desert? Did remote control fail? You should at least have tried to reach the ocean."

"I landed here on purpose, General."

"*What?*" Pounder's face resembled an overripe tomato. "What do you mean, on purpose? Rhodan, you're not trying to tell me that—"

"I'm not trying to tell you anything, at least not what you seem to believe. I'll try to explain."

"I'd like to know what there is to explain," Pounder roared. "Destroy the *Stardust* at once, with the automatic destruct system, and surrender to the forces of the Asiatic Federation. Is that understood?"

An icy glint became visible in Perry eyes. "I understand you perfectly sir; but I will not follow your instructions."

"You will not *what?*" Pounder presented a frightening sight. His face had turned a shade darker still. Reg ducked down involuntarily, as though afraid that the head on the screen would suddenly burst. "Major Rhodan, I am ordering you—"

"May I inform you, sir, that I am no longer a major and therefore no longer under your command," Perry said calmly. "As you see, I have removed my insignia of rank. If you will permit me, I shall explain everything once and for all."

Professor Lehmann's face abruptly appeared beside Pounder's. There was curiosity in his expression. "Rhodan, are remains of an atmosphere present in the moon craters and perhaps traces of—?"

"Silence!" shouted the general, and shoved the scientist aside. "Speak up, Rhodan." He stroked his chin. "And you'd better be convincing, because your words will decide whether or not we'll have a war on our hands within the next ten hours. The Asiatic Federation is absolutely convinced that the *Stardust* is a strategic outpost of the United States, established very much on purpose. Unless this 'strategic outpost' has been given up by tomorrow, diplomatic relations will be severed. I don't need to tell you what that will mean."

"Has it gone so far already?" Perry whispered, fear in his voice. "Then, indeed, every second is precious. Now, listen carefully, General. We landed as planned on the moon and discovered there the remnants of an extraterrestrial civilization. What it is I cannot tell you in detail now, but a few indications will be sufficient for Professor Lehmann's peace of mind. The moon has never been inhabited, but long ago the exploratory vessel of an interstellar race landed there. It is untouched and contains an arsenal of weapons with which one could destroy not only Earth, but our entire solar system. Death rays and force fields, gravity neutralizers and antineutron screens that can prevent any nuclear reaction and, what's more, hand weapons of an effectiveness that you can hardly imagine. You will realize, General, that we could scarcely hand such tremendously powerful weapons over to any nation on Earth."

Suddenly Pounder's voice turned cold sober.

"But you are in Asiatic Federation territory. You landed there, and since this conversation is being monitored, all the world knows now what you've found on the moon. Expeditions will begin, and a race will determine who gains possession of ultimate power. It would have been better if you had remained silent."

"I want the world to know," Perry replied. "And no one will land on the moon unless I so desire. Don't worry, General. Neither the Asiatics nor the Russians *nor you* will obtain those weapons. These weapons are in my hands. I shall take care that no one starts the war that will destroy us all."

"*You?*"

In this one word were hidden such contempt and disbelief that Perry turned red with rage. He stepped forward and glared coldly at the general. "Yes, *I*. Please understand the politics have failed. For decades you have tried to prevent the hot war. Threat followed threat. Conference followed conference. Not only are the Eastern Bloc and the Asiatic Federation to be blamed, but the Western Bloc as well. No one would give in. Everyone kept rearming. Today, everywhere on our globe guided nuclear missiles are poised in readiness. The push of a button will launch them into the sky. Automated guidance systems will steer them along their course. But even before they can reach their goal, on the other side retaliatory missiles will blast off. Almost simultaneously the nations on both sides of the world will cease to exist. We have faced this ghastly vision already for decades now. No one is capable of banning the danger. Only a precarious balance of power has thus far prevented the war. But woe if one or the other side became too strong! In order to live in peace, they would have to destroy their opponent. In order to live in peace, that is, they would have to die in war! You would do this yourself, the same as the Asiatics would. Can you understand at last why none of you must ever gain possession of the *Stardust*, as long as we have the extraterrestrial—"

"You would perform the greatest service to your own country if you—"

"If I would bring these weapons to Nevada Fields, is that what you mean? You're wrong, General. The Asiatic Federation and the Eastern Bloc would immediately feel so threatened that they would have to decide to launch the slaughter of the Western Bloc. The end of our civilization would come. No, I persist in my plan, whether you approve of it or not."

"And what plan is that?"

"I will form a neutral third power between the Eastern and Western blocs. We have the ability to render harmless any nuclear warhead launched. Any atomic weapons will be safely disarmed at great altitude, as if they were simply fireworks that had fizzled. I will repel any attack on the *Stardust*, from whichever side it may come. I will—"

Perry stopped talking. There was a noise behind him, and he turned around. Reg had grasped Clark G. Fletcher's sleeve as he burst into the broadcasting room.

"Don't listen to him, General!" Fletcher shrieked hysterically. "He's gone mad! The Arkonides, with their degenerate ideas, have made him lose his mind. I refused to land here. He threatened me with a gun, General. Rhodan is a renegade!"

Perry had given Reg a signal to let Fletcher finish his speech. Now he approached him, putting his right hand on his shoulder.

"Listen, Fletch. The General can hear what I've got to say to you. Perhaps I would act the same way if I were in your position, but I'm not. You can leave the *Stardust* at any time you wish. I'm holding no one back. But first confirm for General Pounder that we've found these weapons on the moon—these weapons with which we can control the whole world. Don't tell him anything else. Only that."

Fletcher hesitated. He looked into Reg's threatening face. In the technician's hand was the silver rod of the psychoradiator. Perry looked at him almost kindly. The intensely interested face of Pounder was staring at this scene from the screen.

Fletcher nodded. "That's right. Rhodan can destroy the world if he wants to."

He hung his head, turned around, and went out into the corridor.

Perry breathed a sigh of relief and turned to the general. "Together with you, sir, the heads of state of the Eastern Bloc and the Asiatic Federation will also hear my words. I want first of all to state the situation as follows: The realm of the Third Power may be very narrowly limited from a geographical point of view, but don't let yourself be fooled by that. Respect my wishes and take care not to let your mutual mistrust drive each of you to a point of no return. The *Stardust* is not an American military base. That ought to be clear by now. Neither did she land here to become the willing prey of the Asiatic Federation. The Eastern Bloc should now bury its hopes of becoming the third party who will profit by the discord of its two adversaries. Now, apart from that, you can always reach me on this frequency, and should I have anything further to say, I'll do so by the same means. I'm very sorry, General. Perhaps you will understand me one day. For the time being I can only ask you to forgive me."

Pounder confronted the steel blue eyes. Then he nodded slowly. "I will try, Rhodan. One can only hope, by God, that Mercant does the same. You know him as well as I do."

A bitter smile flashed across Perry's face. He knew the meaning of this warning, but nothing frightened him any longer. Mercant was, after all, nothing but a human being.

And human beings were no longer a source of awe for Perry Rhodan.

"Washington to Peking:

*Contact with the* Stardust *has been established. Commander Rhodan claims to have come into possession of incredible weapons, which had been abandoned on the moon by an alien civilization. We no longer have any influence on future events. We urge you to reply.*"

"Peking to Washington:

*Video conversation between General Pounder and Rhodan was monitored by us. His claims incredible and too farfetched. The ultimatum is still in effect. You have seven hours.*"

134

"Moscow to Washington:

*"We concur with the opinion of the government of the Asiatic Federation and regard the American military base in the Gobi Desert as a threat to world peace. In the event of armed conflict, however, the Soviet Union will remain neutral."*

"Moscow to Peking:

*"We concur with the opinion of the government of the Asiatic Federation, and regard the American military base in the Gobi Desert as a threat to world peace."*

"Washington to Moscow [idem Washington to Peking]:

*"We assure you once again that the United States government knows nothing of an American military base in the Gobi Desert and that the crew of the* Stardust *has been asked to surrender. We propose an immediate emergency session of the heads of state."*

There was no reply to this note.

The seven precious hours began to pass swiftly. In Asia the towers of the continental launching platforms were turning toward east and toward west. Monsters of silver glittering steel shone menacingly in the glow of the searchlights. Men scuttled back and forth, and then it became quiet again.

One could see the same picture in the defense installations of the Western Bloc.

The Eastern Bloc aimed its deadly atomic weapons so that they faced the four corners of the Earth.

In each of the three parts of the world, a man was sitting in a room deep underground, in front of giant control panels and electronic computers. He was connected to the command posts by video screens. His hand rested quietly on the table, close to a red button.

This button seemed to wink ironically and say, "Well, go on! Why don't you push me? Are you afraid someone else will do it too? Or do you fear that the end of the world will come if you push me?"

Three red buttons, each an invitation to Inferno!

Khrest was sitting up in bed, leaning back against the messhall wall upholstered with cushions. Eric Manoli had given Clark Fletcher an injection that put the astronomer into a deep sleep. Reg was now in the center with the doctor, monitoring radio traffic. Every half hour he informed Perry of what was going on in the world.

Gradually Khrest began to grasp the implications of his arrival on Earth, even though its populace did not realize that he had come.

He nodded slowly. "It is incredible, Mr. Rhodan, that your race can stand this mental stress. You tell me that your world has already existed for decades in such a tense atmosphere, where the touch of a single button could unleash wholesale destruction. Why has not someone arisen and put an end to such an intolerable state of affairs? Why have they not formed a universal government? Why have they not pooled their weapons stockpiles as a protection against possible extraterrestrial aggressors?"

Perry Rhodan sighed. "Your question isn't easily answered, Khrest. If we had an answer, we wouldn't be living constantly between life and death. Perhaps there can't be an answer, as long as mankind is convinced of being alone and unique in the solar system. One will respect only a more powerful force; but each of the two great nuclear powers on Earth is just as mighty as the other. (The third one plays only a subordinate role.) Everyone knows that if war breaks out, the annihilation of both adversaries, and probably the rest of the world, is the inescapable result. Only this knowledge has heretofore prevented a catastrophe."

"I am beginning, little by little, to understand the problem. When my race was still young, they were confronted by the same difficulties. For more than 200 years they lived in fear of total destruction. Then a warrior insect people from the outer reaches of the galaxy found us and attacked us. In less than half an hour both opposing governments had formed a coalition and successfully conquered the common enemy. However, since the danger remained everpresent, the coalition survived as well. Thus we became a single race and began our evolution toward maturity."

Perry Rhodan slowly nodded his head. Into his eyes came a hard glint. "Although I've never heard it before, your story is nothing new to me. It's the only logical solution to those problems which evolve whenever intelligent creatures discover the ultimate weapon. You will understand now why I'm acting the way I am, why I *have* to act this way. It's not pleasant to be considered a traitor by one's own friends and superiors. But if I give in to sentiment, the world will be lost. Your weapons would fall into the hands of one of the power blocs, and they would destroy the other. But before it could succeed in that, its opponent would release a suicidal vengeance. No, I see my way clearly ahead of me, Khrest. Your problem is the answer to my questions. You want to get well; all right, I'll help you with that. You want electronic replacement parts; I'll obtain them for you. You will again be able to take off in search of the planet of eternal life. Perhaps you will forget us. But I'll use your brief presence here to bring peace to our world. A peace with the help of power, with force. It's no longer possible otherwise. Only the fear of the great powers in the face of a still greater one will bring them to their senses. I believe you will be able to help me with it."

"Whatever is in my power will be done. For the time being, though, it does not look as though your actions are successful. The ultimatum will expire very shortly, and what then?"

"Thora must intervene. The force field and the gravity neutralizer apparently did not convince the Asiatics that they're dealing here with gigantic extraterrestrial inventions. My people in the West, on the other hand, believe that we intend to deceive them. Therefore, something must happen that will make it clear to all parties concerned, with a single stroke, how really strong the Third Power is. Your ship is on the moon, Khrest. What can you do from there, to make all mankind understand its grave danger? Could you, perhaps, loosen the Rock of Gibraltar from its foundation, and let it fall into the ocean 1,500 miles away? Or could you move the Statue of Liberty from New York to Peking or paralyze worldwide radio communications?"

"I could do all of those, and it would be good to give mankind such a dramatic exhibition. Think it over and inform me of your decision. *I* would suggest that we use an energy beam, choose a centrally located but uninhabited area, and warn all humanity. Say that in about two hours— that would be three hours before the ultimatum expires—you will burn into the desert a funnel with a diameter of 30 miles. But emphasize that the second time around, you would use this ray in populated areas, should your wishes not be respected. That should be enough to convince them."

Perry smiled coldly, but behind his apparent heartlessness there was hidden a genuine concern for the future of mankind. He knew that no argument would ever be sufficient to bring the guardians of diverse ideologies into agreement. Only a shock could accomplish this. And he was ready to administer the required shock therapy to the world.

"I can believe that. Do you think Thora will help us with this?"

"Whether she wants to or not, she has to. In her arrogance toward the lower races, she forgets that once upon a time we too were in the same stage of development, level A to D. That was perhaps our most productive period. We were young and enterprising then. We loved everything new and advanced. How different all this has become today! We have degenerated and become self-satisfied. Total standstill. Hmm . . . To be quite frank, Rhodan, sometimes I have odd ideas when I think how much we resemble each other in a physical respect. Your mind blended with our own, your youth combined with our knowledge . . . we could conquer the universe!"

Perry's eyes lost their hard cast. His gaze went off into the unknown distances that could be spanned only by eternities. Quite unconsciously, his hands clenched in fists, then opened again. With lightning speed a vision of the future revealed itself before his eyes. . . .

Human beings and Arkonides—*one* race . . . The spirit of enterprise and the quest for adventure would be coupled with age old knowledge and amazing technology. Faster than the speed of light, spaceships piloted by men and women eager for conquest would penetrate into the farthest reaches of the galaxy, finding new worlds, founding colonies and new empires. Interstellar trade would bring indescribable wealth, and perhaps a great galactic civilization would result. A new race would develop.

Khrest seemed to guess what was going on in Perry's mind. He smiled a wise smile. "We are only at the very beginning, Perry Rhodan. You are the representative of mankind; I am the representative of the Arkonides. You need our help; we need yours. An alliance of sorts, it might be called, born of mutual necessity; but later on I can imagine the product of a coalition of reason and the common advantage. Is Earth perhaps the planet of life that we are looking for? Every rejuvenation means a new life."

"At first we must prepare the beginnings, Khrest. Then we can continue to talk about it. This world, which can bring you the complete recovery of your health, contemplates its own destruction. Hatred and fear, pettiness and egotism, intolerance of diversity of opinion, rigid defense of traditional maxims—all this had led to the current situation. Formerly it was the fear of God that forced man to conduct himself properly and allowed him to become civilized. Today the same result can be achieved only by material force and fear. All right then, Khrest. Ask Thora to direct her energy beam onto North Africa, onto the northern part of the Ahaggar Mountains. I'll send out a warning to clear the area at once, but as far as I know it's as good as uninhabited."

"This demonstrtion should not fail to be effective," promised Khrest. "But emphasize in your warning that this is one of the more harmless demonstrations we can deliver."

The radio receiver of Lieutenant Durbas's desert patrol picked up an array of disquieting broadcasts from all over the world, but all frequencies were suddenly overlaid, with overpowering loudness, by an unknown broadcaster. In vain did the radio operator try to adjust his apparatus. Even when he turned it down as low as possible, Perry Rhodan's voice could still be heard as far away as 200 yards.

"This is Perry Rhodan speaking for the Third Power on Earth. Since the world is preparing for war and the end of civilization is therefore close at hand, I shall try to give you a last warning. This is to demonstrate that I can annihilate at a moment's notice that nation which dares to launch the first nuclear warhead. Exactly 115 minutes from now there will appear in the Sahara, north of the Ahaggar Mountains, a crater thirty miles in diameter. This phenomenon will be caused by the action of an energy ray that has its point of origin on the moon. All persons now in that area are advised to remove themselves as far as possible from the center of the target. As soon as the demonstration has ended, all the world powers will have three hours to reconsider their points of view. That is all."

The radio operator stared, speechless, at his radio set. Lieutenant Durbas, who had risen and come toward him, did the same—he too stared at the radio, speechless.

"What in the world was that?" Durbas asked finally.

"Perry Rhodan—isn't that the moon pilot who landed in Asia? He's supposed to be collaborating with the Asiatic Federation, or so they say. They also talk of new weapons that he's brought back from the moon."

The men of the desert patrol gathered indecisively. Their full track vehicle stood in the shadow of an oasis. The driver looked toward the east.

"Over there are the mountains. Are we far enough away from it?"

Lieutenant Durbas made a gesture of annoyance. "You really believe that nonsense, Hassan? An energy ray from the moon, ha! What next?"

The radio operator shook his head thoughtfully. "There must be some truth to the matter, Lieutenant. I've heard the news. They say that this Rhodan has a bell of pure energy surrounding his spaceship. Even atom bombs have no effect on it."

"Old wives' tales! That's all! You can't believe everything people say, especially where the yellows are concerned. Melt a crater into the desert? What nonsense! What do you hear from Fort Hussein?"

"I'll get in touch with them right away."

Hussein advised them to heed the warning.

"All right," sighed Durbas, and looked longingly at the shaded oasis. "Then let's retreat farther to the west. This old tracker will make about twenty-five miles an hour. That should be enough."

Fifteen minutes before the announced demonstration they were lying behind a deep ridge, looking expectantly toward the east. They wondered about the many airplanes that suddenly appeared and began to circle high above. Nearby, the helicopter of the Eastern Information Center landed with its communications equipment. Beside it the television relay station of the Asiatic Federation stood peacefully. But

140

from the Americans, nothing was to be seen. Perhaps they were stationed farther to the north.

Another ten minutes.

A wide ring had formed around the endangered area. No one could really believe what was perhaps due to occur here in a short while, but no one, nevertheless, wanted to miss the opportunity of observing a spectacle of nature—a spectacle of nature, however, that was produced and announced by a still very secret power.

Another five minutes passed.

Durbas nudged Corporal Abbas. "It will be getting dark in a other hour. Rhodan should hurry up. And by the way, we have been given the command to return to Fort Hussein right away. Something must be going on."

"War?"

"How am I supposed to know? If you really think about it, we have been in a state of war since 1945."

The corporal glanced at his watch. "It's about time now," he whispered, and looked toward the east; but in the same instant he closed his eyes like everyone else, blinded by the intensity of the light.

From out of the clear sky there fell a broad curtain of light that bathed the sandy desert some eighteen miles from the observation front. The spectators could see the bright light even through their closed eyelids. The origin of this ray, becoming progressively narrower with increasing altitude, lost itself deep in the blue sky—to be exact, where the crescent of the moon was standing invisibly.

A heat wave swept over the frightened group, but the radio broadcasts continued and the TV cameras kept operating, never ceasing to report the phenomenon live to all the world. On the screens of the news centers of all nations, the ray could be seen blazing. One of the airplanes that approached the danger zone too closely was seized in a tremendous vortex and carried directly into the heart of the flame storm. It was instantly transformed into a giant drop of molten metal that evaporated by the time it had fallen only a few yards.

For one minute this ray played down upon the desert. Then it was extinguished. All of a sudden, night seemed to fall. The sun, which before had been so brightly shining, now stood like a dying star, pale and reddish in the sky, still high above the horizon. One could look into it with open eyes.

Where the beam of energy had struck the earth, there was no longer any desert. A deep abyss lay agape in sand and rock, bottomless and with glowing borders. Within its interior there was a reddish luminescence, a fiery incandescence. Vapors rose from the depths of this newly created hell.

Only from an aerial perspective could one observe the crater in its entirety. It was gigantic in its dimensions and exactly circular, as if drawn with a compass.

The world held its breath.

For three hours.

The time of the ultimatum came and went.

Three red buttons remained untouched.


## CHAPTER FOUR

Lieutenant Klein arrived in Peking by a roundabout route. He made contact with Number Two, in accordance with his instructions, and received further briefing from him. The assignment he had begun seemed impossible, but he had to attempt it. Perry Rhodan meant danger for the whole world. Whoever could remove this danger would gain undying fame, regardless of the nation of his origin. It was a task that demanded the highest personal commitment and the greatest courage.

There was, however, one circumstance that seemed to make it easier. Allan D. Mercant himself had given this important hint to Klein before sending him on his journey.

"Listen carefully, Lieutenant Klein. This Rhodan could never be removed by ordinary means. There is only one possibility—treason. Don't worry unnecessarily about the morality of the matter, because Rhodan has betrayed us. You must succeed in penetrating the force field. How you do this will remain your own problem. And something else —you are not alone. Agents of the Eastern Bloc as well as of the Asiatic Federation are working toward the same objective. It is not entirely impossible that the common crisis will bring about a certain understanding among ourselves. Until the *Stardust* has been destroyed, the agents from

Moscow and Peking are our colleagues. So, now, good luck."

Good luck. That was what Klein could really use, and so far he had actually had it.

In Kalgan, some seventy-five miles northwest of Peking, he had bought a truck. There he noticed a Chinese he had already seen three times in the same day. This fellow observed him and never let him out of his sight for a moment.

The truck was apparently a good cross country vehicle. Along with it he had bought supplies and provisions, in addition to a tent and all equipment necessary for starting a small expedition. The roads were good, even if they were closely watched.

On the side of his truck, in large letters, he painted words that would place him above suspicion: TRIAL RUN FOR THE ARMY. His papers declared him to be an engineer. He was to determine whether the vehicle was suitable for troop transport through desert and mountains.

As Klein drove the truck out of the city, he watched in vain for the suspicious Chinese he had observed previously. Perhaps the fellow had understood at last that he could find nothing of value here to steal.

"They're on the lookout for foreigners," mumbled the agent, evading a vehicle that came toward him. "But I don't look as rich as a foreigner. What could you steal from an engineer?"

In the evening hours he passed the city of Kwai-hwa while driving along a new road that led alongside the Great Wall. He had no way of knowing that at the same time, Mao-Tsen, Asiatic Federation Minister of Defense, was sitting in faraway Peking, hunched over a radio device that announced the precise location of the presumed test vehicle. Beside him was the grinning Major Buta'an, his chief agent.

"Lieutenant Li Shai-tung is one of my best men," said Buta'an proudly, as if this were of his own doing. "He found the American right away and has not left his side. I am eager to test the validity of your theory that the others will cooperate with us. If this be so, then, as we have reason to believe now, the *Stardust* is really not an American military base. Indeed, were the Western Bloc to possess a weapon such as the ray from the moon represents, we would not be alive any more. Does Li know that the *Stardust* must fall into our hands intact?"

"He has received his instructions," Mao-Tsen agreed thoughtfully. He was listening to the shrill voice that emanated from the loudspeaker. "Ah, the American has driven on. He will soon reach the Hwang-ho and perhaps even Pau-tou, if he does not prefer to stay overnight in the open."

Klein did not know that his route had now been recorded on a map of the Asiatic security high command, as accurately as if he were broadcasting his position at every turn. He would learn this only when he stopped.

The crescent of the moon was already approaching the horizon below which the sun had long ago disappeared. To his left glittered the surface of a slowly flowing stream. Bushes lined the road to the edge of the shore.

Klein found an opening and drove the truck through it. He rolled a few yards farther until he had come to a suitable place to park. Here the truck stood protected among rocks, trees and bushes. Nearby the stream was flowing.

The lieutenant stretched and got out of the truck. Although it was warm, he thought a fire might help. He would not make camp tonight, but some hot coffee would do him a lot of good. Then he could stretch out on some blankets in the back of the truck and sleep.

"Are we stopping for the night?" someone asked in English with a terrible accent. "Take it easy, my friend, don't move! I am not unarmed. Turn around. Yes, all right. But slowly."

Klein had just thrown a few pieces of dry wood into the campfire, whose flames hungrily devoured their meal. Their growing glow allowed him to recognize the face of the speaker. It was, of course, the Chinese he had already noticed in Kalgan. Apparently he had managed to stow away in the back of the truck. All this would not have been quite so bad, but he held a heavy machine gun cradled in his arm. Klein looked directly into the menacing maw of this most dangerous weapon, whose explosive bullets could cripple even a medium sized tank.

"What do you want with me?" asked Klein. "If you're a beggar, then you're certainly a well equipped beggar. But watch out! This is a vehicle of the government."

"Of which government?" Li Shai-tung smiled his enigmatic smile. "The American government? Let us lay our cards on the table. What are your instructions? Perhaps we could reach some sort of agreement."

Klein gestured toward the fire. "Let's sit down."

"Do you have a weapon?"

"Do you want to come to an agreement or not? Are we going to keep talking with gun in hand?"

Li was hesitating. "I have the advantage now, but I would gladly give it up without regret if I only knew that you are sincere. Answer one question before I can trust you, before I consent. What are your instructions? What is the name of your superior? I know the answers already through my chief. If your answers coincide with mine . . ."

He slowly climbed down from the truck but kept the gun pointed at Klein. Klein reflected a moment, and then, remembering the words of Mercant, he suddenly knew how right the chief had been. The developments had already begun to take shape. It was starting at the very bottom, on a small scale, but one of these days it would encompass all nations. If they did not succeed in destroying the *Stardust* . . .

"My superior is Allan D. Mercant, Director of the Western International Intelligence Agency. My instructions are to destroy the moon rocket *Stardust*. Is that quite enough?"

Li nodded. Lowering his weapon, he kept it in his hand for an indecisive moment before he threw it into the back of the truck. Then he walked over to the fire and extended his hand to Klein. They shook.

The lieutenant swallowed hard. His every action expressed amazement as he sat down with Li. A pleasant warmth came from the fire. The water in the kettle began to boil.

"Our assignments differ in one respect," admitted the Chinese after a long pause. "You are supposed to destroy the *Stardust*, but I must prevent this under all circumstances. However, I think we will see eye to eye in time. At any rate, for the moment we have the same goal. Perry Rhodan must be prevented from forcing his will upon the world. Do I understand you correctly?"

Klein nodded.

"We can therefore collaborate until the time when we will have rendered Rhodan harmless," the Chinese said. "What happens then remains to be seen. Let us arrange a compromise. You will state your terms, please."

Lieutenant Klein could never know how grotesque it really was. Two agents of hostile powers cooperating to eliminate an even greater power. Only a few days before, the speed of a bullet would have decided who would still be alive in the next instant. Today all this was changed. Fear and trembling before an unknown and incomprehensible third power had made reluctant allies out of former deadly enemies.

"You promise not to give me away to your people, even after we've reached our goal? For this guarantee, I'll te'l you how I intend to pass through the force field when we've reached the *Stardust* later. Agreed?"

Li offered the American his hand. Again they shook.

Five days later they left the road near Hang-shou and proceeded in a northerly direction into the Gobi Desert. The mountains and the river fell behind them. Now there were only a few salt lakes, small brooks and, with every mile, less and less vegetation. The desert became increasingly prominent. Some thirty miles from their destination, they were stopped by a tank patrol of the Asiatic army. It was Li who saved the day. A radio message to Peking worked wonders. With many apologies, both agents were released. The commanding officer of the patrol bowed a thousand times before Lieutenant Klein and wished him and his Chinese companion the best of luck and much success.

The situation became more and more strange. There seemed never to have been a conflict between East and West. The fear they shared molded even the most contrary ideologies into unity.

They had to cross the military cordon twice more. Klein began to wonder why he was still driving the camouflaged truck. He could just as easily have gone by an army helicopter, and apparently it mattered little whether it was the army of the Asiatic Federation or the Western Bloc.

But then he considered that after all, he had to bluff Perry Rhodan.

If he could be bluffed.

Captain Reginald Bell shut off the motor of the helicopter.

"Well," asked Perry, "everything okay?"

"Of course. It should be easy to make the twelve hundred or so miles to Hong Kong, if I can land and get fresh fuel along the way. Next stop is Borneo. Then I have to make do until Australia."

Clark Fletcher stirred restlessly. He wore a vacant expression. He had long since forgotten the *Stardust,* which stood scarcely a hundred yards behind them. He saw only the helicopter that would return him to civilization. From there, there would be the possibility of returning to the United States, where his wife was expecting him.

How he had got here, he did not know. He knew his name and the name of the city in which his wife was living. That was all. The hypno block that Khrest, with the help of the psychoradiator, had erected like an armored barrier around his memory had erased all recollection of the past from his mind. No one would be able to get anything out of Fletcher that he could no longer remember.

Reg jumped to the ground and shook hands with Perry. "You can rely on me, old man. I can put Fletch down in Hong Kong or Darwin, and then I'll get the necessary spare parts and the antileukemia serum. I'll be back in one week. Say goodbye again to Manoli and Khrest for me."

"Don't let them shoot you down, Reg."

"The helicopter belongs to the army, and besides, I've got the antigrav with me. Its effective range extends as far as six miles. Quite apart from the fact that the hand radiators and other gadgets will help me too. With those, I can trade in whole continents, if need be. Just think of the little power generators! No bigger than a cigar box, and still they can supply 200 kilowatts continuously for a hundred years. Fletch, get aboard."

While the astronomer climbed into the back seat and sat down among the many boxes, Reg once again grasped his friend's hand.

"Release the force field in the very instant I've climbed up high enough. A few seconds should be sufficient. Then close the barrier again. I'll be back in a week."

Perry returned to the control center of the *Stardust.* As the helicopter gained altitude and approached the dome of the invisible energy bell, he thrust back a lever for five seconds. Then Reg was outside.

With relatively moderate speed, the helicopter moved toward the south, flew over a few armored divisions at fairly low altitude and soon afterward crossed the Richthofen Mountains along their eastern limits. Then Reg turned toward the southeast and remained at an altitude of about 2,000 feet.

Late in the afternoon, without any warning, he was attacked by a fighter plane.

This incident was inexplicable, even if it were possible that someone had observed his departure. It seemed unlikely that they had left him undisturbed for so long, only to attack now.

The small plane approached from the front and fired at him. The tracers were too far to the left, but before the pilot could make correction he had already shot past. He banked in a wide circle and attacked again, this time from the side.

By now Reg had overcome his initial surprise. He held the helicopter to its course while setting his hand radiator on medium intensity. Then he directed it at the returning plane.

"Now let's see what you can do," murmured Reg, and added intensely, "Pull up! Pull the engine straight up. Cease fire."

At once the small tongues of flame darting from beneath the wings were withdrawn. The enemy aircraft began climbing on an almost vertical ascent into the clear and cloudless sky.

Reg slowly put the hand radiator down. It was already too late when he thought of issuing another command to the pilot. The distance of some two or three miles could not be bridged by the radiator.

The fighter plane continued climbing, vertically and senselessly. Even when Reg could no longer see it, it continued its ascent, already much slower. The fuel had been exhausted. Nevertheless, the pilot, now half suffocating, faithfully followed the command he had received from thin air. He kept climbing upward until the last drop of precious fuel had been consumed in the sputtering turbine.

For a second the plane seemed to stop in midair. Then it

began to fall. Madly spinning in a descending spiral, it fell for miles, to shatter on the rocks of the Tsingling Shan.

Reg was shaken. He had only now begun to realize what fearful power this innocent looking ray caster meant, if one knew how to use it properly. Perhaps he should have given the pilot another order; but how could he have decided that in a fraction of a second?

He landed on the small military airport near Chun-king. From there, it was another 600 miles to Hong Kong.

At first no one took any notice of him. But when he simply stopped and remained in the helicopter, a jeep arrived. A high officer climbed out and came toward him.

"Why haven't you announced yourself?" he demanded. But then he saw Reg's face, which could not under any circumstances be mistaken for that of a Chinese. "Who are you?"

Reg grinned, if only because he had heard that it was the thing to do in this part of the world. "I don't understand a single word," he said in English. Pointing the radiator at the others, he continued, "I am Marshal Roon, and I need fuel. Please do whatever is necessary, but hurry up, will you, please?"

The driver of the jeep had been included in the treatment.

The officer saluted smartly, climbed back into his jeep, and whizzed off.

Grinning, Reg waited. He turned around toward Fletcher who had been witness to the occasion. Fletcher sat with eyes half closed, uncomprehending.

"Poor guy," muttered Reg.

Five minutes later, a tanker came and stopped beside the helicopter. It was getting dark but no one bothered with the two men in the cabin anyway. The fuel tank was filled. A few reserve fuel cans were placed in the hold. The leader of the group then signaled the end of the transaction.

Nodding graciously, Reg started the engine. He could still seen the wide eyed expression on the faces of the Chinese as he took off into the copper evening sky.

The real Marshal Roon would never be able to explain to his satisfaction how Captain Fin-lai, who knew him so intimately, could swear throughout the court-martial proceedings that he had encountered him that night at the

Chun-king air force base. Surely one could not be in two places at once.

It was strange.

At a distance of exactly seven miles from the *Stardust*, on the Koshun salt lake, a Mongolian firm (with the permission of Peking) had begun to set up facilities for the production of salt.

Bulldozers pushed mighty gaps into the shore, and earth moving machines bore away the sands. Thus were formed, not more than a yard in depth, pans into which brine could flow. When the sluice gates were closed, the sun would evaporate the water and only the salt would remain. Whole columns of trucks stood by, ready to bring the salt back to Mongolia, which belonged to the Moscow sphere of influence.

Lieutenant Klein and Li Shai-tung were forced to rest awhile, lest they become too conspicuous. As strange as the busy group of workmen may have seemed to them, there was no reason not to expect them here. The official battle against the *Stardust* had been ended when the futility of military tactics had finally been established. The low yield hydrogen bombs had left behind no fallout and no harmful aftereffects. The troops had been moved away from the immediate vicinity of the lunar vessel.

The chief engineer of the firm, Ilij Rawenkow, welcomed the unexpected guests with special cordiality. He spoke Chinese fluently.

"What brings you to this forlorn land?" he inquired, after inviting them to a cup of tea. "We didn't expect to see another living soul for many months. By the way, gentlemen, may I introduce Peter Kosnov, the manager of our firm."

Both Russians made a good impression; yet something in—or rather, behind—their eyes warned one to be cautious.

"We are testing a transport truck for the army," Li said very convincingly. "I think this is just the right region for that. Engineer Klein is accompanying me. He's lived in the Asiatic Federation for the last fifteen years."

Rawenkow and Kosnov exchanged quick glances.

"Oh, very interesting indeed." Rawenkow smiled charmingly. "Isn't it odd how Europeans or even Americans will join us and work side by side with us? After all, I suppose, all fences go down when it is a question of economic advantage."

Li almost blinked. "Really? Only economic advantage?" he replied tentatively, expectantly.

The Russian (one could see even at a distance that he, like Kosnov, was no Mongolian) looked inadvertently in the direction in which the spaceship lay, beyond a slight knoll.

"What do you mean by that?" He stalled for time.

Li did not change his expression. He followed their gaze and added, "There are no potential salt production areas over there, if I am not mistaken. Why did you not have the idea of making use of the Koshun lake any earlier?"

"What are you insinuating?" Rawenkow became impatient. He could hardly contain his distress.

"Let us drink to the reconciliation of old enemies." Li smiled and slowly drank his tea. "You don't mean to tell me that you are here just by accident, or do you? Over there, a scant six miles from here, stands the *Stardust*. She is much more valuable than all the salt lakes in the world. Now, since when do Russians work for a Mongolian firm? You are Russian, aren't you, Rawenkow?"

Kosnov made an injudicious movement and found himself looking, not very intelligently, down the barrel of the pistol that Klein waved directly into his face.

"But who would be in such a hurry?" Li said in mild remonstrance. "You are among friends! Kosnov, forget the revolver in your shoulder holster, and you, Klein, make sure your gun stays out of sight. It would be ridiculous if we could not come to terms, in the face of such a terrible opponent. Am I not right, Rawenkow?"

The Russians nodded slowly in agreement.

"How could you find us out so quickly? So far, no one has thought to assume in us anything but the fictitious firm."

"Perhaps because we are colleagues," Li said amiably. "Is the name of your superior, by any chance, Ivan Martinovitch Kosselov?"

Both startled Russians nodded.

"Well, then we are in agreement. May we finally introduce ourselves? This is Lieutenant Klein of Western Security; I am Lieutenant Li Shai-tung of Asiatic Security. Thus, finally, three representatives of the three great powers are sitting around one table, even if it is only a shaky wooden barrel in the Gobi Desert. Speak honestly—is there still any reason why we should remain enemies?"

Rawenkow shook his head. "You are right, Lieutenant Li. I think we should call a cessation of all hostilities. We have the same objective, do we not?"

Klein gnawed on his lower lip. Suddenly he asked, "What happens once we've achieved our goal?"

No one could answer that.

Port Darwin lies on the western edge of Arnhem Land. It is the most important port of Cambridge Bay on the northern coast of Australia.

Although Australia belonged ideologically and economically to the Western Bloc and had its embassy in Washington, a large portion of its population was in favor of continued neutrality toward the continent. They also favored military independence.

Reg knew, nevertheless, that he was not landing in friendly territory when he set the helicopter down near the coast on a sandy plateau. Evening was approaching. The lights of the city had begun to shine brightly.

"Fletch, are you coming to town with me? You can stay there overnight in a hotel. Tomorrow I'll bring you some money, and then there's nothing to stand in the way of your flight home."

"That's all right, Reg. You know I've got to get back to my wife. She's going to have a baby in three months, maybe a little sooner."

"Yes, yes, I know," agreed Reg. This baby story was getting on his nerves by now. If all expectant fathers carried on like this, he could understand why so many jokes were made on the topic.

"Forget your worries. We've got about half an hour's walk into town. Let's hope nobody has observed our landing here. Come along."

Without incident Reg safely established his friend in the Royal Hotel and then took a walk around the town in order to gather some information. He returned to the helicopter shortly. A policeman who had been treated to the effects of the psychoradiator had willingly supplied all requested information.

Dr. Frank M. Haggard lived in the eastern section of the city, in a building near the hospital he had constructed. Here was the laboratory in which he had made his startling discovery two years ago and where he had gone on to develop the serum against leukemia. Reg followed the directions given by the policeman and flew his helicopter along the white shimmering avenue of the freeway until he had reached a fork in the road, where he followed a side road toward the east. Soon he saw the silhouette of the skyline outlined against the lighter hues of the ocean.

He landed in a clearing, put the ray caster in his pocker, tucked one of the inexhaustible generators under his arm, and went on his way.

Frank Haggard had not yet gone to bed. He seemed surprised by his late caller. He drew up his eyebrows in a scowl but asked Reg to enter all the same. He looked curiously at the small package that Reg set carefully on a table.

"What can I do for you?" asked the famous physician.

Reg looked at him. Haggard turned out to be a Hercules with dark blond hair and blue eyes. He might be about forty-five years old. His face wore a kindly expression that would inspire confidence, especially when someone needed help.

"There's a lot you can do," began Reg. "I don't quite know how to explain it. My name is Reginald Bell. I don't suppose you've heard of me before?"

The physician leaned forward. "Do you live in Darwin?"

Reg was disappointed, but he did not show it. "No. I'm from Mongolia. I've just come from there."

Haggard leaned back again, rather quickly. "Oh," he said. And that was all he said. After all, Mongolia was 3,000 miles away. This stranger had just happened to come all the way from Mongolia to see him, of all people, at ten o'clock in the evening. Perhaps a lunatic that had escaped from somewhere. It might be better to watch one's step with him.

"Yes, from the Gobi Desert, to be exact."

"Oh, that's too much!" Haggard exclaimed involuntarily;

but he got hold of himself and asked, full of sympathy, "Did you walk?"

"Only the last 500 yards," admitted Reg. How on Earth could he explain to the scientist what he wanted. "Doctor, I need all your leukemia serum for the treatment of a sick man. Only I am—ah—a bit worried about payment. But I do have a few things I brought along with me."

"You may speak quite freely with me," assured Haggard, his eyes straying across the room to the telephone. "Still, couldn't you have waited until tomorrow morning for this?"

"I'm sorry, Doctor, but that's out of the question. Every minute counts. Would you be interested in a cheap supply of electric current?"

"What do you mean?"

Reg took the little package and put it on his lap. He unwrapped the paper and set a small metal box on the table. There it lay, harmless and unimpressive. Only a few electrical outlets suggested that one might get electricity from it.

"It provides up to 200 kilowatts. You'll never have to recharge it. At maximum use, the supply will last up to 100 years. What do you think of that? Don't keep looking over at the phone! I'm not crazy, and I won't harm you. You have my word."

Now Haggard didn't know what to think. His intuition told him that he was dealing with a normal person, but now he was offered a technical miracle that contradicted all known physical laws.

"Who are you?" he asked.

Reg sighed. "All right, I'll tell you the whole story, but it sounds crazier than a fairy tale. I'm sure you've heard of the *Stardust*, the American moon rocket that landed in the Gobi Desert. Well, I'm a member of its crew. My commander, Perry Rhodan, stayed behind, while I—"

"Perry Rhodan?" Haggard recalled some newspaper articles he had read. "Yes, now I know! Now it comes back to me. Weren't there some political complications?"

"That's putting it mildly. Yes. We have our reasons for keeping the results of the expedition to ourselves. But on the dark side of the moon we discovered an alien spacecraft and its crew. It had been forced to land and couldn't take off again unless spare parts could be supplied them.

The Arkonides—these are the space travelers—are unable to repair their ship themselves because of an advanced state of deterioration. They're extremely intelligent, but physically and psychologically they're wholly debilitated. Their expedition's scientific leader, named Khrest, is suffering from leukemia. He has only a few more years to live, at best. But it's of the greatest importance that he be cured, because the future of his race depends on his survival. And the future of mankind as well. Khrest is our key to outer space and the planets of other solar systems and to a state of technology incredibly beyond our own. Do you understand everything I've said so far?"

Haggard nodded. "I've heard about the big crater in the Sahara, of course. Was it Khrest who did that?"

"Yes." Reg dispensed with unnecessary explanations. "And he can do even a great deal more; but we'll continue along that line later. First of all, my question—will you help us? Will you let me have the serum? I can give you, in exchange, this generator. It comes from the Arkonides."

Haggard lit a cigarette. His hands were trembling almost imperceptibly.

"The serum by itself won't be of lasting benefit. Khrest really should come to my sanatorium for a regular series of treatments."

"That's unthinkable! He wouldn't be safe here for a single moment, Haggard. Agents from all nations would be searching for him."

Haggard nodded slowly. Then he looked Reg squarely in the face. "Then I will have to go with you, Mr. Bell."

"You will? But your clinic, your sanatorium, your research projects . . ."

"They can wait. This Khrest is much more intriguing. I have always had a passion for the extraordinary. You should know that. Do you think I would pass up the opportunity of thoroughly examining an extraterrestrial intelligence? When do we leave?"

It was too sudden for Reg.

"Well, as soon as possible. There are a few more things I have to take care of first. I need some money to buy spare parts for the Arkonide spacecraft. Electronic elements. Perhaps you could offer a suggestion as to how to go about it."

"I'm familiar with several corporations. If you offer them one of these generators, I'm sure you will be able to talk them into giving you a whole assortment of spare parts."

"Very good! Then tomorrow we'll make the rounds of the wholesale dealers. But right now we've got another problem coming up. I have only one helicopter at my disposal, and it won't carry very much. Would you happen to know someone who has a larger vehicle more suitable for transport?"

Haggard frowned pensively. "One of my assistants has a very respectable yacht. I'm sure he would place it at my disposal. There are some 1800 miles across the ocean to Hong Kong, but we could easily manage that in a week."

"Excellent. Once in Hong Kong, we'll see what we can do further. My psychoradiator will be able to help us there."

"Your who?"

Reg brought the silver rod out of his pocket. "A marvelous thing, Doc. With this, you can impose your will on anyone within a radius of two miles. You see, I would have taken you along with me to the Gobi even if you hadn't gone willingly."

"Incredible." Haggard was honestly amazed. "Then if that thing is fuctioning properly, we should have no trouble."

"It's working just fine," said Reg.

The next day brought considerable surprises and worry to the managers of several wholesale dealerships. Only the presence of Dr. Haggard, who was well-known to them all, prevented them from altogether rejecting Reg's demonstration as a malicious deception. Once convinced, however, their attitude of skepticism very quickly became wild enthusiasm. Reg disposed of his little black boxes, and the wholesale dealers, in turn, disposed of several large boxes full of replacement elements of an electronic nature. In addition to that, quite an imposing sum of money changed hands.

Fletcher was given $5,000, and he booked passage to New York.

Haggard had his assistant's yacht come around to the bay near his clinic.

Everything seemed, therefore, to be in the best of order, and three days after Reg had arrived in Darwin the small

156

vessel was loaded and ready to begin its voyage, the helicopter secured to its deck.

The two men went ashore for the last time. Haggard wanted to give a few final instructions to the assistants who replaced him. Meanwhile, Reg waited.

Somewhere in the twilight, sirens were screaming. Searchlights were stabbing into the dark with their bright pinpoint fingertips and bathing the bay in a semblance of daylight. Up in the air, the engines of heavy helicopters were humming. Tanks, scuttling through the bushes on the shore, pointed their guns at the yacht.

Soldiers suddenly appeared between Reg and the pier. In their hands weapons were held in readiness for firing. An officer approached from one side and came to a halt in front of Reg.

"Your name is Reginald Bell?"

"Is that forbidden?"

"You will please answer my questions and say nothing else."

Reg was silent.

"You belong to the crew of Major Perry Rhodan?"

"If you already know, why ask?" Reg thrust his hands into his pockets with a defiant gesture.

"Don't do that," warned the officer. "To resist would be foolish. We have you completely surrounded. Dr. Haggard has already been arrested, and Captain Fletcher is already in our custody."

"Poor guy!" murmured Reg with pity. "He's going to have a baby."

"What was that?"

"Oh, forget it. You wouldn't understand anyway."

During this exchange Reg had succeeded in setting the psychoradiator at maximum intensity. He now pushed the ON button. Carefully he observed the officer's reactions.

*Now, bend your knees ten times,* he thought, concentrating deeply.

The soldiers who had come closer dropped their weapons and stared in wide eyed amazement when they suddenly beheld their commanding officer doing knee bends with outspread arms. Reg was counting along. The man executed exactly ten knee bends.

*Tell your people to disappear as quickly as possible and to return to their barracks.*

The officer turned around and shouted at the soldiers. "What are you idiots still doing here? Get back go the barracks, on the double! Hurry up, before I—"

"What's going on here?"

The cool, calm voice belonged to a civilian who had emerged from the bushes quite unnoticed. His dress was so inconspicuous as to have made it quite obvious to everyone, even one so inexperienced as Reg.

"The soldiers must return to their barracks," said the officer mechanically. "They must disappear."

The civilian turned to Reg. "Are you Reginald Bell?"

"Everyone seems to be asking the same question today. How odd! Once upon a time, no one cared what my name was. But since I've returned from the moon all this sure had changed!"

"Ah! Well, then, you admit it."

"Why shouldn't I? But who are you anyway?"

"Secret police. Follow me."

Reg had moved slightly.

"It would be to your advantage to follow me," the plain-clothesman advised him gently. He began to walk toward the clinic.

"Who is in command of the action against me?"

"Police Inspector Miller and his garrison, sir," the policeman replied with a strangely changed voice.

"And who arrested Haggard?"

"I did. He will be transferred to the prison, where he will remain until his part in this incident has been cleared up. Would you like to talk to him?"

"You will authorize the release of Dr. Haggard at once," commanded Reg, and stopped. He had changed his mind. "Bring him to me at the yacht and see to it that Inspector Miller immediately abandons this action. Is that understood?"

"I am to bring Haggard to the yacht and cease the action. Understood."

"All right then, get going."

Reg had to take into consideration the fact that the new arrangement must not be made known so quickly that perhaps one or the other detachments might still try to execute the old orders. He would do best, therefore, to remain on board the yacht. The civilian would manage to bring the prisoners to him, unless he was prevented from doing so by force.

In the cabin of the upper deck, where glass windows afforded a clear view in all directions, Reg set up the antigravity apparatus on a table. Since its radius of activity extended for six miles, the city would also be affected by it.

He waited until the civilian had handed over the utterly bewildered Haggard. Then he switched on the antigravity. The yacht, being the center of the field, kept its natural gravity. The surface of the ocean, unruffled by the slightest wind, remained like a huge bowl of lead. Only where a fish jumped playfully up into the air could a strange sight be seen. Fish and ocean spray were borne slowly aloft and soon disappeared in the dusk of evening.

Reg said regretfully to Haggard, "Too bad we can't see what's happening in the meantime. Everything within a radius of six miles, in any event, is weightless. Can you imagine how the whole police force must be floating up in the air?"

"But my patients . . . !" worried Haggard.

"The area of your clinic has been excluded. And now it's about time for us to flee the scene. I'll leave the antigrav switched on. Of course, it's also effective vertically, toward the sky, so no one can approach us at a distance of less than six miles."

In a protective bubble wherein the gravitational pull of Earth had been completely nullified for miles around, the yacht left the natural harbor. The yacht, bearing the very appropriate name of *Zephyr*, moved out toward the open sea, floating droplets of water in its wake.

Reg might not have been quite so happy had he been able to see what he had done with his light hearted playfulness. There was utter chaos in Darwin. Men and vehicles found the ground escaping from beneath their feet and rose without gravity into the night sky. If they were lucky, they reached the upper limits of the gradually diminishing antigravity zone, reacted with the opposite impulse, and landed gently on Earth again. Others were less fortunate.

This night, the news of this incredible event circled the globe. Again the whole world was on alert. Naval flotillas changed their course, sailing now toward the Celebes. There they expected to find a member of the crew of the *Stardust* on a secret yacht.

The following day two aircraft carriers and seven destroyers of the Asiatic Federation Navy had left their usual element. When, devoid of gravity, they were lifted up to a height of one and a half miles and then were allowed to fall slowly back into the ocean, they discontinued their efforts. They fired long range missiles from a safe distance.

But here too they had no success.

None of the missiles hit its target. They all detonated quite uselessly at either great altitudes or below the surface of the ocean. Reg was very well versed in how to alter their course by changing the amount of gravity in whatever way it suited him. But he also knew that the real dilemma still lay ahead of him.

Now that the whole world was at his heels, he could hardly succeed in landing without notice in Hong Kong. If he ever wanted to see the *Stardust* again, he would need a great deal of luck.

Captain Clark G. Fletcher stared insensibly into the bright light. His eyes were open wide.

"All you have to do is answer," said a hard voice behind the lamp. The face beyond the voice could not be seen. It was concealed in the darkness of the room. "Why did you want to return to the United States?"

"My wife, she's expecting a baby."

"Yes, you've already said that. But you must have still another reason. No one would risk his life for a baby."

"How would you know that? Are you married?"

The disembodied voice cleared its throat. "Why did you not remain with Perry Rhodan?"

"I don't know what you're talking about. I don't know anyone by that name. I don't know anything about a moon rocket either. Why don't you stop torturing me once and for all with your stupid questions? I don't understand what you mean."

"What are Rhodan's intentions?"

"I don't know."

"What did you find on the moon?"

Fletcher tried to move his arms, but he could not, for

steel bands held him fast to the arms of his chair. Sweat stood in great beads on his forehead. He was thirsty. He closed his eyes, but the bright light bored into him even through closed eyelids.

"I don't know!"

"Listen, Captain Fletcher. We've only begun. Unless you tell us the truth, we will be forced to resort to far more unpleasant methods."

"I can't tell you anything if I don't *know* anything!"

Behind the bright light there was soft murmuring. The light was suddenly turned off. The naked bulb on the ceiling seemed dark and dim. The steel bands were released, and firm hands pulled Fletcher out of his chair. Without protest, he let himself be led away. He saw neither the doors to the room nor the walls of the corridor. Not once did he see the faces of his inquisitors throughout it all. He thought only of the airplane that should have brought him back home by now. Even the brightly illuminated operating theater could not impress him in his delirium.

They placed him on an operating table. Men in white coats bent over him and bound his arms. He willingly submitted to everything. Copper plates enclosed his wrists and ankles. Cables with electrodes were cool against his temples. Somewhere a large motor began to whir.

The first color reflexes appeared on a video screen. Several men sat waiting intently in front of it. Their tension was clearly evident on their faces.

"Do you believe we can learn anything this way?"

"The mental projector is infallible, Inspector. Unfortunately, its application might, in certain circumstances, pose a danger for the malefactor. But so long as he is talking—or rather, I should say, *thinking*—nothing much can happen."

"And his thoughts are translated and made visible on the screen?"

"Correct. We are dealing here with a further development of the lie detector that has heretofore been in use, but there is hardly any basis for comparison of the two any more. If we ask questions of the subject in the machine and he does not wish to answer them, at least he cannot refrain from thinking about them. These thoughts form on the screen in a picture that exactly corresponds to whatever he is thinking."

"I believe I see what you mean."

"Then let us begin."

Fletcher kept his eyes shut tightly. He lay very quietly, as if he wanted to go to sleep. His chest rose and fell rhythmically.

One of the civilians bent over him. "Can you hear me, Fletcher? You don't need to answer if you don't want to. But I would like to ask you a few things. Speak only when you so desire. What was it that you wanted in the United States?"

With fixed attention the men stared up at the video screen. A clear picture began to form there for the first time. The face of a still young and pretty woman appeared. She smiled and beckoned. On the table Fletcher moaned. The picture changed. Beds, nurses, doctors, and then again the young woman. She was lying in a hospital bed, a baby beside her.

"Would you believe it?" muttered the inspector. "He really is thinking only of his baby. An *idee fixe*. Continue the questioning, Chief."

The chief nodded and turned to Fletcher. "Fletcher, what happened on the moon? We must know what happened on the moon."

At once the image of the woman with the baby disappeared. Colors flashed in a kaleidoscopic pattern, formed abstract figures and blended in an unrecognizable blur. Then a vortex began to form, turning faster, ever faster, until it had become a whirling disk.

"What do you know of the *Stardust?*"

The disk spun around with increasing speed. Amid this, lightning raced across the screen. Fletcher was groaning. His breathing grew more rapid, until he was panting. Perspiration ran in streams across his forehead.

One of the men in white coats stepped forward and nudged the chief. "You must stop for a while," he urged. "The prisoner is under too great a strain. His heart may not be able to stand that much."

"But we've scarcely begun!" interjected the inspector. "Just a few more questions."

"But can't you see that he doesn't know anything at all?

162

The symbols indicate total amnesia. . . . All right, I'll give you two further trials, but I will hold you personally responsible."

The spinning vortex on the video screen had disappeared. Once again the young woman was visible. She walked through a blossoming garden, leading a little girl by the hand.

"Fletcher, what is the course of action that Perry Rhodan is pursuing?"

Instantly the image of the woman with the little girl faded out. Once more the vortex began to whirl madly. Lightning was crackling. Color patterns arose and were extinguished.

"It's senseless to continue," said the doctor. "He doesn't know anything."

"But he must know something!" roared the inspector uncontrollably. "He hasn't lost his sanity, has he?"

"Perhaps his memory."

"But we must know what has happened! Isn't there any possibility of forcing his power of recall to return?"

"If you had time, perhaps we could succeed in doing so, but you would have to leave him alone for months, possibly even let him go."

"Impossible! He's a danger to the whole world. Just think of this Reginald Bell. Remember what he did to our whole town yesterday? Swimming up in the air, as though there were no longer any gravity . . . ! No, not for a single moment is Fletcher permitted to remain without supervision."

The doctor sighed. "Well, then, put your last question to him."

The chief nodded. Obviously he did not agree with the inspector's undisciplined behavior. He brought his mouth quite near to Fletcher's ear and asked, "Who is Khrest?"

That was the name Haggard had unwittingly yielded up during the interrogation that had lasted only a few minutes. The Inspector had caught the name, but did not know quite what to do with it.

"Listen, Fletcher. Who is Khrest?"

Fletcher reared up within his bonds. His eyes, now opened wide, stared into those of the civilian. In them there was fear but also something like recognition. His hands clenched into tight fists, and his lips mumbled inaudible words.

On the video screen there was chaos. The multicolored vortex turned faster and faster, until no longer were there any colors but a monotonous gray. Then everything burst asunder. Splinters of color slid in all directions and seemed to leap through the glass of the screen.

Then the glass became dark and remained so.

One of the physicians leaned forward to look into the rigid gaze of Fletcher's open eyes. He felt his pulse; then he stood upright.

His voice was somber. "Gentlemen, he is dead."

The inspector turned pale. "Dead? How could he be dead? His heart was strong enough."

The doctor shrugged. "His heart may have been in perfect condition, but he died of a cerebral stroke."

No one said anything further.

Fletcher lay motionless on the operating table. Never would he learn of the birth of his child. Never would he know his little girl.

Lieutenant Klein stood at the invisible barrier. His hands felt the obstacle his eyes could not see. A mile and a half within the confines of the barrier stood the *Stardust*, once the pride of the whole Western world, then an opportunity that had failed to materialize, now the horror of all mankind.

A lone figure came toward the lieutenant. It was Major Rhodan, whom he recognized from the many film clips taken of him. The major stopped some six feet from Klein. In his hand he held paper and pencil.

*What do you want? Who are you?* Klein read what had been written.

Klein had not thought of it, but of course, if the force field could hold even atomic energy at bay, why not sound waves too? He searched his pockets and found a pencil and some paper. This way, at least, some form of communication was possible.

*Lieutenant Klein. I come in behalf of Mercant and Pounder, to negotiate with you.*

Perry Rhodan smiled and wrote, *Get undressed and I'll lift the force field for five seconds.*

*Undressed?*

*Yes—because of weapons.*

Reluctantly Klein looked around in all directions. No one was in sight. He knew that Li and Kosnov, who sat behind the shore line on the other side of the riverbank, would disapprove, but that was of little concern to him now. The main thing was that he would be able to get through the force field, something no one else had yet been able to do.

Klein took off his clothing, placing everything neatly folded in a little heap. Perry nodded to him. He raised his right arm and gestured toward the *Stardust*, and Klein could suddenly hear his voice.

"Hurry. Come over to my side."

Klein left the humid air mingling with the cooler air when the force field had been removed. Then he was standing next to Perry.

In the same breath everything became totally still again. Klein could feel no wind. The invisible barrier had again been drawn around the space ship, and thus he was entirely cut off from the rest of humanity.

"Well, you come from Pounder, do you?" asked Perry, shaking hands with him. "I thought the old boy would get around to sending an envoy. How did you manage to get through hostile territory?"

"It wasn't so difficult," admitted Klein. "Their efforts at surveillance are diminishing."

"Really?" Perry said doubtfully. "But come along with me. I'll lend you some trousers."

They walked slowly toward the *Stardust*. Klein felt a strange sympathy for the man walking beside him. Yet his instructions were to kill this man at all costs, if he did not assent to Mercant's command. Well, for the time being, anyway, there was no sense in thinking about it. He could hardly kill him with his bare hands, and how should he destroy the *Stardust*? Of course, he knew about the self-destruct system, but there were still three men in the crew. No, it would not be quite so simple. Not even if he *wanted* to kill him.

And did he really want to?

On a flat rock directly at the side of the ship, both sat down.

"Now, please be quite honest, Lieutenant Klein. What are your orders? What word do you bring me? Did Pounder really send you?"

The agent shook his head. "Not directly. I'm with Mercant's defense division. My orders are to persuade you to destroy the *Stardust* and return with me to Nevada Fields. In case you refuse, I'm supposed to kill you and destroy the spaceship myself."

Perry called something to Manoli, who had meanwhile appeared at the hatch. Soon afterward the doctor returned, bringing with him a pair of light trousers from some uniform. Klein put them on.

"This is Dr. Manoli. Lieutenant Klein, from the Division of International Defense. Stay with Khrest, Eric. Tell him that we have a visitor." He waited until the doctor had gone before replying to Klein's words. "Well, then those are your orders? Why have you told me all this?"

"Because I have confidence in you, Rhodan. Because in the last few days I have had an experience that has moved me deeply."

"And what was that?"

"Later, Rhodan. I'll tell you in time, but first I want to ask you one question—"

"That will occur during the course of our discussion. You will answer my questions, I will answer yours. The picture will then form by itself. Is General Pounder very disappointed in me?"

"Why, of course. He cannot understand your motives. But at least, he *tries* to understand them, whereas Mercant's opinion is absolutely fixed. In his book you're a traitor."

"Pounder doesn't think so? And how about you? What's your opinion?"

"You're a traitor in Pounder's eyes, perhaps also in the eyes of most of the peoples of the Western Bloc. In their judgment, it was your duty to hand over the discoveries you made on the moon. You were obligated to do so, if only economically, for without the financial backing of the United States government you would never have been able to reach the moon in the first place. Still, there may be reasons that transcend our morality; but they must certainly be very good reasons."

"Indeed they are," replied Perry decidedly. "My conscience, all my reason and logic, forbid me to surrender to any one terrestrial power the tremendous technology that was our discovery on the moon. What would be the consequences of that, Lieutenant Klein? Think well before you reply."

"There isn't very much to think about. Before the Western Bloc—and I presume it to be the first choice—could test its new weapons, fear and panic on the other side would already have caused a nuclear attack. War, and with total annihilation, would have been unavoidable. I can understand very well what it is that you seek to avoid, Major Rhodan, but will everyone else?"

"They will have to," said Perry in a hard voice. Uncompromising resolve was visible in his eyes. "In reality, it is a question of much more than just avoiding a war. You are aware that on the moon we found an alien technology; but you are *not* aware that the creators of this technology, the Arkonides, are still alive. One of them, a scientist, is here with us, aboard the *Stardust*."

Klein needed a full minute to recover from the shock. "They are not dead, they are not extinct? They are alive, and they can, if they wish, produce more of these weapons?"

"Not only weapons of destruction but also constructive things. For example, tremendous sources of energy in the form of handy portable generators with which you can power vehicles of every sort. . . . You can extend the list of achievements almost indefinitely. Now you will begin to understand more fully why I really had to land here and why I am forced to defend myself against everyone—*everyone*. You are the first exception to this rule."

"Why me?"

"Because you come from Mercant and Pounder. I value these two men, and I would like for them to understand my motives. But you, Lieutenant Klein—you will be able to convince others only when you can follow my reasoning with your own intelligence. This is why I will not explain it for you."

Kein smiled. "I understand very well, and I believe I know your intentions. Look beyond the force field, over here at the river. Two colleagues are waiting for me. No, not Americans or western Europeans. An agent of the Asiatic Federation and an agent of the Eastern Bloc. We are cooperating in order to meet a common crisis. Just a few days ago we were threatened by the outbreak of war among ourselves but today the deadly enemies of yesterday are

already working side by side in the fight against the sti
greater threat of your Third Power."

Perry nodded and smiled back. "Yes, it seems that w
understand one another. Continue."

"Nothing more, Major Rhodan. Only you could confir
my suspicion that this event is only the beginning of
great upheaval."

"Yes, that is so. I represent a serious threat to th
world—but not a threat to its uneasy peace. Fear of m
and the might of the Arkonides will unite the nations (
Earth. When that has happened, nothing should prevei
the acquisition of the galactic technology by a stable worl
government. That, Lieutenant Klein, you may report t
Mercant and General Pounder. Now I'd like to introduc
you to my guest, the Arkonide Khrest. Please follow m
into the ship."

Two long hours later, when Lieutenant Klein returned t
his colleagues waiting at the river, there was no longe
anything that could have changed his decision. He ha
become a defender of Perry's dream, a dream that woul
become the moral foundation of a future empire encom
passing the galaxy.

"Well?" asked Kosnov, and stood up.

"What has happened?" Li inquired.

Klein stood between them. On his right, the Russia
walked with long, strong steps. Little clouds of dust wer
kicked up by his heavy boots. On his left, the Chinese I
shuffled quickly along. In his slanted eyes could be see
a great deal of distrust.

"Well, please do say something, Lieutenant. What hav
you accomplished?"

"Really everything. My assignment has ended, and I thir
yours as well. I'll try to explain it to you, Li. We've becom
comrades, haven't we? We understand each other ver
well. And you, Kosnov, can you imagine why we shoul
kill each other simply because we have different answers
the same questions? Both of you shake your heads as if t
say no. Fine. Then tell me, what would happen if th
spaceship over there, with all the fantastic weaponry
brought back from the moon, should suddenly cease to exi

or if it should fall into the hands of any one of the great powers, no matter which?"

They did not reply.

"Then I will tell you. In that same instant we would turn our weapons upon one another again; once more we would be deadly enemies, and that only because a greater threat would no longer exist. And just as it would happen among ourselves, so would it be with our nations. The end of the *Stardust* would mean the end of peace on Earth. Do you understand? Only so long as there exists the Third Power, the power of the Arkonides, will our world continue to exist. We three now have the chance to preserve the peace of our world, by returning to our countries with the report that there is no way to the *Stardust*. Then we will remain three good friends, and our three nations will do exactly the same."

Li smiled his enigmatic smile. "Six days ago I already had similar thoughts, but I did not dare to express them. Now I fully agree with you."

Klein and the Chinese looked hopefully at the Russian. Kosnov had stopped. He returned their gaze.

Then he suddenly smiled.

"I fear that extracting salt from brine would be much more profitable at the Black Sea. We will soon be moving out of here. Soon we shall break camp and leave."

All three men laughed heartily.

Then all three clasped their hands and shook them in friendship.

## CHAPTER FIVE

Hong Kong bore some resemblance to an army camp when the private yacht *Zephyr* arrived in the harbor.

Reg had turned off the antigrav but kept it ready for use, fully prepared in the event of an attack. Haggard had given orders to the crew of the yacht to steer for a vacant berth. Both men were standing on the forward deck.

"Still looks a bit risky, I'd say," murmured the doctor skeptically. "How can we go ashore without getting caught? All the world knows by now of our arrival."

"Well, so what?" Reg answered in amazement. He toyed

with the psychoradiator. "With this contraption I can put the whole city to sleep, and I can make it sleep soundly. To every single inhabitant, to every soldier, I can issue a command that must be obeyed unconditionally. No, I don't see any reason to be concerned. Not at all. Particularly when they won't be able to employ tactical nuclear weapons, the only thing that might become dangerous for us."

"And how shall we bring my laboratory ashore? How shall we unload your spare parts and get them finally to the Gobi Desert?"

"We'll cross that bridge when we come to it," Reg said in the most soothing manner. "For now, let's have the port commandant come by as soon as we dock. By the way, why did you have to bring such an extravagant lab with you? I haven't had time to inquire into the matter until now."

"Extravagant? This is hardly more than a small portable lab, equipped with the more modern diagnostic aids, surgical instruments, machines to analyze basal metabolism, and samples of a wide variety of medications. You must consider that we are dealing here with a biologically divergent being who will likely as not respond to treatment in a manner entirely different from what we are used to. An X-ray console is also here, for which—"

"And I thought," Reg interrupted with a sigh, "that we could do with an ordinary surgical syringe and a few ampoules of serum."

"That's where you are mistaken, my dear Mr. Bell. But look over there at the armored tanks on the quay. They're just waiting to sink our yacht."

"Nonsense. They could already have tried that a long time ago. They know very well that I will leave them up in the air, in the exact sense of the words. Okay, now the yacht is at anchor in port, and I can try a few of my magic tricks."

Reg directed his radiator at medium intensity toward the low lying building on the main quay and began to concentrate deeply.

*The port commandant is to report at once to Pier Seven. Port commandant to Pier Seven. Most urgent. Yacht* Zephyr.

If he could have seen what he achieved with his telepathic command, he would probably have burst out laughing. In the administration building, almost 200 employees were busily at work. Each and every one of them suddenly felt it his most momentous duty to direct the port commandant's attention to the fact that he must go at once to pier number seven where the yacht *Zephyr* was awaiting him. But the commandant was already on his way there, following the impulse that had arisen in his innermost being, and all along the road he had to fend off the entire work force of the administration building, who seemed only to delay him with their incessant reminders to "Report at once to Pier Seven."

"I know, I know!" he shouted, so loud that everyone could hear him.

He rushed out onto the quay, pushing his way through the crowd of dock workers. He reached the yacht quite out of breath. Along the way he was joined in silence by the commander of the armored division employed in the area. Together the two men climbed up the small gangway that had in the meantime been rolled out for them.

By now, Reg had stationed the switched on psychoradiator in such a manner that its radius of activity included the pier and the upper deck. The apparatus couldn't be seen, but it was nevertheless very effective.

Haggard could not conceal his uneasiness but Reg confidently strode out toward both visitors.

"I am so glad to see you," he said with honest conviction, "and I thank you for the magnificent parade you've put on in my honor. That really wasn't necessary. Sir, in two hours I shall require twenty longshoremen to unload my ship. Will you please see to it that I have these workers? Thank you so much. You may leave now."

The port commandant saluted smartly and departed. The commanding officer of the armored division remained where he was. He seemed to be waiting for something.

"Who is in command of the troops assembling in Hong Kong?" asked Reg.

"Marshal Roon is personally in charge."

"Roon? Wasn't that the officer who floated way up into the air in the most marvelous spiral when Perry switched on the antigrav? Of course! The same to whom the helicopter belonged. Tell him that he can pick it up again at his earliest opportunity."

"Very well. I shall inform Marshal Roon immediately."

Ten minutes later, a group of high ranking officers proceeded from the main quay to the narrow pier. A pair of golden stripes shone in their midst. That would be Marshal Roon himself.

The psychoradiator lay well hidden beneath a huge coil of rope. Its rays played over the whole group, but no one would notice their effect so long as he was not addressed directly.

After a brief discussion, Roon and two officers came aboard the yacht. Roon had long since forgotten why he really had come here, and only the compulsion to fulfill the command still motivated him.

Reg puffed out his chest, which made him appear a bit less potbellied. His short hair was standing upright like a hairbrush. He saluted smartly. "Marshal Roon, I am delighted that you could come so quickly. Gentlemen, welcome aboard the *Zephyr*. May I ask, Marshal, how you liked your little trip through the air not so long ago? I am sure you remember it."

"Why, of course. I remember it well. A very strange phenomenon. An invention of the white devils. Besides, my helicopter was stolen. You are Captain Reginald Bell, if I am not mistaken. I urge you to surrender."

"But Marshal, we are such good friends! Of course you're only joking. You will have your helicopter returned, and that will be the end of the whole affair. You'll just forget all about it. Agreed?"

"Agreed," consented Roon without the slightest hesitation.

"In addition, you will withdraw all your troops from Hong Kong and release instructions to the army. The *Stardust* must not be disturbed, not in any respect. You will also guarantee safe transportation to Reginald Bell and afford him all possible support. Agreed?"

"Agreed."

"Well, then. You will send me three overland trucks within an hour. One of them you will man with ten high ranking officers. Let them take along blankets or sleeping bags. The other two vehicles must be empty, to carry our own freight. Agreed?"

Marshal Roon saluted. "Your orders will be executed. Is there anything else, sir?"

"Yes, Marshal. In the future you will refuse to submit to any command that concerns action against the *Stardust* or its crew. Pass this on to your subordinates."

Turning around with a flourish, Marshal Roon marched off the deck. Back on the pier, the other officcers began to question him, but he shouted them down so furiously that they pulled in their heads and kept silent. After all, he was the field marshal; he ought to know what he was doing.

And Roon suddenly did.

Haggard eventually stopped gaping. "It's most amazing—" he began, but Reg interrupted him.

"You'll be even more amazed, once you've talked to Khrest. Didn't I tell you that we'd make it?"

They waited calmly in silence. They saw how the armored tanks assembled on the other side of the quay and then rolled off toward the eastern exit of the city. The infantry, which had by then begun marching, followed them. The police, however, hesitated. Reg showed them no mercy. He took the psychoradiator in his hand and commanded, "All members of the police, whether official or secret, lie down flat on the ground!"

It was astonishing to note just who abruptly stretched out on the ground, as directed. Even very dignified old gentlemen who seemed to be walking around with a bored expression on their faces suddenly threw themselves into the mud and lost their yak hair beards. Workers and fishermen who appeared quite harmless joined them on the ground. And of course, there were the policemen in uniform.

"Crawl along the ground," ordered Reg with secret joy. He swore that from this day forward he would never let go of the psychoradiator. "Crawl on the ground until you reach your quarters."

Squealing children accompanied the procession of once feared policemen as they made their way through the streets, crawling on their bellies like snakes. No one could explain these circumstances, but everyone felt that this was the way it should be, for all had been witness to the command without recognizing its source. But those who did not belong to the police were not unduly concerned about it.

The port was completely depopulated.

Shortly, the twenty workers and three trucks arrived as requested. Ten officers were sitting expectantly in the last vehicle.

"Just keep quiet and wait for further instructions. You are our military escort. You'll have to defend us with your guns against attack. That is all."

The unloading of the yacht and the loading of the trucks did not take very long. Just one hour, and all was done. The yacht raised anchor, moving out to sea. Reg wished the crew a happy and safe voyage home.

He had taken a seat next to the driver in the first truck. Haggard was sitting in the second one, which carried his valuable laboratory equipment. The column started to move and was soon bouncing over the rough road. Only at the edge of the town did the condition of the road improve, so that one could finally drive a bit faster. No military forces nor policemen could be seen.

In Canton they reached the overland road, wide and well paved, leading to the 1,200 mile distant Lan-chou. Once they had arrived there, they would have to turn north through the valley of the Hwang-ho, past the Alashan Mountains, and then along the 38th Parallel westward across the desert. Altogether, it would take a three day journey at the most.

If only everything went all right . . .


"Peking to Washington:

*"Various incidents seem to indicate (contrary to the minority opinion that Major Rhodan's claims might possibly be true) that the Stardust with which we are dealing is nothing but a Western military base. Our scientists are of the opinion that the nullification of gravity could easily be a Western discovery. We therefore repeat our demand that you remove the base in the Gobi Desert forthwith."*


"Washington to Peking:

*"How do your scientists explain the still active new volcano that has appeared in the Sahara Desert? We reaffirm that we have nothing whatsoever to do with the Stardust. We are just as interested in removing this menace as you are."*

174

"Peking to Washington:

"*The crater could very well be a diversionary tactic entirely unrelated to any so-called energy ray. Our belief that the Stardust is an American military base has been confirmed by the fact that your people have prevented our agents from approaching the lunar spacecraft. Your agents, on the other hand, have been able even to enter the Stardust. We therefore repeat our warning.*"

"Washington to Peking:

"*We have no corroboration of your charges. We are unable to verify that even a single one of our agents has been able to contact Major Rhodan. There obviously must be some misunderstanding. There must be some explanation for this incident.*"

"Moscow to Washington:

"*We demand the immediate removal of your military base in the Gobi Desert.*"

"Moscow to Peking:

"*We demand the immediate removal of the American military base in your territory.*"

The assault took place three days later.

The truck column had passed the Alashan Mountains and had just turned westward. The former caravan road was very poor and forced the trucks to drive at an extremely slow speed. Huge holes in the road had to be carefully evaded, and deep ruts made it constantly necessary to detour.

It was to their advantage that at the moment of the attack, they were crossing a rather low depression. Otherwise, the first round of fire would surely have found its mark. But this way the heavy barrage passed over their heads and detonated on the northern foothills of the Richthofen Mountains.

Reg had everything stop on the spot and ordered the vehicles to line up in close formation on their right. There they were protected from direct hits by a steep slope facing the north. He then took the gravity neutralizer under his arm and looked for a good place to climb up and assess their position. Arriving atop a bluff looking out over the desert, he put down the box.

"Dammit, the yellows have learned a few things since the last time."

The Asiatics were now at a distance of at least six miles and had set up a regular emplacement there. One of the officers gave Reg a pair of binoculars.

At least eight heavy cannon were over there. Further to the right, there was a battery of lighter guns. In between them were machine gun nests.

The enemy was no longer vulnerable to the effects of the neutralizer.

Once again a salvo passed above them, this time already a bit lower. The hits were coming closer.

"Haggard, the radio instruments are in the front truck. Take one of the officers and try to get in touch with the *Stardust*. Wavelength, 44 meters. Let me know as soon as someone answers. But hurry up! Otherwise, those guys over there will finally hit their target. There's nothing I can do to prevent it."

Haggard found a radio officer. It was nevertheless ten endless minutes before the instruments received the *Stardust*'s reply. Reg slid down the slope and asked Haggard to take his place. They had to protect themselves against a surprise infantry attack.

"Perry, is that you?"

"Reg! Hi, fellow! You're still alive! Where on Earth have you been keeping yourself? Did everything come off all right?"

"So far, so good. I'm less than sixty miles from the *Stardust*. We have three trucks full of material for Khrest. With me is Dr. Haggard, the discoverer of the antileukemia serum. And now the Chinese are giving us a nice fiery reception."

"Well then, so far you've been able to manage?"

"Don't forget that the others are learning too. They've already found out that they can't come any closer than six miles. They're not even using any long distance missiles any more, because they know I can change their course. But I'm not immune from the chance hit of a grenade, much as

I'm trying to deflect them. You must help us, and very quickly at that."

"What is your exact geographical position?"

"Just a moment. Hey, driver! The map."

In a few minutes Perry knew the exact position of the column and where the enemy artillery was. He promised to ask Khrest for immediate assistance. Reg stayed tuned to the radio.

The shell bursts were falling closer and closer. Several smaller shells were already whistling very near above their heads. One of them even exploded on the southern crest of the ridge, but that was pure accident.

Perry came on again. "Khrest wanted to ask Thora to use the energy ray, but the moon is still too far below the horizon. It's impossible, Reg. There's nothing we can do from the *Stardust* either. But there's still one possibility. Have you traded away all the power generators?"

"No, I'm returning with two of them. Why?"

"Then thank the Lord! Which do you want to use, the psychoradiator or the antigrav?"

"But the distance is too—"

"Don't get all upset—it's not good for your health. All right, which do you prefer? You can choose both if you have two generators left. The situation is this—the power reservoirs of the psychoradiators and the antigrav are too weak to bridge more than the specified distance. Attached to the generator, however, they can multiply their range tenfold, but only for a few minutes. Then you'll have to wait awhile, to avoid an overload. Do you follow me?"

"And how are they supposed to be connected?"

"Between generator and antigrav, a cable will do. The psychoradiator has a little cap in its reverse end. Unscrew the cap. Underneath it you'll find a plug. You'll know how to insert it into the generator and—"

"That will do, my lord and master. And thanks a lot. Too bad you can't watch what's going to happen here in a little while."

"As a matter of fact, I can. That's even worth the risk of switching off the force field. You'll be arriving back here tonight, I hope?"

But Reg was no longer listening. Now that he knew what to do, he did not want to lose a second in doing it. The drivers and officers were ordered to keep as quiet as possible. Haggard was given the antigrav with the attached generator, while Reg held on to the amplified psychoradiator.

Perry Rhodan, who along with Khrest and Manoli, was sitting in front of the screen of a small closed circuit television set, had surely the greatest fun watching the spectacle that followed. They observed the scene from above, via a miniprobe hovering above the enemy's position at about two miles altitude.

At first nothing seemed to be happening. But then, when the heavy guns fired another round, a rather bizarre tableau was offered the spectators. Unhindered by any earthly gravity, the shells whizzed off in a straight line and disappeared in the vicinity of the faraway mountains. The guns, however, recoiled with the corresponding reaction, sailing off at a lesser speed and slowly rising in the opposite direction. The gradual descent that later occurred suggested that Reg had left them perhaps one-tenth of normal gravity, so that all involved would reach the ground again safely, without losing their lives in a sudden fall.

Khrest made note of all this with a nod of approval. The smaller guns did not fare any better.

But the main event was still to come. As if in obedience to a silent command, all the soldiers were suddenly executing an abrupt about-face—officers, drivers and artillerymen alike —and running off toward the north. Like giant fleas, they proceeded with great leaps, touched the ground after several hundred yards, then bounded off again. The distance spanned by the jumps became shorter. Reg had to decrease the power of the antigrav gradually. Eventually the poor devils were only running; but they ran and ran, as if the very devil were after them. They would probably have kept on running if Reg had not given them the command to take a refreshing bath in the nearest salt lake of the Ninghsia Desert.

Perry adjusted the dials on the control panel. The miniprobe descended. In higher magnification, Reg appeared on the screen and, next to him, a giant of a man with dark blond hair. Both were laughing until tears streamed down their cheeks. They slid down the slope and climbed into their vehicles again.

When the trucks started off, Reg was still laughing.

Perry turned off the set and looked at Khrest.

A fine amusement was visible in the eyes of the Arkonide. He nodded slowly. "I stand in admiration of you and your race," he said. "But possibly I am mistaken and you are an exception. Your friend could easily have killed all his enemies. Why did he not?"

"Because he was in possession of far superior weapons."

Once again Khrest nodded. "Ah, I thought so. Now I am certain that our destiny could not rest in better hands than your own. You will achieve it, Perry. You will realize your dream."

"Thanks," replied Perry warmly.

Four hours later the two trucks were rolling through the force field, which had been lifted especially for them. The third truck, however, had already turned around, and it drove off in an easterly direction with its three drivers and ten officers.

They had been given instructions to report to the security high command in Peking with the information that the Third Power wished to take up diplomatic relations with the Asiatic Federation.


## CHAPTER SIX

"Peking to Washington:

*"The latest incident has proved that your government does not intend to comply with our request. Therefore, if this affair has not been cleared up by noon tomorrow, our time, we have decided to officially sever diplomatic relations with the Western Bloc. The Asiatic Federation possesses means sufficient to defend itself against attack."*

"Peking to Moscow:

*"We are expecting a definitive statement from Washington regarding the presence of the American military base in the Gobi Desert. The answer should have arrived by ten o'clock tomorrow morning. . . ."*

"Peking to *Stardust*:

*"Your demand that we take up diplomatic relations*

*with a single spaceship is absurd. We ask you for the last time to announce your surrender by radio. You will please switch off the force field and leave your ship, unarmed. Should you send us a negative reply, diplomatic relations with the Western Bloc will be officially terminated tomorrow at noon."*

"Washington to Peking:

*"We assure you once again we have no explanation for the current crisis and therefore urge an immediate emergency session of the heads of state concerned."*

"*Stardust* to Peking:

*"We repeat our offer. Furthermore, we wish to make known that we will, with all means at our disposal, prevent any warlike act between nations of Earth."*

"Moscow to Peking:

*"We acknowledge receipt of your communique."*

The waning moon now followed the sun in its descent below the horizon. Because of its favorable position, a direct line video connection with Thora was possible.

In spite of his iron self-control, Perry could not suppress the somehow strange feeling that seized him when he saw the singularly beautiful woman. Her light, almost white blond hair made a pleasant contrast with the red golden eyes that looked at him so coldly and matter of factly.

With an arrogance that made Perry's face flush with anger, she said, "Why are *you* calling me?"

"Khrest would like to speak to you," Perry replied just as icily.

"Then will you kindly get him?"

Perry did not reply. He looked at her once more and turned away. With an unemotional expression, Khrest took his seat in front of the video screen and began to speak in an unknown but melodious language. His voice suggested urging, sometimes commanding, then again imploring. Occasionally Thora offered a question or made a reply. Finally she said something further and nodded in agreement. The screen grew dark.

Khrest remained seated at the set for several moments, unmoving, before finally rising.

He sighed. "For the moment she will do what I have ordered her to do. But I already have a presentiment that later we shall run into difficulties with her. She blindly defends the old laws, without recognizing the necessity of change. She will resist when it comes to the question of bringing about a *rapprochement* of our races."

"Perhaps I should talk to her for a few minutes with a psychoradiator in my hand," Reg suggested sharply. "Then she'll behave as nicely as the officers of the Asiatic army."

"We are immune to the effects of the radiator," Khrest said. "No, one of these days she will *have* to understand where the future of her race now lies. At any rate, now she is informed of our situation. She suggested that I return in a small space capsule she would send for me. It was her intention to let the energy ray wander in a criss-cross pattern over the whole globe. I was finally able to convince her that nothing would be gained by this. I made clear to her, first of all, that my cure and recovery is the most important thing—and not only my own, because I assume that our entire race is suffering from leukemia as the result of some genetic decay. I must therefore remain here alone. Tomorrow Thora will personally supervise all the events from an auxiliary vessel of our space sphere, revolving around Earth in a stable orbit at an altitude of about 600 miles. A constantly renewed neutron field will prevent any nuclear reaction. Magnetic fields will divert rockets from their course and let them fall harmlessly into the ocean. Special mechanisms for draining energy will interrupt your power supplies and paralyze your communications systems. Gentlemen, you may rest assured that there will be no war, even if all the world should want it. By tomorrow afternoon we will already be negotiating with the various governments, and they will be forced to recognize us."

"And what until then?" asked Perry.

"There is nothing to do but wait."

Eric Manoli laid a hand on Khrest's shoulder. "Please, Khrest, won't you lie down again? You must avoid any unnecessary strain. Tomorrow, when everything is over,

Dr. Haggard will examine you. I'm convinced that he will be able to help you."

Khrest smiled in gratitude. "If he can't, then no one can."

They all regarded him fondly as he turned to leave. Reg followed him and helped arrange the blankets of his bunk.

Haggard glanced questioningly at Manoli. "What is your conclusion? Have you had an opportunity yet to examine him and make a proper diagnosis?"

"Come with me into my cabin. There, in complete peace and quiet, I'll tell you what my observations have been so far. Together we should succeed in helping Khrest recover completely. For the time being he is in no danger."

Perry remained alone in the center. Through the observation dome he studied the nocturnal sky. The stars were shining with a rarely seen clarity. The waning moon sank toward the horizon. In one or two hours it would have set.

Tomorrow would be the day of ultimate decision. If nothing thus far had persuaded the world of the might of the Arkonides, only the terror and consternation of the following day would convince them. There was nothing more difficult than to prevent a war that a desperate humanity had freely chosen.

He remained until the moon had vanished completely below the horizon.

Then he suddenly felt the cool night air. It was as if, with the moon, the face of a woman had also withdrawn into darkness. The beautiful face of a woman with light, almost white blond hair and red golden eyes.

The awesome machinery was set in motion.

For years it had lain awaiting this moment. Thousands of test runs and exercises had proved that in time of crisis, the mechanism would function without error. One touch of a button was sufficient to release the chain reaction that nothing could ever stop.

Peking, twelve o'clock noon.

The Premier of the Asiatic Federation nodded to Marshal Lao Lin-to, who had assumed command of the armed forces in place of the deposed Marshal Roon.

Lao lifted the receiver of the telephone that was connected by a direct line to the security high command.

"*Pleiades*. The squadrons are to take off at once. Step number one. Missile launching pads, target: West. Fire with radius seven. Fleet, navigate waters: East. In ten minutes it must all be over. All ground troops into the fallout shelters. Await counterattack. Endit."

Somewhere a hand was balanced over the red button. The hand hesitated for a moment that seemed to last eternities. Then a yellow thumb fell upon it and pressed it hard, ruthlessly, all the way down.

A continent was trembling.

From barrels hidden beneath the sea, in submarines patrolling international waters, slender atom torpedoes broke through the surface of the waves and raced high into the radiantly blue sky, as if in pursuit of the sun. They turned toward east and toward west. Hundreds, thousands, tens of thousands . . .

In every base there was maximum activity. Squadron after squadron, heavily laden with their deadly cargo, rose into the air, entered formation, and followed the prearranged course high into the stratosphere.

The fleet followed close behind, to deliver the *coupe de grace* to a destroyed world and perhaps also to avoid the annihilation that must inevitably fall upon their own shores.

All this happened according to plan.

Only one unanticipated move was made, somewhere in the barracks of some installation in the Asiatic Federation. A Western agent fingered a telegraph key with furious haste. Morse code raced around half the world, requiring but 1/20th of a second.

Exactly one minute and eighteen seconds after the yellow thumb had touched the red button, the same thing happened in Washington. The same machinery was set in motion. This mechanism could not in any respect be distinguished from that in the Far East. In a hair trigger instant, ICBMs were hurled into the black night sky, leaving behind them a train of fiery gases. They were lost as glowing specks among the stars.

Perhaps they were a bit faster than those of the Asiatic Federation. In that case, death would not make a difference of seventy-eight seconds but might strike both sides simultaneously.

Only the missiles of the nuclear submarines, which were stationed in every ocean all over the world, would be faster, for they would have to bridge smaller distances.

How much longer still?

Ten minutes, perhaps; possibly even fifteen.

Then the end of the world would begin.


Moscow waited all of two minutes.

Then there as well someone punched the red button. The missiles stormed into the morning sky and remained on course. There were thousands of them. Now the differences between this and the attacks that had begun elsewhere became obvious.

The ICBMs of the Eastern Bloc all had only one target. Their trajectories all converged at one point. This point designated the spot where the *Stardust* stood beneath its protective bell of energy, isolated from the world and the imminent disaster.

The sun shone brightly in Moscow.

The radar installations along the borders of the gigantic country revealed that the missiles of the Asiatic Federation had passed them by, high in the upper atmosphere, and still had a long flight ahead of them. None of them would come down in the territory of the Eastern Bloc.

The first rockets of the Western Bloc showed a similar disinclination.

Marshal Petronsky nodded toward the Prime Minister with open triumph. "We've done it! In half an hour there will no longer be any Asiatic Federation, nor will a Western Bloc or a United States exist. This damned base in the Gobi Desert will have been obliterated. There will be but one power remaining. *We* will remain."

"The art of survival my dear marshal. Merely the art of survival. It is only possible for a neutral power."

Then a mood of silent expectation descended upon the two men. But not onto them alone. It fell like a shroud upon the whole world.

The last minutes before the end seemed never to pass. They crept along to become eternities.

Mankind held its breath. The first Polaris rockets, gliding into lower layers of the atmosphere, approached their targets. Their angle of trajectory grew more and more acute, and finally they simply began to fall vertically toward Earth.

They buried themselves deeply in the ground, leaving nothing but small, inconsequential craters.

No detonation, no nuclear reaction, no mushroom cloud.

The wave of ICBMs had meanwhile traversed the Pacific. The explosive power of each was so great that they could each have destroyed all life within a radius of sixty miles. Therefore, they diverged from one another during their flight, until they reached the western coast of North and South America like a single long and narrow line of fire. When they failed to detonate on the intended targets, their own momentum drove them further inward before making their descent on mountains, jungles or plains. Only one missile in the second wave fell prematurely. It went right through a seven story apartment house in the western district of Los Angeles, plummeting through each floor in turn and finally lodging in its foundation.

The fate of the American missiles was just as inglorious. Not a single one detonated or went down in densely settled areas. As could be confirmed later, they caused only insignificant material damage.

On the oceans of Earth a preposterous set of circumstances was taking shape.

At a distance of more than 120 miles from the Asiatic coast an American bomb squadron sighted the fleet of the Asiatic Federation. The aircraft carriers and heavy cruisers, smaller destroyers and PT boats—yes, even submarines—drifted as if at anchor on the calm ocean waves.

Air force Colonel Bryan Neldiss gave the signal to attack. Although he could find no explanation for the attitude of his suddenly materializing opponents, he nevertheless had no intention of letting this fat booty get away from him.

The radio went dead. He could not get confirmation of his command. Without his having to lift a finger, his plane started to dive. The whole bomber squadron followed rank. Not far from the enemy fleet, the squadron of American bombers plunged *en masse* into the water. Everyone hastened to abandon the rapidly sinking aircraft. Rubber liferafts helped the swimming crews to safety.

Admiral Sen-toa did not give the command to fire, as he had at first intended. Instead, he initiated rescue procedures. Lifeboats were put down into the water. Helping hands pulled the airmen out of the softly undulating ocean. Within half an hour, all was finished. The American squadron had sunk. The fleet of Asiatic vessels lay motionless, as if held fast in the light breeze by an invisible hand.

Bryan Neldiss and Sen-toa sat silently and icily opposite one another in the officers' quarters. Their mutual animosity had given way to the fear of something still more threatening, something unknown.

Some ninety miles off the West Coast of the United States, the same events had occurred, but with the roles reversed. And here one of the pilots drowned when he could not leave his sinking plane in time.

The Russian ICBMs, pulled out of their trajectories by some unseen force, made 180 degree turns and returned to their own bases. With only minor deviation, they bore straight down into the ground almost where they had begun their flight. None of them detonated.

The nuclear war was over before it had even begun.

There were actually some peasants in China and farmers in the American Midwest who never even knew what had happened. After they heard of the rockets that had gone down, when radio communication was restored, they loudly declared their displeasure with what they at first thought were futile attempts to send another man to the moon. But upon learning the truth of the matter, they suddenly grew silent.

Someone had prevented the war. A single individual had been greater than all the great powers. He had opposed them and had forcibly wrung peace from them.

Perry Rhodan!

But not for long did Perry remain the hero of the common folk. Too great had been the insult that he had inflicted upon the overlords of Earth, too great their anguish when they found themselves displaced from the thrones of their power.

And if none of them, alone, was able to end the sinister reign of Perry Rhodan, then perhaps all together, in a common effort . . .

With this conviction, a fever of diplomatic activity ensued.

"Peking to Washington:
*"Herewith we express our regret over the misunderstanding that almost resulted in global conflict. We propose an immediate conference of all concerned parties. We leave it to you to select an appropriate site where the conference may be held."*

"Peking to Moscow:
*"The Prime Minister of the Eastern Bloc is requested to participate with the Premier of the Asiatic Federation and the President of the Western Bloc in a conference of world powers to be held in two days."*

"Peking to Washington:
*"Cairo will be satisfactory as the site of the conference."*

"Washington to Peking [idem Washington to Moscow]:
*"The government of the Western Bloc has declared the crew of the Stardust principal enemies of the state. We therefore invite the Asiatic Federation to prepare a joint lunar expedition when the present world political crisis has been resolved."*

"Peking to Washington:
*"Agreed."*

"Peking to Asiatic Federation Space Explorations Command:
*"*(Highly Classified Information.)
*"Step up all efforts to launch a new moon rocket immediately. Preparations are to be kept secret."*

"Cairo to Washington/Peking/Moscow:
*"Arrangements completed. We await the arrival of the respected representatives of the three great powers and consider it a great honor to have been chosen as the site of your summit conference."*

Two days later:
"They've officially excluded us from the community of na-

tions," whined Reg. If one had not known him better, one would have thought him ready at any moment to break into tears. "Enemies of the state, that's what we are. Criminals! And why? Because we prevented World War III."

"Are you surprised by that?" Perry drew up his eyebrows. "By preventing the war, we demonstrated that we are stronger than they are. In Cairo they finally speak with unanimity. The great nations have united to destroy us. I couldn't ask for anything more."

"For anything more! What do you mean by that?"

"No nation—only man as a citizen of the world—must conquer space. The alliance against us is really only the first tentative movement toward a unity of purpose for all mankind. Fear has welded all mankind in an identity. With the help of the Arkonides, we have realized the great dream. Reg, we have united the world."

"And therefore they exclude us?"

"That is the price we have to pay."

Reg scratched his reddish hair. "I wonder if Fletch has returned home safely by now."

"I don't know. Anyway, his name has not been mentioned. Only Manoli, you and I—we are enemies of the state. They don't know anything yet about Khrest. That is a surprise that still awaits mankind."

Reg pointed toward the blue sky. "It was really marvelous how Thora went along with us, I must admit. Without her we'd be in a fine mess."

Perry slowly shook his head. "No more so than we are now. The difference is that we might very well now be the last human beings on Earth."

Suddenly Khrest was standing in the doorway of the control center. "In the fate of your race I recognize the rebirth of my own," he said thoughtfully. "Now I see the future before us. Of course—and this you must not forget —there may still be incidents. The danger has not been entirely removed, but the first steps have been taken. Sometimes fear is the best therapy."

"But it must not remain this way forever," warned Perry earnestly. "Someday the unity of mankind must be the result not of fear but of an edict of conscience—a result of reason, reflection, perhaps even an affair of the heart.

This cannot be achieved from one day to the next, but I do know that someday it will come about, whatever I may contribute to it."

Khrest put his hand on Perry's shoulder and said gently, "You have already done this, my friend. Perhaps you are already become the first human being that I—who do not belong to your world and who have origin in the wilderness of space—could call a Terran. Yes, of course! You are the first Terran, Perry Rhodan."

"And what am I?" asked Reg sulkingly. The perennially silent Manoli this time did not fail to make a very fitting remark: "One must become a human being before one can become a Terran."

Reg sniffed with disgust and started his massive body in motion toward the exit. "I'm going swimming in the lake," he announced.

Manoli let him pass, whispering softly to him, "Very well. Take a bath in the salt lake. Let them pickle you."

Khrest smiled silently.

Perry Rhodan seemed not to have heard anything. He stood near the astrodome, gazing up into the cloudless sky. Somewhere up there the moon was pursuing her lonely orbit around Earth.

# DON'T MISS THIS GREAT SCIENCE FICTION
# SPY SERIES!

---

### 01040   AGENT OF T.E.R.R.A. #1:
*The Flying Saucer Gambit* by Larry Maddock

Hannibal Fortune and his symbiotic partner Webley come to Earth to investigate the murder of T.E.R.R.A.'s Resident Agent in the 20th Century.

### 01041   AGENT OF T.E.R.R.A. #2:
*The Golden Goddess Gambit* by Larry Maddock

Fortune and Webley fight a desperate battle against time-tampering by EMPIRE agents in the dawn of Earth's history.

### 01042   AGENT OF T.E.R.R.A. #3:
*The Emerald Elephant Gambit* by Larry Maddock

Fortune and Webley must battle to insure the destruction of a great civilization, while vicious looters from the far future upset the balance of history.

---